THE
CIRCLE

K.M. Montemayor

Copyright © 2013 Kathleen McGaw Montemayor
All rights reserved.

ISBN: 1483970787
ISBN-13: 978-1483970783

Library of Congress Control Number: 2013906331
CreateSpace Independent Publishing Platform
North Charleston, South Carolina

DEDICATION

To Noah—My blessing from God. I love you.

To Andy—My template for Charlie. If there were such a thing as a soul mate, you would be mine.

To Brandy—My friend, fellow writer, and beta reader. Your input has been invaluable.

CONTENTS

Prologue vii
1. Lilly 1
2. Charlie 9
3. Fall Semester: August–September 17
4. Homecoming 63
5. Coffee and Pumpkin Bread 81
6. Thanksgiving 89
7. Revelations 99
8. Christmas Break 119
9. Strained Reunion 137
10. Secrets and Lies 149
11. Apart 159
12. Spring Break 175
13. Prom 187
14. Course of Action 205
15. Henry 225
16. Together Again 237
17. On the Run 249
18. Hopeless 261

PROLOGUE

Clear Lake

"You were born in the wrong time. You should have been born in, like, 1900," Claire told Lilly.

The two girls had just finished watching *Jane Eyre*, the black-and-white version with Orson Welles. Claire was Lilly's so-called best friend. So-called because they would only hang out together when Claire wasn't speaking to her boyfriend, Matt. The temperamental couple had had a huge blowout that afternoon, so Claire decided to take Lilly up on her invitation to sleep over and watch movies.

"I mean, my *grandmother* likes *Jane Eyre*," Claire said between bites of popcorn. "Seriously, you have the mind-set of an eighty-year-old."

Lilly rolled her eyes. She wasn't crazy about Claire's movie choice either: *Sixteen Candles*. There was no way Sam's infatuation with Jake could compare to the epic love story of Jane and Mr. Rochester.

Claire reached across Lilly, ejected *Jane Eyre* from the VCR, and inserted *Sixteen Candles*. Lilly groaned and put a pillow over her head in a futile attempt to drown out Farmer Ted and the rest of the geeks. Summer was essentially over. It was the August before her senior year, and marching band practice was starting Monday. Lilly didn't like thinking about it. She liked marching band just fine, but she was dreading her senior year. So far her high school experience had been suboptimal in the social activities department. She was almost eighteen and had never even been asked on a date. Granted, there was no one in her high school she was particularly interested in, but still it would be nice to go to at least one homecoming dance, or hopefully, senior prom.

Claire started snoring, so Lilly ejected the movie. She stared up at her Superman poster before flipping off the light switch. Perhaps she was better off with her fictional characters and superheroes, sublime beings so perfect that even their faults seemed like assets. Real men in the real world would only be a disappointment.

Sentria

"Pack your things. We're leaving tonight," Mr. Gray said. There was no discussion; they didn't have a choice. The young man was accustomed to these short-notice moves, but that didn't mean he liked them. He walked to his father's study.

"Where are we going this time?" the young man, whose Earthan name was Charlie, asked.

"Clear Lake, Texas," Mr. Gray replied.

"When?" Charlie input the information into his personal communication device, or PCD for short.

"1988."

LILLY

The phone rang, and Claire rushed to grab it out of Lilly's hand. "Matt?" Claire smiled broadly. She began chatting animatedly.

Right on schedule, Lilly thought. Claire and Matt never stayed mad at each other for long. The girls had made plans to go back-to-school shopping today. Lilly knew that would not happen now.

"OK. Love you, too. Bye," Claire said. "Lilly, you don't mind if we go shopping some other time. Matt is ready to apologize and take me out."

"Of course not. You go ahead," Lilly knew how it worked. She would just fade into the background until Claire needed her again.

"Thanks, Lil. You're the best," she said and ran out. Unlike Lilly, it took hours for Claire to get dressed. For Claire, being presentable in public involved a complex ritual of styling gel, curling irons, and a vast array of cosmetics. Lilly didn't know why she put so much effort into it; she already had Matt wrapped around her little finger.

While Claire ran upstairs to change clothes and get her overnight bag, Lilly thought about it. Although she did long for some romance in her life, Lilly didn't want the type of fickle relationship Claire and Matt had. To Claire, a boyfriend was something she could wear on her arm that proclaimed to the world, "Look at me. I have a boyfriend. We are a couple." It wasn't that Claire didn't love Matt, but if he left her tomorrow, she would be head over heels in love with someone else by the end of the week. She couldn't speak from experience, but Lilly thought she would prefer to be alone than to be with someone out of sheer desperation. It didn't really matter. To the guys at the school, it was as if Lilly didn't even exist.

Lilly wasn't supermodel gorgeous like some of the drill team girls, but she was pretty. She was petite—four feet eleven and ninety-five pounds. Her features were well proportioned and she had clear café-au-lait skin. She had dark brown eyes and long chestnut-brown hair that her mother called naturally wavy, which was really just a euphemism for wild and out of control. But it was the eighties. Big hair ruled. If she had to be cursed with such a volume of hair, at least it was in style. Lilly thought her lack of interest from the opposite sex had more to do with the fact that she was shy and kind of an outsider. Although she had lived in Clear Lake since her freshman year, she was still considered the new kid.

Claire bounded down the stairs two at a time. She was twisting her long, unnaturally blonde mane into a ponytail. "See you later," she said and ran out the door.

Lilly sighed. She had most of the day left and no plans for her last weekend of summer. Well, she still needed clothes for school, so she would have to go shopping at some point. She could wait until her mother got off work from her second job, but she knew her mom would be really tired.

Lilly's mother, Michelle, was a workaholic. She worked the evening shift at the local hospital as an ICU nurse and had a weekend job as well. With their house paid off, they really didn't need the extra money. Lately, Michelle had justified her killer work schedule by claiming she was saving for Lilly's college. While Lilly accepted that was part of it, she knew the real reason her mom worked so much was to avoid social interactions, especially with men. The unfortunate truth was that her mom was still hung up on her dad.

"No use putting it off," Lilly said. She ran upstairs and got dressed.

Lilly finished her shopping and was sitting in the food court. At least it hadn't taken long. If she had gone with Claire, it would have been an all-day affair. Claire had to try on everything in the store. Twice.

"Hey Lilly. I'm kind of surprised to see you here." Lilly turned to see Dana, a pretty, popular senior on the high school drill team. Even though she was one of the cool kids, Dana wasn't stuck up. She always said hi to Lilly and the other outcasts in band and drama.

"Yeah. Shopping's not really my thing, but I needed some clothes," Lilly said. She felt the need to justify her presence at the mall.

"Let's see what you got." She was digging into the shopping bag before Lilly could object. "This blue blouse will look terrific on you," she said putting it up to Lilly's face.

"C'mon, Dana. Let's go," her friend Nikki complained. Dana was nice; her friends were a different story. Like Dana, Nikki was beyond perfect in the looks department, but her personality ruined the effect. If Lilly were the judge, she would have to give Nikki the award for Snottiest Girl at Clear Lake High.

"Well, OK. Just a sec." Dana lowered her voice. "Sorry about Nikki. She's just…"

"It's OK," Lilly said.

"Maybe we'll have some classes together this semester."

"Yeah, that would be great," Lilly agreed. Dana waved at Lilly and then ran to catch up with Nikki and her friends. Lilly threw away her half-eaten slice of pizza, took her Diet Coke, and dragged her shopping bags to her car.

When she got home, Lilly took her radio and went out to her backyard pool to swim and read. "Owner of a Lonely Heart" began to play. *How appropriate*, Lilly thought. She adjusted her sunglasses and leaned back on the float. One mediocre summer down, one monotonous school year to go.

When Lilly woke up the next morning, Michelle had already left for work. She practiced her French horn, cleaned her room, and read a book. At ten thirty she decided it was late enough to call and get the Claire/Matt update.

"And guess what he did next," Claire said.

"I can't guess," Lilly said, stifling a yawn.

"He took me to the mall to buy me a new heart charm bracelet!"

"Wow, that's great. So what have you got planned for today?" Lilly asked hopefully.

"Matt said we could go to the movies, and I get to pick."

Lilly assumed as much. Matt was paying a steep price for checking out that girl at the beach. "Just don't stay out too late. We've got band practice tomorrow."

"How can I forget?" Claire asked. "Hey, did you hear? We're getting a new trumpet player. A transfer student. He's supposed to be really good."

"That's kind of unusual," Lilly said. High school transfers were rare. Well, at least *she* wouldn't be the new kid anymore.

"Yeah, and he's a senior."

"A senior? That's awful. Making your kid move his last year of high school."

"What? Oh yeah. No kidding," Claire said. She sounded distracted. She was probably looking at herself in the mirror. "Well, Lil, I gotta get going. I'll talk to you later."

Lilly sighed. "OK. See you at band practice."

―――

August band practice in Texas was insufferably hot. Even wearing her light cotton shorts and with her hair in a ponytail, Lilly was drenched in sweat.

As she walked to the field, she noticed a new band member. That was hardly remarkable. Most of these freshmen she had never met before, but this guy kind of stood out. While the rest of the band was wearing T-shirts and shorts, he was wearing blue jeans and a button-down plaid shirt with a white T-shirt underneath.

Man, he must be burning up in that, Lilly thought. He was short, probably only a couple inches taller than she was. His clothes weren't in style, but it wasn't like he was unable to coordinate solids and stripes. It was more like he was dressed in period costume from the fifties or sixties. He wore these awful, black, thick-framed glasses. Lilly's abuelo—well, her great-grandfather—had had a pair just like them. They were very unattractive, in Lilly's opinion. The glasses made the new kid look as if he just stepped out of an episode of *Happy Days.*

Lilly decided she had better things to do than fret over a freshman's lack of fashion sense. She hurried over to the field. Many of the band members were already warming up. A smile rose to her lips, and she was somewhat surprised by how glad she was to be back with the band. She would never win any popularity contests, and she didn't even have a lot of close friends, but these were her people. She belonged here.

"Nice of you to join us this evening, Garcia," Mark complained. He was the first chair French horn and easily the most gorgeous guy in band, or would have been, if he had half a personality and ever cracked a smile. The mundane marching band practices were beneath him, and being section leader was such a burden. If he were on a soap opera, Lilly thought it would be titled *The Bored and the Beautiful.* He had a girlfriend, a flute player named Jill who looked like a goddess. It wasn't as if Lilly was interested in Mark, but if she forgot the fact that he was a total downer, she could at least enjoy the view.

"Coming," Lilly said. She quickly found her place in the French horn section next to Beth and Ian. Lilly had sort of taken the two sophomores under her wing when they were just freshmen in the band, so Ian had nicknamed her "French Horn Mama." They just called her Mom most of the time.

Ian was shorter and smaller than most of the tenth graders, but he always attracted attention. He was extremely outgoing and loved to talk to everyone. His first job was to be Lilly's French horn son. His second job was to keep Lilly in the know. If there was a bit of gossip, he usually knew about it.

By contrast, Beth preferred to remain in the background. She was a small Goth/new wave girl with maroon-and-black spiky hair. She always wore heavy black eyeliner. She didn't speak much, but she was *very* perceptive. Even though Beth was younger, Lilly came to respect her insight on most matters.

"OK, folks," Mr. Patterson, the band director said. "We'll be performing Copland's 'Rodeo' this year. It's going to be challenging, but I know we're up to it, and we're going to do great at competition. We have great music and a great marching show. It's going to be exciting, folks. We'll start with the music tonight, then tomorrow we'll start running through the first few marching sequences."

It was your typical introduction to marching band speech. This would be the fourth such speech Lilly had heard, and it amused her that Mr. Patterson always called the band "folks." He overused the word.

Michael, the drum major shouted out, "Chorale number eight." He counted them off and led the band in the warm-up. At its conclusion, Mr. Patterson picked up his bullhorn. "All right, folks, let's go. Brass in the band hall. Woodwinds in the choir room."

Lilly absently flipped through the pages of the marching music as she headed for the Jeep. Ian and Beth followed close behind. She glanced up to see the new kid with the awful glasses get into the driver's seat of a light-blue classic Mustang. "How is that freshman able to drive? Does he have a hardship license?" Lilly asked Ian.

"Charlie's not a freshman, he's a senior. Just moved here from New Mexico or somewhere."

"Oh, so he's the trumpet player Claire was talking about," Lilly mumbled to herself. "Poor guy."

"What?" Ian asked.

"Oh, nothing. I just think it must be difficult to be the new kid, a senior, and be such a little guy."

"Look who's talking, short stuff." Ian patted her on the head. He then broke into a chorus of "Short People Got No Reason to Live."

"Oh, hush, Ian. Unless you prefer to walk home." He was right, though. It was embarrassing, but Lilly was often mistaken for a freshman herself.

Lilly unlocked the car doors, and Ian and Beth climbed in. Ian called copilot, and Beth crawled into the backseat.

Beth, who had said nothing during this entire exchange, suddenly piped up.

"Hey, Mom, we are going to McDonald's, aren't we?"

"Don't we always?' Lilly had started the tradition of stopping at McDonald's after band practices to get supersize drinks, and her underclassmen passengers had come to expect it.

"You're such a good French horn mama," Ian said.

"Uh-huh," Lilly said. She turned on her New Order tape as she pulled out of the school parking lot.

CHARLIE

Charlie only had a few weeks to acclimate to his new environment before beginning his senior year of high school. This was not his first time on Earth, but it was his first time in Texas. On the prior mission, they had been stationed in Roswell, New Mexico. The purpose of this current mission was essentially the same: find out what the Earthans knew regarding space exploration, find out what kind of technology they had, and prevent them from learning of the existence of the Sentrian civilization.

To accomplish this task, the Sentrians needed to infiltrate the NASA facility. They would live among the Earthans and interact with them as ordinary neighbors, coworkers, and students. As far as Charlie could tell, there was only one major difference between this mission and the last. This time the elders wanted the Sentrian families to have *more* interaction with the Earthans. The adults were ordered to join some sort of social club, and the children had to be involved in extracurricular activities at their schools. Charlie was annoyed by this new requirement. He did not want more interaction with the Earthans. The less he had to deal with them, the better.

"Why do the elders want us to befriend the Earthans all of a sudden? Aren't they the enemy?" Charlie asked his father over dinner their first night on Earth.

"Yes, but they want us to fit in, and Earthans are social creatures," Louis answered. "On the 1978 mission, the Sentrians raised a lot of suspicion among the Earthans with their asocial behavior. The elders thought the best way to combat this problem was to have our people assimilate with the Earthan culture. It will also make it easier to observe them and find out what they know."

"Swell," Charlie said.

"Charlie, I don't like this any more than you do," Louis told him. "Just find some sort of activity you can do, or I'll find one for you." That was the end of the discussion.

Reluctantly, Charlie researched his options. He used his PCD, a device that could play music, games, and most important, be used for research. Sports were out. Sentrians were both faster and stronger than Earthans. If he competed to the best of his ability, it would draw too much attention to him, and the idea of throwing every sporting event was no fun. He had no interest in drama or choir.

Then he noticed that band was an option. Charlie was an accomplished musician, and the Earthan instrument called the trumpet was very similar to the instrument he played on Sentria. With some self-tutoring on reading Earthan music and some practice, he was sure he could do it. The fall semester was marching band, so he would have to learn to march as well. Sentria had wonderful orchestras, but no marching bands. At least it would be something different, Charlie thought.

Charlie did very well on his audition—maybe too well. The assistant director, Mr. Newsome, wanted to make him first chair, but because he had no experience in marching, the director decided he should be third chair instead. Charlie was relieved. He didn't want to cause any problems with the other band members. It was bad enough he was knocking the third chair player out of his spot.

At least the now fifth chair trumpet player seemed to take the seating shake-up well enough. He actually came over and congratulated him. "Way to go, man," he said, holding out his right hand. Charlie hesitated before he realized the boy wanted to shake hands, a strange Earthan custom.

"Thanks," Charlie said. "I'm sorry. I didn't catch your name."

"It's Matt."

"Charlie."

"That was a great audition," Matt said, looking over at the rest of the trumpet players. Most were either stunned or sulking. "And don't worry about these guys. They just weren't expecting such stiff competition from the new guy."

Charlie glanced over his shoulder at them. The one named Dan was fuming. He kicked a chair, knocking it over. Charlie couldn't understand Dan's reaction because, as first chair, his seat had been unaffected by the audition. Charlie decided it would be a good idea to get out of there.

"Thanks, Matt. I'll see you later."

"OK, Charlie. And don't worry about marching. It'll be a cakewalk for you."

Charlie didn't understand the expression but nodded at Matt and walked out to the parking lot. When he was sure no one was looking, he pulled out his PCD and looked it up.

CAKEWALK: SOMETHING THAT IS REALLY EASY TO DO.

That was a relief. Charlie made a mental note to brush up on Earthan idioms. He had become rather good at them when he was in New Mexico, but that was several years ago, and he had forgotten a lot of them. Also, these Earthans were always coming up with new expressions. At least he wouldn't have to return until next week. Maybe by then, Dan would have cooled off.

Charlie put his trumpet in the trunk of his 1960 light-blue Mustang, the car he fell in love with when he had been to Earth the first time. He looked up to see the freshmen arriving for their marching practice. It was ninety-five degrees, and they were all wiping their foreheads and fanning themselves.

Perspiration. Charlie wrinkled his nose in disgust. It was only August, and he would have to spend the entire marching season side by side with these sweaty Earthans. Perhaps he should have researched his choice of extracurricular activities a little better.

His mother was sitting at the kitchen table when he got home. Helen Gray had decided to join the Clear Lake Garden Club as part of the social club requirement. She was reading up on the care of various varieties of roses when Charlie walked in.

"How was the audition?" she asked.

"Fine," Charlie said simply.

"Did you make the team?"

"Yes, Mom. I made the *band*."

"Oh," she said. She closed her gardening magazine. "I'm brewing some coffee. Could I get you a cup?"

"That would be great, thanks," Charlie said.

Coffee was one of the things the Sentrians liked best about Earth. The first Sentrian explorers who came to Earth brought coffee plants back to their home planet, eager to share this wonderful drink with their people. Unfortunately, Sentrian soil was utterly unsuitable for coffee plants. They also tried importing coffee beans, but Sentrian water did not brew well. Their scientists invented a synthetic substitute for coffee, but it had a bad aftertaste and was completely inferior to Earthan coffee.

Mrs. Gray poured Charlie a large mug, the size of a soup bowl, full of strong black coffee and refilled her own mug. It was only eleven, but the Grays had already consumed three pots of coffee this morning.

"What plans do you have for today?" Mrs. Gray asked.

"I was going to study up on marching maneuvers."

"That's nice, dear. Your father will be home early tonight, and I know he'll want to hear about your day. I'm making your favorite for dinner: stuffed bell peppers and pancakes."

"OK, Mom," Charlie said and excused himself. His mother still sounded like a fifties housewife on a TV sitcom. It was going to be hard for all of them to make the adjustment from the fifties to the eighties. He had already decided that he wouldn't mention upsetting the seating arrangement in the trumpet section. That would be an unnecessary thing for his mother to worry about, and it wouldn't please his father, either.

Charlie went upstairs and turned on his Sentrian computer. He reviewed videos of championship-winning marching bands and drum-and-bugle corps. He was surprised that he actually enjoyed watching them.

He was a little concerned about returning to practice on Monday, but Matt was right. The other trumpet players were as friendly as he could expect, considering he was the new guy. Only the first chair, Dan, was still hostile. Charlie just kept to himself and tried not to bother anyone.

After the warm-up, they broke into sections to practice "Rodeo." Dan walked down the trumpet line handing out the marching diagrams, while the drum major told them to start learning the moves. "If you can't get it, you can always come up tomorrow morning and practice with the fish," Dan said to Charlie and motioned to the freshmen struggling to learn the basic marching maneuvers.

"If he marches half as well as he plays the trumpet, he's gonna make you look like the fish, Dan," Matt said.

Some of the other trumpet players touched their index fingers to their tongues and made a sizzling sound. Dan turned red and scowled at Matt. Charlie wasn't sure what the fingers on the tongue meant, but he gathered that Matt had taken a shot at Dan.

"Just make sure you know your stuff," Dan said, shoving the diagrams into Charlie's hands.

Charlie went home and practiced the marching moves until he had them down cold. He didn't need to give Dan any reason to bother him. It wasn't until the next day at practice that he realized his diligence had backfired.

"Hey, Chuck, where are your diagrams?" Dan asked.

"It's Charlie, and they're at my house," Charlie replied. By the look on Dan's face, he knew he should not have left them there.

"Well, *Charles,* having them at home isn't going to do you much good. What are you going to do when we start the marching sequences?"

"I have them memorized," Charlie said. All the other trumpet players snapped their heads back to look in his direction.

"Oh really," Dan said sarcastically. He called over to the drum major. "Hey, Mike."

"What's going on?" Michael asked. He started walking over to where the trumpet players were standing.

"It seems Charlie doesn't need to bring his marching diagrams, because he's got the whole thing memorized."

Charlie looked at the ground. These darn Earthans. He took it literally when they said start memorizing the maneuvers and the music, and he was still in trouble. Why didn't they say what they mean and mean what they say?

"I think he needs to prove it," Dan said.

Michael took Dan aside and whispered into his ear. "He's not a fish; he's a senior. I don't see any reason to humiliate him." No one else could hear, but Charlie could. He was a supersonos. A small number of his people had superhearing, and he was one of them.

"Aw, c'mon," Dan said. "This dude needs to be taken down a few notches. He's never even marched before."

"All right," Michael agreed. "But get it over with and don't embarrass him in front of the whole band."

Dan nodded. He could live with that. He called the trumpets to attention. "All right, listen up. Charlie's got this first section memorized. He's going to show us how it's done."

Charlie knew he should just let Dan be right. He should say, "You were right. I don't know this at all," but he just couldn't do it. Maybe he was just sick of putting up with stuff. It was bad enough the rulers on his planet tried to run his life; now he had to deal with this insufferable Earthan punk. Or maybe it was because he did know it, and he wanted to prove it.

Whatever the reason, Charlie took his trumpet and walked over to the hash mark on the football field to mark off his position. Dan counted

Charlie off, and he played and marched the entire section flawlessly. When he finished, there was a mixture of cheering, clapping, and laughing. Matt especially whooped it up. Now Charlie realized why Matt had been so nice to him after the audition last week. Matt had wanted Charlie to unseat Dan.

Dan's face turned red again, and his scowl reappeared. Michael called the band to attention then, and Charlie was glad for the interruption. The rest of the practice, Charlie just tried to keep out of Dan's way. If there was one thing Charlie understood from life on his planet, it was pecking order. You had to know your place in the world, or in his case, the universe.

As soon as Michael dismissed the band, Charlie headed straight for his car. He glanced up and for just a second caught the gaze of a pretty Earthan girl. She smiled at him, and he found himself wanting to smile back. Instead, he frowned and turned away. She was lugging a French horn case, and it was almost as big as she was. She was tiny, maybe five feet tall, but probably less. She could easily have passed for a Sentrian female. He suddenly felt homesick. He wished he didn't have to be here. Charlie started the car and drove home.

Helen and Louis were sitting in the living room drinking coffee when he arrived. "How was practice?" Helen asked cheerfully.

"It was fine," Charlie said glumly.

"Let me get you a mug of coffee, and you can tell us all about it."

"Not tonight, Mom. I'm really tired." His parents looked disappointed. He was an only child, so his parents focused a lot of attention on him. Ordinarily he loved to talk to his father, but tonight he just wanted to be alone.

Charlie changed clothes and crawled into bed. He tossed and turned for a while. He hated Earth. Why did his father have to be so valuable to the Sentrian government? Why couldn't he have been a janitor or something? If he had, then Charlie would never have had to go on these Earthan missions to begin with. When he finally did fall asleep, he dreamed about Sentria.

FALL SEMESTER: AUGUST–SEPTEMBER

The sound of Duran Duran's "Planet Earth" blaring from her clock radio woke Lilly up. She wanted so badly to hit the snooze button on her alarm clock, but she resisted. It was only the first day of school, and she could not get motivated. This did not bode well for the rest of the year.

After ten minutes in a hot shower, she finally started to wake up. On her way out the door, she grabbed a cereal bar and a Diet Coke, her preferred method of caffeine ingestion. She was already regretting letting Ian and Beth sucker her into taking them to school this year. By picking them up, she was sacrificing an extra fifteen minutes of sleep.

First period was band, so at least she could ease into the school year. They went through "Rodeo" a few times and then practiced the songs for the drill team. Next was English: a real class with real homework. Lilly loved to read, but she could do without the research papers. She met up with Claire and walked with her toward their second-period classes.

"Homecoming will be here before we know it, and I have no idea what kind of dress to wear," Claire fretted. Lilly thought she must have spent hours choosing her first day of school ensemble. Her teal shirt and blouse were color coordinated with her hair clip, purse, and nails. She might as well have tattooed "high maintenance" on her forehead. "Matt better not go cheap on the mum like last year," Claire grumbled. "I had the smallest, cheesiest mum in the school. What do you think that says about a guy's level of commitment when he gets you such a small mum?"

Lilly didn't really want to get involved. She liked Matt and Claire both, but she thought they could fight about the most juvenile things. "I don't know, Claire. I've never been invited to a homecoming dance."

"That's true, but still, you are a girl. I'm sure you have an opinion," Claire said.

"I don't know. It would depend on other factors," Lilly said.

"Other factors? What does that mean?"

The girls realized they had company. The new trumpet player was walking behind them. Suddenly he stopped, tilted his head to one side, and looked up at the ceiling. A moment later he started moving again and headed into Mrs. Hartman's class.

"That is *so* not normal," Claire said. Lilly had to agree. Claire looked back to Lilly. "You were saying?"

"Uh, yeah. It's like how he treats you. Is he thoughtful and considerate, or selfish and self-centered? Maybe he's a wonderful guy who just doesn't have a lot of money."

"I still think if he cared enough, he could find a way to get a decent mum," Claire said.

"Maybe so."

"I gotta go." Claire was frowning, and Lilly got the feeling Claire was mad at her for not agreeing wholeheartedly with her.

"See you at lunch," Lilly called out, but Claire was gone.

Lilly was the last one to enter the classroom, and Mrs. Hartman gave her a dirty look. She quickly sat in the only seat still available. It was right next to Charlie. Lilly sighed. It really didn't matter. There wasn't anyone in this class she knew well anyway.

"Let's get started," Mrs. Hartman said. "Tomorrow, be sure to bring your spiral notebook. We are going to start every class with five minutes of brainstorming."

Some of the class groaned. *Great,* Lilly thought. Over the summer Mrs. Hartman must have attended some stupid workshop that endorsed the idea of brainstorming. Now they would have a year's worth of useless journal entries. What a waste of a spiral notebook.

Mrs. Hartman ignored the groans and continued. "Reading assignments: the first three chapters of *Brave New World* by Friday. There will be a quiz." More of the class groaned this time. "Now, open your literature books to page ten."

Lilly glanced over at Charlie. He was wearing the usual: plaid shirt, jeans, and white tennis shoes. And, of course, those awful glasses. "He should really consider contacts," Lilly said under her breath. She thought she had spoken softly but was surprised when he turned his head toward her.

Whoops, Lilly thought. She felt her face get hot.

"Ms. Garcia, would you care to read the first lines of sonnet eighteen?"

"Yes, ma'am," Lilly said. She looked down at her book and started reading.

At lunch Lilly went through the salad bar line, as she did every year. As far as Lilly was concerned, salad was the only edible option in the cafeteria. She got her drink and walked over to sit with the band. Ian nodded at Lilly as she walked past. "I can, too. I reached level ten twice this weekend," Ian challenged. "Wanna bet?" He was talking about a video game with Gary, a saxophone player. They were both gamers.

"Hey, Lil," Claire said, scooting over to make room. She was no longer annoyed with Lilly, and she was in quite a talkative mood. "English class stinks this year," Claire complained. She had Mrs. Hartman right after Lilly. "And *Brave New World* sounds totally lame. I don't want to read it."

"Join the club," Lilly said, munching on a carrot. "I wish we could read a love story."

"Like *Jane Eyre*?" Claire suggested.

"Well, we read that one last year," Lilly said. "Oh, that's right. You only skimmed the Cliff's Notes."

Claire took a carrot stick out of her own salad and crunched loudly, giving Lilly a dirty look in the process. Claire also preferred the salad bar, but that was because she was constantly on a diet. She didn't want to gain an ounce on her size-four frame. After all, some people had homecoming dresses to fit into.

Claire turned and started talking to Matt. They were bemoaning the fact that they only had one class together and trying to figure out their weekend plans. Lilly felt like a third wheel. She let her eyes wander across the cafeteria. She noticed Charlie sitting by himself. He picked up his sandwich; then suddenly he froze and looked up at the ceiling. A moment later he snapped out of it and continued eating.

Lilly shook her head. He was so strange. She had known Charlie for a little over four weeks, and in that time she had never seen him smile. He kept to himself, and the other band members pretty much ignored him. Lilly felt kind of sorry for Charlie, but then again, he put out a leave-me-alone vibe. It was as if he had a dark cloud hanging over his head. The bell rang then, startling her out of her thoughts. She took another bite of her salad, a sip of Diet Coke, and headed off for her next class.

Charlie's day was just as bad as he imagined it would be. Since he had last been to Earth, it seemed as if the kids had become more unruly. They would ignore their teachers or just be plain rude by talking through the entire class. His Sentrian teachers would never have tolerated that behavior. And their appearance was odd to Charlie. The boys all had yellow-orange hair and wore these ugly slip-on checkered shoes. The girls wore their hair in a big poof in the front. They wore too much eye shadow and eyeliner and had giant hoop earrings in their ears. All the teenagers dressed so casually. Back in the fifties, many of the girls and all of the female teachers wore dresses or skirts. Now, the girls wore jeans, and even the teachers wore slacks.

When he entered the cafeteria, he saw Henry—or actually, the top of Henry's head. He was immersed in a book and didn't even look up when Charlie passed by. Charlie briefly thought of sitting with his fellow Sentrian but then thought better of it. He and Henry had nothing in common, and besides, Henry was a total bore and kind of strange. He found an empty table by the window and ate his lunch alone.

Hopefully, this afternoon would go smoother than the morning. He at least had classes that he found somewhat interesting: chemistry, calculus, and government. Government especially fascinated Charlie. He knew the Earthans had more freedoms than Sentrians, and he had been taught that this was the reason they were such violent brutes. According to the elders, all people needed strict guidance from their government so that they could live in peace and harmony. Charlie had always believed that was the reason for so many Earthan wars—the people had too many freedoms.

Michael, the drum major, was in his chemistry class, and both Matt and the petite French horn player were in government with him. He remembered her from this morning in English class. When the teacher took attendance, Charlie paid more attention, so he could catch her name.

"Liliana Garcia?" Mr. Austin called out.

"It's Lilly," she answered.

After roll call, Mr. Austin started right in. "We're going to start the year studying the different branches of government. Can anyone name the three branches of government for me?"

After the last bell, the band had exactly fifteen minutes to get to the field for practice. The guys changed into shorts quickly and were ready to go. The girls had more difficulty. They had to change into shorts, pull their hair up, and freshen their makeup. Many were racing to get to the field on time. Charlie, who hadn't changed clothes, wondered why the girls bothered reapplying their makeup. They would just sweat it off.

Marching band practice lasted two long hours. A lot of it was kind of boring, because the director would work with one group of the band at a time. The only groups that were constantly busy were the drum line and the color guard, who were practicing on the parking lot next to the field.

When Charlie had chosen band, he didn't realize all it involved. Band was a huge time commitment, with practice every day after school and all the football games and marching contests. He could have joined the Latin club, which met twice a month and still complied with the Sentrian requirement. Of course, band practice would be a lot more fun and go more smoothly if these teenage boys would pay attention to the director and do what they were supposed to do.

"Bones," Mr. Patterson called out to the trombone section. "You were completely out of step. Let's run through that section again. Just the bones. C'mon, folks."

Charlie sighed and knelt down on the field with the rest of the trumpets. The first-chair French horn looked bored and annoyed. He sat by himself, picking up bits of grass and rolling them between his fingers. The girl named Liliana, who went by the nickname Lilly, had moved out of formation and was sitting in a circle with some of the other horn players. Dan never would have allowed that. Unlike Mark, Dan kept his section on a tight leash.

Finally Mr. Patterson picked up his bullhorn again. "Folks, listen up. We're going to run through this from the top."

Lilly was waiting for Ian and Beth at her car after band practice. Ian, Mr. Personality, was always dawdling. He had to say good-bye to the myriad friends and admirers he imagined he had. Beth was trying to hurry Ian up. "C'mon, do you want Lilly to leave us?"

"She would never leave me. She loves me too much."

"OK, get in. Let's go," Lilly said.

"Yes, Mom," Ian said and snickered at Beth. "Here, let me get that for you." He picked up Lilly's horn case and put it into the back of the Jeep.

"Suck-up," Beth said under her breath.

Charlie had parked near Lilly and was walking up to his car, when he suddenly froze. He tilted his head to the side and looked up at the sky.

"What's he doing?" asked Ian.

"I don't know," Lilly said, "but he does that a lot."

A moment later Charlie started walking toward his car again. "You know," Beth said, "maybe he has epilepsy. My cousin does the same thing when she has a petit mal seizure."

Charlie laughed out loud and shook his head. He put his trumpet in his car and drove off.

"That's not epilepsy. That's just freakin' weird."

"Be nice, Ian," Lilly said.

"What? I'm just saying what you guys are thinking. The dude's probably having a really interesting conversation with the little green men inside his head."

Lilly started the car, and Ian reached over to put in a New Order tape. "Wait, Ian," Lilly said. "I want to hear this." "Circle in the Sand" was playing on the radio.

He put down the New Order tape. "Since when do you prefer this girlie pop to New Order?"

"I don't like girlie pop," she said. "I just happen to like this song."

When Charlie returned from band practice, his mom had dinner on the table. Sentrian food was remarkably similar to Earthan food, but the combination of food served would seem odd to Earthans. This evening his mom had made spaghetti and beets. And instead of water or a cold drink, they had steaming mugs of coffee.

Louis was sitting at the table but not participating in the conversation. Mentally he was still at work.

"So did you make some friends today?" his mom asked Charlie.

"No, Mom." He was annoyed. What did his mother expect? Most of these kids had gone to school together for years. Their friendships had been forged long ago. Charlie was the interloper.

"Well, I think it would be nice if you did. After all, this is your senior year."

Louis suddenly looked up from his work papers. "Leave him alone, Helen. He joined the band. Isn't that enough?"

Charlie could sense a fight brewing. He decided to change the subject. "How was your day, Father?"

"Tolerable, I suppose. Mr. Conner has assigned us a lot of unnecessary charting that takes up a lot of time, but that's pretty typical for him. The dolts I work with think anything he says is just great. They're falling all over each other to please him." Louis sighed. "It would be nice if we had some Sentrian *friends* here."

Charlie knew what he meant. Even though they came to Earth with other Sentrian families, they had very little in common with them. The other families were too busy trying to please the magistrate and the elders. There was no one they could actually trust.

In the fifties, with Daniel's family, it had been different. Daniel's father and Louis would sit on the back patio and take advantage of the fact that no one was listening in on their conversations. They discussed their jobs: what they liked and didn't like about them. They would often criticize the Sentrian government, something they couldn't do at home. But mostly, they would just discuss life, what they would do if only they had the freedom and the opportunity.

"I wish Daniel were here," Charlie said.

"Yes," Louis agreed. "Last trip was nice. But we can't afford to be so lax this time. Most of the families on this mission are completely brainwashed by the state. I heard Mr. Jones tell Mr. Lassiter a few days before we left that whatever the state wanted him to do, it was his duty to comply. If it meant spying on his teenage daughter, he would do it. And if she was involved with the troublemakers, he would be the first to hand her over to the political police."

"Surely, he was joking," Mrs. Gray said.

"No, he wasn't. He would probably send his One to the dungeons, if he thought it would please the state."

Louis was exaggerating, but not by much. Charlie had watched his father get passed over for promotion after promotion. Louis was a brilliant scientist and an extraordinary worker, but he was a poor actor. He had difficulty concealing his contempt for those in charge. They recognized this, and that is why, after many years of exceptional service, he was still a technical worker. He never moved up, while other, inferior workers rose higher in the government ranks. The current magistrate was one of these people. A few years ago Louis was staying late, correcting Mr. Conner's mistakes, but because Mr. Conner was a yes-man for the state, he was now Louis's boss.

"Oh, no," Mrs. Gray said, her hand going to her throat. "I was telling Mrs. Jones just before we boarded the ship that I was looking forward to grocery shopping on Earth without the state knowing how many bananas I have in my cart. Do you suppose she told her husband?"

Mrs. Gray started hyperventilating. She was on the verge of a nervous fit. Louis had to talk her down. "Helen, it's OK. She probably thought you were joking. Anyway, she's not that bright. She probably forgot all about it before she had a chance to say anything to her husband."

Helen seemed to calm down then. Louis always knew how to diffuse an intense situation with his wife. She turned her focus back on Charlie then. "You know, dear, I hope you at least *try* to make friends."

Charlie sighed. "Mom, what would I have in common with a sweaty Earthan?"

Helen turned to her husband then. "Louis, I told you we should have let him stay on Sentria. Find his One."

"Helen, we've already discussed this. Charlie's place is here with us."

"Louis, you can be so stubborn," she said.

"And you can be such a nag," Louis added. The tenderness that Louis had just shown his wife a few moments earlier was gone now. His parents didn't argue often, and they never raised their voices. They believed in civil discourse. But like most of his people, they had mastered the art of saying the vilest things to each other in the most pleasant tones.

"May I be excused?" Charlie asked.

"Yes, you may," Helen said.

Charlie put his plate in the sink, topped off his coffee mug, and headed upstairs to his room. His parents spoke softly, but Charlie could still hear everything they said. Even they did not realize just how keen Charlie's sense of hearing was.

"If we had stayed on Sentria, Charlie would already be settled down," Helen whispered.

"You don't know that, Helen. He had an opportunity to marry last spring, and he didn't do it. And you didn't even like the girl."

"That's not the point," Helen said.

"Then what exactly is the point?" Louis countered.

"He's eighteen now; he'll be almost nineteen when we return. It's not that easy to find your One when you're that old. He can't get close to anyone, because he's always afraid he'll be uprooted again by your work."

"Now, Helen, that's not fair…"

That's when Charlie filtered out their conversation. It wasn't always great to overhear others when they were talking about you. He turned on his radio. One of the first things he did when he got back to Earth was find a station that played fifties music. He pulled *Brave New World* out of his backpack and began reading. He couldn't put it down. Charlie read the entire book in one sitting. He still wasn't tired, so he flipped open his PCD and insta-searched books like *Brave New World*. The title *1984* popped up, and Charlie started reading it. He was shocked. If a Sentrian author dared to write anything so incendiary and blatantly critical of the government, he would be thrown into the dungeons. Charlie was learning through his reading and research that Earthans were much different from what he had been taught. They weren't dim-witted feral animals. There was another side to them. It was a proindividual, independent mentality. They had the freedom to go where they chose, say what they wanted to say, and make decisions about their own lives. Their freedom, especially from an intrusive government, was very important to them.

By contrast, his people only had two aspects of their lives that were free from government control. The first was that God chose your One, your soul mate, and the government could not interfere with God's master plan. The second was privacy in your own home, but that only extended to your immediate family. If you congregated in your house with a group of friends, and the leaders found out about it, chances were good that someone was wearing a bug. With so many Sentrians eager to please the state officials, it was hard to know whom to trust.

There used to be a third law regarding the day of rest. It was designated a holy day to worship the Lord. Unfortunately, the current government infringed on this right whenever they needed the people to work longer hours for the good of the state.

Charlie supposed they were fortunate to still have two of the three rights. That was likely due to King Augustan. He was king of Sentria several centuries ago. King Augustan noted that if the people had a few rights that were guaranteed, things they could control, they worked harder and cooperated with the state rather than trying to rebel. That's when the privacy laws were enacted. There had been no war on Sentria since.

However, things were about to change. Charlie could see the signs of unrest among his people before he left for Earth. The younger Sentrians were growing weary of all the restrictions on their lives. A group known as the troublemakers was making its presence known. Small uprisings were occurring throughout the Sentrian provinces. Charlie knew that was the real reason his father had insisted he come on this mission with them. If the government decided to round up a group of its enemies, Charlie would be targeted simply because he was eighteen and not married. Being an older single on Sentria would automatically place him under suspicion. It would matter very little that Charlie knew no one in the troublemaker's movement.

By Friday Lilly had gotten adjusted to her new schedule. The teachers were already piling on the homework, but that was to be expected. On the way to school, Ian was frantically finishing up geometry homework, and Beth was reading *The Scarlet Letter*. Lilly wished she could read something else. *Brave New World* was getting on her nerves.

Lilly was calm as she walked into English class. Most of her classmates were not. They were rushing to finish up the chapters and cramming for the quiz. Charlie was the exception. He observed the Earthan female's demeanor. Liliana did not seem like the stereotypical Earthan teenager he had always heard about. She was not ignorant or unsophisticated. She was quite studious, spending her free time reading a book or working on schoolwork. When any of the teachers asked her a question she knew the answer, and it wasn't just something she regurgitated from a textbook. There was true thought behind it.

He was the first to finish his quiz, with Lilly a close second. This gave Charlie time to ponder things while the other students were still fumbling through the quiz. Liliana, he saw, had fished a paperback out of her backpack and was reading. She was a pretty girl, and intelligent: a desirable combination in any galaxy.

Yes, Liliana was different than other Earthans and would be quite a catch on Sentria, except for one thing. Sentrians would never entertain the thought of courting a low-class, sweaty Earthan. Even the thought of it was repulsive. Charlie frowned. Such a strange thing to pop into his head. He supposed he was just really tired of being alone.

There were no band practices on Friday afternoons because of the football games. For Lilly, it was hardly worth going home. She and her French horn children had already decided to get something to eat and just come back and hang out at the band hall until the game started.

Out in the parking lot, Lilly saw Charlie walking to his car. He looked as glum as ever. She hesitated. Inviting Charlie *would* be the nice thing to do.

"Charlie, wait," she called out to him and waved. He turned at the sound of his name. It was Liliana. She was walking toward him.

"What's up?" he asked, hoping that was the appropriate Earthan greeting.

"Um, I was just wondering…I mean, we have a couple of hours before we have to be back for the game, and some of us were going to get something to eat. Do you want to come with?" she asked meekly.

Charlie was surprised. "Oh," he said. He really should decline. His house was just a few minutes away, but she was being nice. She wanted to include him. It might hurt her feelings if he turned her down. A voice in Charlie's head told him, "I don't think this is a good idea." Charlie told it, "I know what I'm doing."

"Sure. I'd like that, but I need to call my mom. She's expecting me home," Charlie said.

"Yes, of course. We'll wait."

Charlie walked to the band hall to use the phone. He wished he could whip out his PCD and send his mother a message, but that technology was not available on Earth in 1988.

"What's the holdup?" Ian asked. He was already sitting in the front seat, blasting the air conditioning and fiddling with the radio.

"I invited Charlie. I need you to sit in back with Beth."

Ian's head jerked up. "Freakshow? You can't be serious."

Lilly rolled her eyes. "Look, I feel kind of bad for him. He's always by himself. How would you feel if you were the new kid?"

"Great. Now we're picking up strays," Ian grumbled, but he got out of the front seat and moved to the back.

"It won't kill you to sit next to me." Beth smiled.

"It might. Scoot over," Ian said.

Charlie picked up the phone and dialed his parents' house. After the second ring, his mother answered. "Mom, I won't be home before the game. Some of the band members are going to eat at a local restaurant and have invited me to join them."

"Charlie, that's wonderful. You've taken my advice, I see, interacting with your Earthan peers. I know they aren't like your friends on Sentria, but they can't be that bad. Try to enjoy yourself."

"I will," Charlie said.

"Your father and I will be at the game tonight to see you march."

"You don't have to do that," Charlie said.

"Sure we do. We at least need to show up to one game or the Earthans might grow suspicious." Like most Sentrians, his mother was hyperparanoid.

"OK, Mom. I really need to go. They're waiting."

"OK, Charlie. Love you," she said.

"Bye, Mom." Charlie hung up the phone and walked out to Lilly's Jeep.

"Charlie, this is Ian and Beth," Lilly said.

"Hello," said Beth politely. Ian said nothing. He was still miffed he got booted out of the front seat.

"Nice to meet you," Charlie said.

"We were going to McDonald's, if that's all right," Lilly said.

"Absolutely," Charlie said. McDonald's restaurants were just starting up in the fifties, when he had been in New Mexico. He had never been to one, but he knew it was a popular place for Earthan teenagers. Lilly pulled out of the school parking lot and headed down the road.

"So, are you liking Clear Lake?" Lilly asked.

"I like it," Charlie lied. Again, he did not want to hurt Lilly's feelings. "And marching band is different. I think I'll like it more once we march in a few games. I'm still trying to get the hang of it." Charlie hoped he was using Earthan idioms appropriately.

"You seem to be doing great so far," Lilly said. She caught sight of Ian in the rearview mirror. He was mocking her, mouthing everything she said. Then he put his index finger in his mouth like he was going to puke. Lilly shot him a dirty look. "I hear you're a great trumpet player."

"Thanks," Charlie said. He didn't know if he should return the compliment, since he didn't actually know anything about her French horn playing. He decided to change the subject. "I noticed you read a lot. What was that book you were reading after the quiz in English today?"

"It was *Pride and Prejudice*." Lilly was surprised. "So you like to read?" Most of her friends read for school, not for pleasure.

"Oh yes," Charlie said. "How do you like *Brave New World*?"

"It's not really my style," Lilly confessed. "You like it?"

"I think it's fascinating. Huxley paints a very bizarre and dark future. The people just go along with it. They think they have it so great, but nothing could be further from the truth."

"That subject matter can be interesting, but if I'm going to read dystopian stuff, I prefer *Atlas Shrugged* or *1984* to *Brave New World*," Lilly said.

So Lilly had read *1984*. He was liking this girl more and more. "Yeah, I really enjoyed *1984*, but I've never heard of *Atlas Shrugged*. What's it about?"

"The individual over the collective. That creativity must not be stifled by an oppressive government. I have a copy of it at home. I'll bring it to school on Monday and let you borrow it."

"Thanks," Charlie said. They sat in silence for a moment.

"I like your car," Lilly said, trying to keep the conversation going.

"Thanks. It was my father's," Charlie said.

"Classic Mustangs are really cool," Beth added. "Say something," she hissed at Ian.

"Does it give you any trouble? I know those older cars break down a lot." Beth elbowed him in the ribs.

"No, it runs fine," Charlie said. Lilly wondered if Charlie noticed how rude Ian was acting. If he did, he didn't show it.

"Mom, can we go inside? I don't want to eat at the band hall," Ian whined.

"Yes, of course. Then you can go to the playground and hang out with kids that are more on your level," Lilly said. She was only half-joking.

"Good one, Mom," Beth said.

Charlie was confused. "Why do they call you Mom?"

"Because I'm a senior, and I kind of look out for the younger horn players. Like a French horn mom. I know it's kind of lame," Lilly explained.

"No, I think it's cool," Charlie said, incorporating some eighties' slang.

Ian and Beth jumped out of the car as soon as Lilly parked, beating Charlie and Lilly inside. Charlie held the door open for Lilly, and she had to admit she liked it. They walked up to the counter, where Beth and Ian were already paying.

"What do you like to get here, Liliana?" Charlie asked. Only Abuela had called her Liliana, but she didn't mind. Lilly liked the way he pronounced her name. The L sound rolling off his tongue was almost lyrical.

"I usually get a Quarter Pounder with Cheese, plain and dry. And a supersize Diet Coke," she told him.

"Can I help you?" the cashier asked in an utterly bored tone.

Charlie nodded. "We'll have two Quarter Pounders with Cheese," Charlie said. He looked at Lilly to make sure he was getting it right.

"One of them plain and dry." Lilly spoke up.

"Yes," Charlie continued, "and a supersize Diet Coke and a supersize coffee."

The cashier gave Charlie a strange look. "Did you say a supersize coffee?" Charlie nodded.

"Hey, Jason," the cashier called over her shoulder. "Do we do supersize *coffees*?"

"I guess so." The guy named Jason shrugged.

"It'll be a few minutes," the cashier said. "We have to make a fresh pot."

Lilly tried to hand the cashier her money, but Charlie insisted on paying. As they walked to the table to sit with Ian and Beth, Lilly told him, "Thanks for getting my dinner, but you didn't have to. What I mean is, I didn't expect you to…"

"You're welcome, Liliana," Charlie interrupted.

"Her name's Lilly," Ian said.

"You're right. I'm sorry," Charlie said. "I just really like the name Liliana."

"It's OK. You can call me Liliana if you want."

Beth's and Ian's jaws dropped. For as long as they had known her, she had gone by Lilly and corrected anyone who called her anything different. The cashier brought over Charlie's supersize coffee. "Do you want cream or sugar?"

"No thanks." Charlie took a sip.

"So you don't drink Coke?" Lilly asked. Ian and Beth were wondering the same thing.

"I have sensitive teeth," he said, trying to make a plausible excuse. "The cold bothers them."

"Dude, that's weird," Ian said as he dipped a French fry in catsup.

Look who's talking, Charlie thought. French fries and hamburgers did *not* go together. And who would dip French fries in catsup when grape jelly was the obvious choice? Charlie looked over at Lilly's plain burger. "That's really how you like to eat your hamburger?" he asked.

Lilly nodded between bites. "I'm kind of a meat, cheese, and bun girl."

After they ate, they returned to the band hall to get ready. Many of the girls styled their hair in French braids or ponytails so that they could more easily tuck their hair under their hats. The drum line was already lined up and practicing their cadences. Lilly could feel the excitement building for the first half-time show of the year. Michael had the band line up to file out to the bleachers. The drum line started a cadence, and the band marched out.

Although he knew of football from his first trip to Earth, this would be Charlie's first opportunity to actually see it played. During the first quarter of the game, he tried to figure out the point of the game. A group of large Earthan males wearing the same uniform tried to keep a brown, oval-shaped ball away from another group of males dressed in a different uniform. They would run into each other violently until an official blew his whistle. Meanwhile, a group of scantily clad females climbed on top of each other, yelling and chanting rhymes about how great their team was. To Charlie it seemed more like some kind of bizarre mating ritual than a sport.

The band exited the stands in preparation for the half-time show. Charlie spotted Louis and Helen in the crowd. They put on a good show of being proud parents supporting their son in his musical endeavors, though Charlie knew this would be the last game they attended.

Michelle was also in attendance for the first game of the year. Even with her hectic schedule, she tried to make it to the home games. She saw Lilly and waved enthusiastically. Lilly gave her a small wave before Michael called the band to attention.

The drill team performed first. The band played as the Lake Flairs entered the field. Charlie tried to keep his eyes on the drum major and not on the females in short skirts kicking their legs up and wiggling their body parts right in front of him. It's not as if he didn't know they'd be here. In fact, he'd seen them dance before in practice, but at practice they had more clothes on.

Finally it was time for the marching show. When they started to play the music, Charlie finally got it. So many things that just did not make sense to him during practice made sense to him now. He could see the big picture. He realized how magnificent it was when the music and the design on the field meshed.

The band marched off the field to enthusiastic applause. When they got back to their seats, they removed their hats. With the exception of Charlie, everyone's hair was plastered to their heads from sweat. Charlie was thankful no one seemed to notice. The band boosters began handing out cold drinks. One of the women handed Charlie a Coke, and he wrinkled his nose. "What?" she asked him. "You want diet instead?"

Charlie shook his head no, took the Coke, and went to his seat. Matt was talking to one of the trombone players. "You want this?" Charlie showed him the Coke can.

"You don't want it?" he asked.

Charlie shook his head.

Matt took the can. "Thanks, man."

Dan saw the exchange between Matt and Charlie. "So you don't want a Coke, Charlie Brown?"

"It's Charlie Gray," Charlie said evenly.

"Whatever. Perhaps you'd prefer Sprite." He shook up the can he was holding and opened it, spraying it all over Charlie. "Whoops! Sorry, Charlie," Dan said, imitating the tuna commercials. Charlie just sat there, saying nothing.

Matt got in Dan's face. "That was really uncool, dude."

"Look," Ian said to Beth and Lilly. "Dan just sprayed his drink all over Charlie."

Lilly turned to see. Charlie didn't react. He just sat there, trying to find something to wipe his face with. "What a jerk!" Lilly exclaimed. She couldn't believe how calm Charlie was. He wasn't even angry. Lilly was furious *for* him. He didn't deserve this; he never bothered anyone. She knew Dan was just pushing him around because Charlie was such a little guy.

The football team scored a touchdown then. "Go back to your seat, Matt," Dan said. Matt went back and picked up his trumpet, and everyone stood up to play the fight song.

"C'mon, Mom. Let's go," urged Ian. It was customary for the band members to go to Bennigan's after the game to celebrate.

"Just a minute, Ian," Lilly said. She quickly scanned the band hall for Charlie. She wanted to make sure he was OK.

"If you're looking for Charlie, he already left." Beth told her. Lilly blushed. She would have to be more careful. Beth was far too observant.

"Let's go," she said, trying to hide her disappointment. Ian whooped and ran out of the band-hall doors.

Lilly, who usually loved the weekend, found herself looking forward to Monday. Well, maybe not Monday so much as seeing Charlie again. He was a strange little dude, but still, she had enjoyed talking with him. Best of all, he was a reader like herself. She put *Atlas Shrugged* in her backpack so she wouldn't forget it.

Charlie was no worse off after the Sprite incident. Despite his run-in with Dan, he still looked forward to school on Monday and band practice. He thought it was because now he was actually excited about marching band, but that was only part of it.

When Lilly sat down at the lunch table, Matt and Claire were in a tiff. They refused to talk to one another. Here we go again, Lilly thought. "What's going on?" Lilly asked, hoping that would break the ice a little.

Claire crossed her arms, and Matt turned his back to her. Finally Claire spoke up. "Tell Matt I'm not talking to him until he apologizes."

"You can tell Claire that maybe when she's asleep tonight, she'll hear it in her dreams," Matt answered.

"Enough," Lilly said. The whole situation was absurd. Lilly thought that if they really didn't want to talk to each other, they should give up this "you tell him this" or "you tell her that" game. Besides they really didn't need a go-between. They could each hear what the other said. There was no way she was going to spend her too-short lunch period with these two. If she reveled in immaturity, she could always go sit with Ian. There was an empty seat by Susan, an oboe player and a senior. She and Lilly had been in a few of the same classes last year and Lilly thought she was pretty nice. Then she saw Charlie sitting at his usual table all by himself. She grabbed her tray and walked over.

Charlie heard footfalls heading in his direction and lifted his head up out of the book he was reading. "Liliana," he said, getting up out of his seat.

"Mind if I join you?" she asked.

"No, of course not." He pulled her chair out for her.

Did boys even do that anymore? Lilly asked herself. "Thank you," she said. Charlie just smiled at her. Lilly pointed at his food. "You're smart to bring your lunch. It's way safer than the cafeteria gruel."

"But you're eating the cafeteria gruel," Charlie observed.

"Not exactly." Lilly picked up a carrot stick. "The salad bar doesn't count. Oh, before I forget," Lilly said, rummaging through her backpack. "Here." She laid the tome on the table.

"*Atlas Shrugged*," Charlie said. "You remembered."

"Anything for a fellow bibliophile."

"You know, you don't speak like most Ear—I mean, teenagers," Charlie said. "You seem…"

"Older?" Lilly finished for him.

He nodded. "Well, you don't act like most teenagers either," Lilly said.

At that moment, Ian stood on his chair along with three other guys. They all had French fries hanging out of their nostrils and were pretending to fight with invisible light sabers.

"I guess not," Charlie said. The bell rang. Charlie waited for Lilly to rise, then he stood up, too. "Well, if you're up for some mature companionship, meet me in government. Sixth period."

"Got it," Lilly replied.

Lilly began sitting with Charlie instead of at the band table. They started a book exchange. She lent him some of her favorite titles, and he lent her some of his. Then they would discuss them during lunch. In the afternoons, Charlie would join Lilly and her "French horn children" on their trek to McDonald's for supersize drinks. By the end of the first week, the McDonald's crew knew to have a pot of coffee ready at five o'clock.

Ian also learned to go straight to the backseat in the afternoon. He wasn't happy about it and grumbled when he could. Then Lilly started taking Beth and Ian straight home after getting drinks instead of dropping Charlie back off at the band hall first. That really rubbed Ian the wrong way. One afternoon as they were leaving the school, Charlie reached over to pick up Lilly's horn case to put it in the back of her Jeep.

Ian grabbed it first. "I've got it," he said sternly.

Lilly started the car, and Charlie said, "Oh, I forgot my wallet. I'll be right back." Like a lot of the guys, Charlie locked his wallet in his car during marching practice.

"Great. How long is that going to take?" Ian griped.

"Ian," Beth and Lilly said at the same time.

"Look, if you guys want to go without me…" Charlie began.

"No, of course we'll wait. It's totally fine," Lilly said, smiling at Charlie. When he left to go to his car, she turned to face Ian. "What is your problem? I'm sick of your rudeness. If you can't be nice to Charlie, then you can just find another ride home."

"Chill. I'm just trying to look out for you. I don't want just *anyone* dating my mom."

Lilly nearly choked. *Did he say dating? Is that what he thinks?*

Charlie was back at his car, but he heard what Ian said, and it troubled him. *Dating? Is this considered dating on Earth?*

"We aren't dating," Lilly objected, but she could feel her cheeks get hot. She turned her head forward so that Ian and Beth couldn't see. "Charlie is a friend, and I expect you to be nice to him."

Charlie sighed in relief. Lilly didn't think of him in the romantic sense at all.

"Yeah, whatever," Ian said and looked out the window. The three of them sat in silence until Charlie returned.

"Got it." Charlie waved his wallet.

Lilly smiled. "Great. Let's go."

The next morning, Lilly picked up Beth as usual, but instead of getting in the backseat, she sat in the front seat. Lilly knew something was up then. Beth always left the front seat for Ian. "Ian called me," Beth explained. "He's getting a ride from his dad."

"Oh, OK," Lilly said. Beth looked at her, wanting more of a response than Lilly gave.

"You know," Beth said, "Ian's a dork who is incapable of thinking before he speaks, but he's not a bad guy."

"I know. I know. I just wish he wouldn't act like a little turd around my friend. It's embarrassing," Lilly said.

"Don't you mean *boyfriend*?" Beth asked pointedly.

For the second time in less than twelve hours Lilly felt her face go bright red, and for the second time in twelve hours she felt the need to get defensive. "Not you, too, Beth."

"If you aren't fooling Ian, how in the world do you think you're fooling me?"

"Look, I don't know what our relationship is, or if we have a relationship, even. Charlie's never asked me out. But I do know I like to talk to him, be around him. I don't need Ian to make things harder than they have to be."

"OK. Fair enough," Beth said. "I'll talk to Ian and make him play nice. You know he's just jealous in a 'I don't like the new guy in my mom's life' kind of way. For the last year he's been your main man, and now you're replacing him."

"Yeah, I know. I really don't want to do anything drastic like boot him out of my car. Just let him know he will always be my firstborn band son. He's not getting replaced."

"I will," Beth said. "And Lilly, why don't you just ask Charlie out? I mean it's 1988, not 1958. Clear up all this confusion."

"No. No way," Lilly said shaking her head. "If he can't figure it out, I'm not going to figure it out for him."

They got to school early, since they didn't have to stop for Ian. Lilly went in the band hall and waited for Charlie, and Beth went to go find Ian.

At lunch Charlie thanked Lilly for letting him borrow *One Flew Over the Cuckoo's Nest*. "Wow, I just gave you that book two days ago, and you've already finished it?"

"Yeah, well, it was interesting. That Nurse Ratched kind of scares me. She's got way too much power."

"She's definitely one of those people who feel the need to control others," Lilly said.

' "I was kind of surprised. It's so unlike any of the other books you've lent me," Charlie said.

"Well, sometimes I veer out of period romance into other genres," Lilly said.

"There's nothing wrong with period romance. I liked *Jane Eyre,* and *Wuthering Heights* was pretty good," Charlie told her.

"I thought the same thing about *A Separate Peace,* but *The Lord of the Rings* did nothing for me," Lilly admitted.

"To each his own," Charlie said amiably. "Actually I tend to veer toward sci-fi myself."

"Then how come you haven't lent me any sci-fi? You've been holding out on me."

"No, not really. Most of the sci-fi I was talking about are movies and television. Like this show I like from the fifties. *Twilight Zone.*"

"I love the old *Twilight Zone*," Lilly said.

"You're kidding. How would you know about that show? It's so old."

"And just as relevant today as the day it was made, probably more so," Lilly said. "I wish I had known you like sci-fi. That adds a whole other level of books and movies we can discuss."

"Liliana, I wanted to talk to you about something else." He glanced over in Ian's direction. "Maybe I should discontinue the trips to McDonald's with you after band practice. I don't want to cause problems with you and Ian."

"Don't worry about *that*." Lilly laughed. "Ian will have to understand that he's not the only friend I have in the world. Trust me, he'd drop me in a heartbeat if he ever got a real girlfriend."

"So you don't think he's jealous? He's awfully possessive," Charlie said. Being Sentrian, that was one thing Charlie knew a lot about. Sentrians had turned jealousy into an art form.

"No, not the way you mean. Besides, guys don't think about me that way," she said and bit her lip. She wished she could unsay it.

"What do you mean guys don't think about you 'that way'? Any guy in this school would be lucky to go out with you."

"No, I'm not, like, putting myself down. Look," she said, pointing at Nikki Thompson, the snotty-but-beautiful brunette with a perfect figure. "That's what guys want."

"Some might," Charlie agreed. "Yes, she's pretty, and she does have a curvaceous body. But Liliana, you have a curvaceous brain." Now it was Charlie's turn to be worried. Maybe he had said too much.

"A curvaceous brain? That's the most unique compliment I've ever received. Thanks." Lilly had to admit she liked that Charlie thought she was smart.

"You're welcome," Charlie said. The bell rang, and they were both relieved. After that exchange, anything they said would have been awkward.

Charlie was completely distracted throughout his afternoon classes. Before now, his feelings for Liliana had just been bubbling under the surface, easy to dismiss. But now there was no denying the attraction he felt for her. The voice in his head told him, "Remember she's an Earthan, strictly off limits." Charlie told the voice, "I know, I know, you don't have to remind me."

Lilly, too, wondered about Charlie. She really liked him; he was fun to be around and interesting to talk to. He definitely respected her, but was that enough to build a relationship on? Didn't there have to be that spark? She didn't know. She had never been in love, but she thought there needed to be some sort of physical attraction. Geez! How shallow could she be? Then she remembered what Beth had said that morning about not fooling anyone. *If they can see it, then why can't I?*

The next period the teacher was just reviewing old material, so Lilly decided to do what she always did when she was trying to put things in perspective. She tore a piece of paper out of her notebook and made a list.

Pros	Cons
Charlie is…	Charlie is…
Well-read	Very short
Intelligent	A fashion victim
Interesting to talk to	OK with his ugly glasses
Dependable	Weird
Attentive	
Loyal	

There were definitely more pros than cons; although, just glancing at the last three attributes in the pros column, it sounded like she was describing the family dog. Lilly looked over the cons. With the exceptions of height and weirdness, these were things that could be corrected. She was being superficial, she knew. But the bottom line was this: Charlie. Was. Odd. If she dated him, people would think she was strange, too. She would like to believe she was above all that, but unfortunately she was just as susceptible to peer pressure as anyone else. Lilly tore up the sheet of paper and threw it in the trash at the end of class.

She walked into the bathroom before fifth period to straighten her barrette and reapply her lip gloss. She stared at her reflection. "Who are you to judge? No one appointed you arbiter of what's cool." She was a freaking band geek, not exactly the elective of choice of the in-crowd.

After thinking about it all during fifth period, she came to some conclusions. Yes, she might not be physically attracted to him, but there was some kind of attraction there. Why else was she looking forward to seeing him again in government and spending time with him this afternoon? She didn't have to make any decisions right now. Maybe she would just wait and see what happened.

Toward the end of the school day, it began to rain. The band was waiting in the band hall to see if it would clear up. Lilly was sitting on her French horn case staring out the window when Ian approached her. "I'm sorry I've been a jerk, Mom."

"Ian, I appreciate the apology, but you don't owe it to me, you owe it to him," she said, motioning to the trumpet section. Ian nodded and walked over to where Charlie was standing. He was staring out the window and hoping Lilly had brought an umbrella.

Ian's ego prevented him from coming right out and saying he was sorry. Instead, he asked Charlie, "Are we cool, dude?"

Charlie got the gist of what he was saying. "Yeah we're cool."

Ian gave Charlie a thumbs up and walked back to where Lilly and Beth were sitting. "We're good," he announced. "Now if they would just hurry up and cancel band practice, we could go to McDonald's."

Ian got his wish. A few minutes later Mr. Patterson made an announcement. "Folks, it looks like the rain is not letting up. Marching practice is canceled. But it would be an excellent opportunity for you to go home and practice the music. Especially the bones." Most of the band didn't even hear the last part. They started packing up the second he said practice was canceled.

Ian stifled a cheer. Lilly peered out the band-hall windows. Now it wasn't just raining; it was pouring.

"I guess we'll have to make a run for it," she said. She didn't mind. A little rain never hurt anyone.

"No," Charlie panicked. "Give me your car keys, and I'll bring the car closer. Ian can come with me. I think I have something we can use for cover in my car."

"It's OK, I don't mind the rain," Lilly said.

"Liliana, I insist." Charlie wasn't just being chivalrous. He *couldn't* allow her to get wet. It meant something different to Sentrian males than to Earthan boys. Charlie was already more attracted to Lilly than he ought to be. He did not need the added temptation of having an image of her wet hair and body seared into his mind.

Ian followed Charlie out of the double entry doors of the band hall. Truth be told, he wanted to get a closer look at Charlie's Mustang. "Here's the plan," Charlie told him. "I've got an old blanket in my trunk, but if we walk it back from where I'm currently parked, it will be soaked through by the time we get halfway across the parking lot. I need you to move my car as close to the band-hall doors as possible before you take the blanket out. I'll move Liliana's Jeep as close as I can to the band hall, then we'll make a run for it."

"Wouldn't it be easier if we just took your car?" Ian asked.

"I can maybe fit all four of us in my car, but there's no way I can fit our instruments, too."

"Dude, I don't even have a driver's license," Ian admitted.

"I trust you." Charlie tossed him the keys.

Ian whooped and ran to Charlie's Mustang. Even though he ran full speed, he was soaked long before he got to Charlie's car. He backed the Mustang into the parking spot so that the trunk was closest to the doors.

Then he jumped out, opened the trunk, and ran with the blanket through the doors of the band hall.

Lilly's Jeep was bigger, and Charlie couldn't get a spot as close as Ian. He was still several feet away. Charlie ran into the band hall. Water was dripping down his face. The girls had moved all their instruments over near the band-hall doors. They picked them up to take them along when Charlie stopped them. "No instruments. Ian and I are already wet. We'll come back and get them after you two are in the car. Charlie picked up one end of the blanket and instructed Ian to pick up the other.

"Ladies, if you wouldn't mind stepping under the blanket."

When Beth and Lilly were sufficiently covered up, Charlie kicked the band-hall door open with his foot. He and Ian walked the girls over to Lilly's Jeep. Lilly opened the door and slid into the driver's seat, and Beth climbed into the backseat. Charlie and Ian ran back to get the instruments and put them in Lilly's trunk. Charlie closed the hatch, satisfied that the girls' modesty was preserved.

Charlie climbed into the passenger seat. He was completely soaked. He couldn't even see through the lenses of his glasses. Lilly hadn't really been paying attention to what he was doing, but she suddenly looked up. What she saw changed everything. Charlie took off his glasses looking for something to wipe them on. Lilly couldn't believe her eyes. Without those awful glasses, Charlie looked like a different person. He was beautiful. And perfect. And she couldn't stop staring at him. His eyes were the color of dark chocolate. With those hideous glasses she had never even noticed before. The transformation was amazing.

He finally found a tissue in Lilly's glove box to dry his glasses. That was when he noticed Lilly staring at him. "Is something wrong?"

"Not even," Lilly said under her breath. Then she shook her head no. Of course Charlie had heard. That response puzzled him, but he shook it off. Lilly just sat there, staring at him, until he finally put his glasses back on.

"OK, let's go," Lilly said, clearing her throat. She put the car in gear, and they drove off.

After dropping off Beth and Ian, Lilly drove back to the school parking lot to deliver Charlie to his car. The rain had slacked off; there was only a drizzle now. Charlie decided then and there that he was going to get two umbrellas: one for his car and one for hers. He wouldn't be caught off guard again.

"I'm glad you and Ian are cool now, but I still can't believe you let him drive your car. I kind of thought the Mustang was your baby," Lilly said.

It was. "Keeping you dry is important," Charlie said. He turned to open the door, and Lilly asked him, "Charlie, do you *have* to wear glasses?"

"Of course," he said. All Sentrians suffered from severe myopia. "That's an odd question."

"What I mean is, can you wear contacts or a different pair of glasses?"

"I suppose," Charlie said. "But why would I? These are perfectly fine."

Lilly sighed.

"What?" Charlie asked.

"Nothing. Forget I brought it up," Lilly said. "I'll just see you tomorrow." She turned the key in the ignition.

"No wait," Charlie said, grabbing her hand and turning the ignition off. "I want to hear what you have to say."

"No, you're going to think I'm really shallow."

"I doubt that," Charlie said.

"OK, I know I'm being petty, but I really don't like your glasses."

"Oh," Charlie said. They were quite fashionable back in the fifties but maybe not so much now.

"And when you came in from the rain and took off your glasses to wipe them off, I kinda noticed that you're, well, you're a nice-looking guy, Charlie," Lilly said, blushing. "I just don't think those glasses do you any favors." She hoped she hadn't offended him.

He started laughing. "They're really that bad?"

"Yeah, they're awful." Now she was smiling, too.

"Well, OK," Charlie said. "I'm open to change."

"I am so glad to hear it," Lilly said animatedly. "My mom knows this great eye doctor, and…"

"Whoa, Liliana, take a breath," Charlie said.

"Sorry," Lilly said. "But I could go with you if you want."

"You want to go, don't you?" Charlie asked.

"I could help you choose another pair," Lilly suggested.

"Then go ahead, make the appointment."

A week later, Charlie had his new glasses. Lilly thought the improvement in his appearance was huge. She even convinced him to get a pair of contacts, although he thought he'd never wear them. He couldn't care less what he wore as long as he could see, but he was happy that these new glasses pleased her.

To Lilly, it seemed like she and Charlie were the couple/non-couple. They were inseparable at school, and she was sure that everyone thought they were together, but they had never even gone out on a date. Heck, they'd never even held hands. Lilly was starting to feel defective.

Beth was getting fed up with their non-romance. She decided to take matters into her own hands. She cornered Charlie one morning before school. "What's up with you and Lilly, anyway?"

"What do you mean? Has she said something to you?" Charlie was concerned now.

"What I mean is that she doesn't know if you two are even together. So are you going to ask her out, or what?"

"I don't know, I haven't thought about it," Charlie lied. Going out with Liliana was *all* he thought about.

"Well, you sure are giving mixed signals. Look, if you don't want to go out with her, fine. Your loss. But be fair to her. She really cares about you. So let her know something one way or the other."

Charlie let that sink in. She really cares about you. Those were Beth's exact words. Was he being unfair to her? He considered Liliana his best friend on Earth. He didn't want that to change. But how could he take it to the next level? It was all so complicated. If he did nothing, would she still want to be friends, or would she want more and decide to look for someone else? The thought of Liliana dating someone other than himself was unsettling. He had to make a decision. The conversation with Beth was the catalyst he needed to move forward. Charlie spent the rest of the day getting his nerve up. After band practice he approached Lilly and blurted out, "Liliana, I was thinking of going to the planetarium on Saturday. Would you maybe want to go with me?"

Lilly jerked her head up. The invitation took her by surprise. "Like on a date or something?" It was a fair question.

Charlie swallowed. "I would like it to be a date, but if that makes you uncomfortable, then would you consider spending a day at the planetarium with a good friend?" There. He said it. Now there was no doubt where he stood.

"Then let's consider it a date," Lilly said.

———

Charlie was fine with his decision until he pulled into his driveway that afternoon. Although he had no intention of telling them about Liliana, his parents were a vivid reminder that what he was doing was wrong.

"Good, you're home," Helen Gray exclaimed. "It seems like these band practices are getting later and later."

Charlie sat down at the dinner table. His father was again absorbed in his paper. "If you don't need me around the house this Saturday, I was thinking of joining the science club for a trip to the planetarium."

Louis put his paper down. "You sure are taking this edict from the elders seriously. First band, now science club. You're really immersing yourself in Earthan teenage culture."

"Band is time-consuming, but I would want to go to the planetarium either way. I just thought it would be more fun going with a group."

"It's fine with me, if it's all right with your mother," he said. Helen Gray nodded her approval. Charlie finished his dinner, went upstairs to his room, and lay down on his bed. The voice in his head told him, "You are really crossing the line now." He ignored the voice and closed his eyes. His thoughts turned to Liliana, the reason for his rebellion.

Lilly fussed with her hair for about an hour before Charlie was to pick her up. She had already changed her clothes three times, finally settling on a pair of jeans and a sapphire-blue shirt. Now, she was sitting in the living room, just waiting for the doorbell to ring. When it finally did, she jumped up immediately to answer it.

"Hello, Liliana."

"Hi, Charlie."

"I suppose I should introduce myself to your parents," he said.

"Well, it's just my mom, and she's at work. But she knows we're going to the planetarium, and she's cool with it." Lilly had told her mom she was going to the planetarium with a *friend*. She never mentioned it was a boy. Lilly decided to put her mom on a need-to-know basis.

"Well, OK. If you're ready, we'll head out." They walked down the drive to Charlie's Mustang. "I like the blue," Charlie said.

"What?" Liliana asked. She assumed he was referring to his car.

"Your blouse. I like blue, and that color looks good on you. You should wear it more often."

"Thanks," Lilly said. It wasn't, "Liliana, I'm enthralled with your beauty, and my heart skips a beat every time you are near." But it was a compliment, and she would take it.

Charlie opened the passenger-side door for her. This was Lilly's first time to ride in Charlie's car. Ian was right; it was an awesome ride.

"I finally get to drive you for a change," Charlie said. He flipped on the radio. An oldies station was playing. He started to change it, but Lilly stopped him.

"Wait, I recognize this song. What's the name of it?"

"'A Summer Place,'" Charlie answered.

"I like it," Lilly said.

"Yes, the song's pretty good, but the movie, I didn't like."

"I didn't even know there was a movie," Lilly said. "So why didn't you like it?"

"The subject matter. Infidelity."

Lilly hadn't been to the planetarium since she was eight years old. She enjoyed the show, but even more fascinating was Charlie's knowledge of astronomy. He told her all about the stars and constellations.

"You sure know a lot about space," Lilly remarked.

"Studying space is one of my hobbies," Charlie said.

Lilly was getting a glimpse into Charlie's life—his interests and preferences. At lunch and in the car after school, he always preferred to talk about her. She knew very little about his personal life, other than he liked to read and enjoyed the music and television shows from the fifties. Charlie lived in her world every day; for the first time, she was living in his.

After being at the crowded planetarium, Charlie wanted to take Lilly somewhere a little more private. "I was hoping you would be up for dinner. There's a place not too far from here that I really like."

"That would be great," she said.

Lilly was not surprised when they pulled up to an old-style diner. The clothes and hairstyles of the waitresses and the decor reminded her of the movie *Grease*.

"Wow, you really do like the fifties," she said to Charlie.

"We can go somewhere else if you prefer. I like the food here, and I thought you might too."

"No, this is great. I've never been here before, and I'd like to try it."

"Seating for two?" the friendly hostess asked.

"Yes, we'd like a booth, if one's available," Charlie told her.

"Sure, follow me," the hostess said, picking up silverware and menus on the way to the back of the restaurant. She showed them to a booth next to a window where they had a view of the avenue. The booths were tall, and when you sat in them it really felt private, as if there was no one else around.

"What can I get you to drink?" the plump, middle-aged waitress asked.

"What would you like?" Charlie asked.

"A Diet Coke," Lilly said.

"And I'll have a coffee, black." The woman nodded and walked off.

"So what's good here?" Lilly asked as she scanned the menu.

"Everything's good here, but I highly recommend the cheeseburger."

"Sounds good to me," Lilly told him.

When the waitress returned with the drinks, Charlie gave her their order. He specified Lilly's burger was to be plain and dry and asked the waitress to substitute chili for the fries with his own cheeseburger.

"You remembered," Lilly said.

"Meat, cheese, and bun girl," Charlie smiled. He reached over the table, "Would it be OK if I held your hand?"

Liliana nodded. This was the first time Charlie had ever initiated any type of physical contact. His hand was warm. It felt nice. Lilly thought she could sit there all night. They chatted about band, their favorite *Twilight Zone* episodes, and everything in between.

Even though Liliana was an Earthan, she was so similar to Charlie. She was very easy to talk to, and Charlie was relieved that most of the things she talked about were familiar to him, and he could keep up his end of the conversation. There was only one topic he didn't know anything about.

"So, are you excited about homecoming?" Lilly asked.

Charlie didn't know what homecoming was, so he didn't know if he should be excited or not. "Um, I don't know. Are you?" he asked.

"Well it's always nice to see the former band members and the game is kind of fun. And of course, there's the dance," Lilly hinted.

"Yeah," Charlie said. Not knowing what to say, he decided to change the subject. "So have you read the last few chapters of *Brave New World*? We have our final quiz on it Monday."

Lilly nodded and smiled, trying to hide her disappointment.

After dinner, Charlie drove Lilly home. He opened her car door for her and escorted her up the walk to her front door. "I really enjoyed our evening," Charlie said.

"Me, too."

"I hope we can do this again. May I call you tomorrow?"

"I certainly hope you will," Lilly said.

Charlie took hold of her wrist and lifted it up. Very lightly he touched his lips to the top of her hand. Then he walked to his car and waited for Lilly to enter her house. Lilly stood at the window and watched as he drove away. With her finger she lightly traced the spot where he had kissed her hand.

For Charlie and his parents, Sunday was a day for worship and rest. They started at daybreak. Charlie and the other Sentrian families met at one of the elders' homes. It was an opportunity to worship in their own language and in the manner they were accustomed to, but it was essentially the same type of service used by the early churches of Earth.

Louis preferred that Charlie and Helen stay home with him on Sunday afternoons. While Charlie and Louis watched the news, Helen Gray would prepare a large midday meal. Usually it was baked chicken with chocolate-covered cucumbers and oat bran muffins. And of course, coffee.

The three of them would sit at the dining-room table after dinner and talk for hours. Sometimes Charlie and his father would play a game of Jamfel, a Sentrian version of chess. That was what they were doing today. Helen Gray sat in her comfy chair cross-stitching, while Charlie and his father played their game.

"It's good to finally spend some time with you. Between my work and your band practice, I hardly get to see you anymore."

"Yes, band does take up a lot of my time," Charlie agreed.

"So how are your studies coming?" Louis asked.

"Great. All As," Charlie answered.

"That's good. I don't want your studies to suffer because of all this band practice. No wonder Earthans are so ignorant; they spend all their time on activities other than learning," Louis said. Charlie didn't respond.

"So, are you liking your job?" Charlie asked.

"As well as can be expected."

Charlie made a move that ended in checkmate. "Good one," Louis commended him. "It's been a while since you defeated me. I'll have to work on my strategy. Why don't we take a coffee break?" It was four in the afternoon. According to Sentrian custom the Sabbath was over. After having coffee with his parents, Charlie asked if he could be excused.

"I need to get my car washed."

Louis nodded. Charlie did need to keep his car up. "Hey, Charlie, why don't I go with you? It's been a while since I've taken a ride in the Mustang."

"That's OK, Father. I know you'd probably rather read your paper or something. Enjoy your day off."

"Well, just be back in time for dinner," Louis said. Charlie retrieved his car keys and walked out the door.

Lilly had finished her homework and practiced her French horn, and she was now organizing her closet. Michelle had invited her out for dinner and a movie, but Lilly declined. She wanted to stay home in case Charlie called. She had just about given up when the phone rang.

"Please be him, please be him, please be him," she said as she ran to the phone. Even though she was right beside it, she let the phone ring one more time so it didn't seem as if she had been waiting for it to ring all afternoon, which is exactly what she had done.

"Liliana? It's me, Charlie."

"Hi," Lilly said. "So, what's going on? What have you been doing all day?" she asked.

"Going to church, spending time with my family, the usual. How about you? What have you been doing?" Charlie asked.

"Homework, horn practice, organizing my closet, the usual," Lilly said.

"You and your mom don't go to church?" Charlie asked, surprised. Worship was so important to his people. It was hard for him to understand why anyone wouldn't go to church.

"No, we used to go to Mass when Abuela was alive, but after she died, my mom started working on Sundays."

"Who's Abuela?" Charlie asked.

"My mom's grandmother, my great-grandmother, but I just called her Abuela. We lived with her for a while after my dad left, so we were very close to her. After she died, my mom didn't want to stay in Spring with all the memories, and that's when we moved to Clear Lake."

"You said your dad left. When was that?"

"Oh gosh, I was just a baby. They were young when they got married, and my dad couldn't handle the responsibility, so he just took off."

"I'm so sorry," Charlie told her.

"It's OK. It's not like I ever knew him."

"You have no contact with your father?"

"No. Not since I was a baby," Lilly said.

"I'm sorry," Charlie said again. He couldn't imagine growing up without his father. "So your mom never remarried?"

"No. You'd have to know her. She's loyal to a fault. She fell hard for my dad, and even though he turned out to be a jerk, she never wanted to remarry. He was her one and only. I know that sounds kind of strange."

"No. Not really. If something happened to my father, I know my mom wouldn't remarry, and vice versa."

"That's so sweet. So your parents are still really in love?"

"You could say that. Commitment is a big deal for us, I mean them," Charlie said.

"Wow, Charlie. Your life is so Norman Rockwell. It sounds idyllic."

"I guess so," Charlie said. "It's all I know. You talk about Abuela, but what about your grandparents? You haven't mentioned them."

"That's because they died before I was born. Car accident. My mom was a teenager, and she kind of flipped out. She started staying out late, skipping school—you know, the whole teenage-rebellion thing. Well, Abuela laid down the law. She grounded her and told her to stay away from my dad. My mom, of course, hated that. Soon after she turned eighteen, they ran off and got married. And, well, you know the rest."

"It sounds like your mom has had a difficult life. She must be a strong person to have raised you by herself, especially with all the personal tragedy she endured." He knew his own mother could not have handled it.

"I guess so," Lilly said. She had always thought that her mother threw herself into work to avoid having a social life, but now that Charlie brought it up, Lilly had to admit it took a certain amount of strength just to get out of bed every day and go to work. "I know she was devastated when her parents died, and getting married so young wasn't a good idea, but things are better now."

"Getting married young isn't necessarily a *bad* thing," Charlie said. Even though Lilly had no idea about Sentrian customs, he still felt the need to defend them.

"Maybe not, but in Michelle's case it was disastrous. Besides, these days, it's just not done. You finish college, live on your own for a while, and then think about getting married."

"Um," Charlie said. Maybe if his people had a seventy-plus-year life expectancy, they wouldn't get married so young, either.

"So how old were your parents when they got married?"

"Uh, eighteen," Charlie said. Actually they were younger than that, but Charlie knew enough of Earthan laws to know that sixteen was considered underage.

"Well, no wonder you feel that way. Your parents are one of the success stories. Good for them," Lilly said.

The car wash employee signaled to Charlie that his car was ready. "Liliana, I've got to go. My father expects me home for dinner, but I'll see you tomorrow."

"Sure," Lilly said. "See you soon." She wished he could have talked longer, but at least he had called. The conversation made her realize something—she wanted to tell her mom about Charlie.

Lilly bounded down the stairs with a smile on her face. Michelle was in her recliner, channel surfing. "Mom, remember when I told you I went to the planetarium with a friend? Well, the friend was a guy. His name is Charlie…"

After Lilly told her mother all about Charlie, Michelle insisted on meeting him. A couple of nights later, Lilly invited Charlie over for Michelle's enchiladas. Charlie was nervous. He had never gotten far enough into a relationship to meet the girl's parents. But Lilly was important. He decided he would do whatever it took to get on Mrs. Garcia's good side.

Charlie looked up Earthan courting rituals on his PCD. He found some tips from an etiquette expert from the fifties. With regard to meeting your sweetheart's parents, she recommended wearing something nice: no jeans. Always be polite and friendly. Try everything, even if you don't like what's being served. She suggested bringing a bouquet of flowers to your sweetheart's mother. He thought these things seemed simple enough to do.

The night of the dinner, Charlie arrived at the Garcia home in navy trousers, a button-down long-sleeved shirt, and tie. He rang the doorbell and waited. When Lilly answered the door in blue jeans and a T-shirt, he realized he was overdressed. "Charlie, wow, you look great," Lilly said. Michelle was standing right behind her, peering over her shoulder.

"Mom, this is Charlie Gray. Charlie this is my mom, Michelle."

Charlie could see the resemblance immediately. Lilly was a younger version of her mother. He extended his hand. "How do you do, Mrs. Garcia?"

Michelle shook his hand. "It's great to finally meet you, Charlie. You can call me Michelle."

"I can see now that Liliana's beauty is an inherited trait," Charlie told her.

Lilly was surprised to see her mother blush. She was even more surprised to hear Charlie refer to her beauty, even if it was indirectly. He never had before. "Thank you," Michelle said. "Won't you come in? Dinner is almost ready."

"Thanks for having me," Charlie said. "These are for you." Charlie handed Michelle a bouquet of multicolored flowers.

"How lovely. And thoughtful. I'll just get a vase, and we'll put these on the dining-room table," Michelle said.

"Is there anything I can do?" Charlie asked.

"Of course not," Michelle said as she filled the vase with water. "You're our guest."

"Actually, Mom, Charlie makes really good coffee. You should let him brew some, while I set the table," Lilly said. Charlie nodded.

"Are you sure you don't mind?" Michelle asked.

"It would be my pleasure," Charlie said. Michelle showed him where she kept the coffee maker and supplies.

"So, you like coffee?" Michelle said. "Most young people don't have a taste for it."

"My parents have always been coffee drinkers. I just started drinking it with them."

When it was time to sit down for dinner, Charlie pulled out first Michelle's chair then Lilly's. Michelle was impressed.

"Mrs. Garcia, this dinner is delicious," Charlie said after taking a few bites.

"Thank you. It's a family recipe. And please call me Michelle. Mrs. Garcia sounds so old," Michelle said as she pulled her hair behind her ear and crossed her legs. Lilly gave her mother a quizzical look. Was she *flirting* with Charlie? Lilly gave her mom a nudge under the table, and Michelle shot her a dirty look.

There was no way Charlie would call Lilly's mother by her first name, but he was curious about something, so he asked. "Your first name is very pretty, but I didn't realize it was Spanish."

Michelle smiled. "It's not. We're not all named after saints, you know. My parents named me after my father's boss's wife. She helped teach him English and was very kind. Papi wanted me to have an American-sounding name, so Michelle it was."

After dinner, they went into the den for conversation and empanadas. Charlie and Michelle had coffee, but Lilly poured herself a glass of iced tea.

"Lilly wasn't exaggerating. Charlie, this coffee is really good."

"So are the empanadas. I've never had them before." He sat down on the love seat across from Michelle's recliner, leaving Lilly alone on the couch.

"Mom, you and Charlie have a lot in common. Charlie loves the movies from the fifties and sixties, too." Lilly would soon regret ever bringing it up. Michelle and Charlie both loved *Psycho* and *To Kill a Mockingbird*. They began talking about the movies in depth.

"Gregory Peck was terrific," Charlie said. "He made an excellent Atticus Finch."

"Oh, yes. If Lilly had been a boy, I would have named her Atticus."

Atticus? Really? Lilly frowned. Her mom was going overboard. "That was a really good book. I read it in tenth grade," Lilly said. They didn't even acknowledge her and started discussing a movie called *Vertigo* that Lilly had never heard of.

After talking movies, they moved on to music. Michelle jumped up and ran to the stereo. She put on an Elvis album, *Love Me Tender*, and started swaying to the music.

"Would you dance with me, Mrs. Garcia?" Charlie asked.

"I'd love to," Michelle told him. Charlie put his arm on her back and took her other hand as they slowly turned in a circle. Lilly rolled her eyes. Her mother was acting like a teenager. But she couldn't help but notice that Charlie was a good dancer.

After "Love Me Tender" ended, Michelle insisted on showing Charlie her record collection. They spent half an hour discussing groups from the fifties and sixties. "Don't mind me," Lilly mumbled. "I'll just sit here and count the fuzz balls on my sweater." She said it softly and under her breath but was surprised when Charlie looked up at her. He stood up and walked over to Lilly. He put his arm around her and brought her over to where he had been sitting with Michelle and tried as best as he could to include her in the conversation.

At nine o'clock, Charlie got up to leave. "Thank you for having me over tonight, Mrs. Garcia."

"I'll walk you to your car," Lilly said and jumped up.

Michelle walked with them to the front door. "Don't be a stranger, Charlie."

Charlie waved good-bye as Lilly was pulling him outside. She would have loved to sit with him in his car and talk with him for a while, but Charlie noted, "Um, your mom's kind of watching us."

Lilly turned to look. Michelle was looking out the window and waving. Lilly groaned. "See you at school tomorrow." She stomped up the driveway to the front door.

"Charlie's wonderful," Michelle said.

"I know, Mom."

"I think that if I were twenty years younger, I'd give you some stiff competition, *mi hija*," Michelle said. Lilly supposed she should be happy that her mother liked Charlie. At least she didn't think he was weird. But then again, Michelle was old. She had no idea he wasn't cool. She probably thought his good manners were charming.

After the successful dinner, Charlie became a fixture in the Garcia household.

A few days later, during second period, a bomb threat was called in. On the way out of the building, Charlie grabbed Lilly's elbow and steered her toward the teachers' lounge.

"Where are we going?" she asked. "We're supposed to be lining up outside."

"And we will. But first we're taking a detour."

"What are you doing?"

"With everyone distracted by the bomb threat, now is the perfect time for a coffee break."

"I have never in my life met someone who likes coffee as much as you do."

"Well, we don't have coff—I mean, this kind of coffee where I come from."

"They don't have Folger's in New Mexico?" Lilly asked.

Charlie shrugged. "You know, you should really give coffee a try. Then we could go out for coffee dates."

Lilly shook her head. "No thanks, I'm trying to limit my caffeine intake."

As they walked out the double doors of the school, Lilly pointed to a poster in the hall. "Look, Charlie. It's a poster for homecoming," she said hopefully.

"Huh? Oh yeah," Charlie said, tucking his coffee under his jacket so the principal wouldn't see. Lilly tried to hide her disappointment at his lack of reaction to the homecoming dance as they walked outside.

"C'mon, people. No dawdling," the assistant principal yelled.

Charlie and Lilly met up with Mrs. Hartman's class. She hadn't even noticed that two of her students were missing. They found a patch of grass and sat down.

He took a sip. "It's OK, but my coffee is better."

"Yeah. My mom says you make the best coffee she's ever had." Lilly picked up a blade of grass and rolled it between her fingers. "Michelle really likes you, but I'm sure you already know that."

Charlie shrugged, embarrassed.

"She wants you to come to the movies with us on Saturday. I was going to call to invite you, but you've never given me your phone number."

"It's best if I call you, Liliana."

"You don't want me to have your number?" she asked.

Charlie shifted uncomfortably. "It's kind of complicated."

"You haven't told your parents about me, have you?" Lilly asked.

"Um, not exactly," Charlie said.

"Why? You don't think they would approve of me?"

"It's not you, Liliana. They wouldn't approve of anyone. My parents are very…strict. They think I need to focus on school. To them, a girlfriend would be an unnecessary distraction for me," Charlie told her.

"What do you think? Am I an unnecessary distraction?"

Charlie brushed back a strand of Lilly's hair that had blown into her face. "Distraction, yes. Unnecessary, no."

Lilly grew quiet. It really bothered her that Charlie kept her a secret from his parents. And it hurt her feelings that they wouldn't even give her a chance. Charlie tried to make her feel better. "This changes nothing. It doesn't matter what they think."

"But I hate the idea of you sneaking around," Lilly said.

"You let me worry about that."

"All clear," the principal shouted. Charlie gave Lilly a hand up, and they returned to class.

HOMECOMING

After band practice Monday, Lilly got caught up in Claire's latest drama with Matt. She was crying in the bathroom, and Lilly was trying to cheer her up.

"It's going to be OK," Lilly said.

"How can you say that?" Claire wailed. "You can't understand. You've never had a boyfriend; never been in love."

Friend or not, Lilly was annoyed at Claire's comments. How dare she assume she was the only one who had romance issues, or that Lilly couldn't relate. But then Claire was incredibly self-centered. Lilly knew this about her. In Claire's eyes, no one's relationships were real except her own.

"As a matter of fact, I do have a boyfriend," Lilly said. She hoped it was true. She had never referred to Charlie as her boyfriend out loud before.

"What? Who?" Claire asked as she fluffed her hair and reapplied the mascara she had just cried off.

"Charlie Gray," Lilly said. Claire looked at her as if she were speaking Greek. Lilly rolled her eyes. "You know. The new trumpet player from New Mexico." It was really sad that her best friend wasn't even aware of whom she was dating.

"That strange, short guy?" Claire asked. Lilly nodded. To each his own, Claire thought. "Oh well, that's nice, I'm sure. But right now I've got a serious problem with Matt, and I don't know what to do…"

While Lilly was sitting with Claire, Charlie was out practicing with the trumpets. Dan decided they needed an extra practice. After they finished, Beth ran up to talk to him. "Lilly told me about your date at the planetarium. Actually, she gushed about it."

If Charlie had been able to blush, he would have. Instead he just shrugged.

"So what's your next move?" Beth asked.

"Next move? You think I should ask her out again?" Charlie asked.

Beth sighed, exasperated. Guys could be so dense, even the so-called intelligent ones. "In case you haven't noticed, we have a very important dance coming up. It's called homecoming. I happen to know that Lilly loves to dance, and she would be thrilled to go with you."

"You really think so?" Charlie asked. He vaguely remembered seeing some posters up around the school announcing the dance, but that was only because Lilly had pointed them out to him. "Liliana's different. She's not like other Ear—uh, girls. She doesn't like to get all dolled up."

"Yes, Lilly *is* different, but she's still a girl. Trust me. She's been hoping you'll ask her."

"You haven't steered me wrong so far," Charlie said.

"No, I haven't," Beth said. "And please get her a halfway decent mum. This is her senior year, and she deserves it." Beth took off for the band hall. Charlie heard her muttering, "Dolled up? Who says dolled up anymore?"

Mum? What's a mum? Charlie asked himself. As he was walking across the field, back to the band hall, he rehearsed how he was going to ask Lilly. Ian was waiting there, hanging out in front of the girl's restroom.

"They're still in there, dude. Beth just went in to check."

A few minutes later, Lilly emerged from the restroom. "I'm afraid I can't go to McDonald's today. It's a long story. I'll tell y'all about it tomorrow. And Charlie, I hate to ask, but can you take Beth and Ian home?"

"We can leave our horns here if there's not enough room," Beth offered.

"Sure, that should be fine," Charlie said. He was a little disappointed. He wanted to ask Lilly to the dance now. Today. Get it over with. But it would have to wait.

"This is what happens when you date a single mom with kids. We're a package deal," Ian said, shrugging his shoulders.

Charlie sighed. "OK, let's go."

"Yes," Ian said. He was eager to ride in the Mustang again.

"Can we go by McDonald's?" Beth said.

"I suppose," Charlie said.

"Can I drive?" asked Ian.

"Absolutely not. That was a one-time deal."

The next day at lunch, Lilly filled Charlie in on the Claire/Matt saga. "So Matt shows her the mum he got her for homecoming, because she demands to see it. And she absolutely throws a fit. She tells him, 'It's not big enough. I want another one.' Then he tells her, 'Forget it. I've already spent enough money on this one.' She starts crying and says, 'You don't even love me.' And he says, 'Fine.' He grabs the mum out of her hand. 'You don't like this one, I'll just give it to someone else.' I think this time he really means it. Claire thinks he might ask Jennifer Cromwell to homecoming."

"Not might ask," Ian said, plopping down beside Lilly, "did ask. And of course, she said yes. Serves Claire right, that snotty b—"

"Ian," Lilly interrupted. "She *is* my friend."

Ian couldn't stand Claire. He had a crush on her when he was freshman, but she humiliated him when she told him to get lost in front of the entire band. Since then, Ian had spent a lot of time reminding Lilly she could do better in the best-friend department.

"Well, what's done is done," Lilly said. "I hope it's worth it when she's sitting home alone for homecoming. She should be thankful she had a date at all. Some people have *never* even been asked."

Charlie smiled. OK, so he hadn't noticed before, but he was definitely paying attention now. Both Beth and Claire were making an issue of this mum thing. Whatever it was, it must be pretty important, and he'd better get it right.

Charlie finally got his chance to ask Lilly that afternoon. They had just dropped off Beth and Ian, and now he and Lilly were back in the school parking lot, sitting in her Jeep. "Liliana, I've been meaning to ask you something," Charlie said.

"What is it?" Lilly asked.

"I was wondering if maybe you would like to go to the homecoming dance with me."

Lilly threw her arms around Charlie and squealed. Charlie put his arms around her shoulders. "Is that a yes?" he whispered into her ear.

Lilly nodded her head.

Homecoming was two weeks away. That didn't give Lilly much time, but it didn't matter. She was just glad to be going. That meant she *had* to go dress shopping this Saturday. She went to the mall and wandered around, unsure of where to start. Where should she go? Should she choose jewelry first, then a dress? Right when she was about to give up and go to one of the department stores, she ran into Dana.

"Wow, Lilly. We meet here again. Are you starting to make the mall a habit?"

"No. I have to find a homecoming dress."

"So you're going with Charlie?" Dana asked. "You two make a cute couple."

That was it. No comments about how weird Charlie was, only that they made a cute couple. Lilly couldn't believe Dana knew about Charlie.

Most of the people Dana hung out with didn't know people like Lilly and Charlie even existed.

She convinced Lilly to steer clear of the department stores and try a boutique called Jasmine's. Dana went with her, and together they found the perfect dress. The store even had a seamstress on hand for alterations.

While Lilly was out shopping, Charlie was making his own preparations for homecoming. Beth said Lilly was a great dancer. Charlie wasn't too bad, but he thought he ought to practice. He went home and insta-searched Arthur Murray dance lessons on his computer. A holographic dancer named Dina materialized. "What kind of dance would you like to learn?" the friendly computer voice asked. After his dance lesson, he used his PCD to find out what exactly a mum was.

Charlie brought Lilly's mum to school with him the Friday of homecoming. When he had gone to the florist shop to order it, the clerk had asked him what his price range was. He told her he didn't care as long as it would make his girl happy. After the ordeal with Claire, he decided it would be better to do too much than too little. The florist was all too happy to comply, and before he knew it, he had spent sixty dollars on a triple-flower mum with stuffed animals, French horns, and long, flowing ribbons. Liliana's name in glittery letters topped it off.

Lilly was shocked when she saw it. It was beautiful, but it was so heavy she had to attach it to her jacket, for fear it would pull her shirt halfway down her chest. The ribbons were so long, she almost tripped on them. When she was out of Charlie's sight, she snipped a few inches off the bottom. It was the most spectacular mum in the school. Claire was positively green with envy. Dan had asked her to the dance, so she had a date, but the mum he bought her was smaller and simpler than the one she'd refused from Matt. Ian thought she was getting what she deserved.

Charlie couldn't understand the whole Matt/Claire situation, and it kind of bothered him. He didn't get this whole Earthan breaking-up ritual. According to Lilly, Matt and Claire had dated for a long time, but now, suddenly, it was over. Even stranger, they both had immediately found dates to the homecoming dance.

Charlie didn't know about Jennifer, but he couldn't understand why Claire was going with Dan. He overheard some of the trombone players say that Dan never asked girls out on his own. Instead he would take advantage of situations like this one. As one of the trombone players put it, "Dan can't get his own date, so he takes everyone else's rejects."

The previous week, right before band practice, Dan had come up to Matt and said, "I hope it's OK that I asked out Claire. No hard feelings." To Charlie, it sounded more like he was trying to rub it in than smooth things over.

Matt was more calm than Charlie would have been. He told Dan, "You know, dude, whatever. Claire's not my problem anymore. If you want to make her yours, be my guest."

How could Matt suddenly stop caring about Claire? It was as if he turned off a switch, and their relationship was over. Claire, too. If she truly loved Matt as she professed, then why was she going with Dan? Where was the faithfulness?

Dan bothered Charlie for different reasons, and it wasn't because of his personal history with him. Charlie heard his opinion about girls in general, and it wasn't nice. Plus, he was a bully; he had a mean streak a mile wide and a really bad temper. Charlie was worried he might be dangerous.

"You have to warn Claire. Dan's not a good guy," Charlie told Lilly.

"You're right," she said. "Dan's a creep. But there's no talking Claire out of it. She's not missing homecoming her senior year, even if she has to go with a total loser like Dan."

On the night of the homecoming game, the band went out as usual for the half-time show. The principal announced the band beau and sweetheart. Of course it was Mark and Jill. Jill smiled graciously and accepted the ribbon. Mark acted like his typical bored self. Lilly glanced over and saw Claire glaring at Jill. Lilly caught up with her after the half-time show.

"Hey, you OK?" Lilly asked.

"Do I look OK? If Matt hadn't broke up with me, we'd be band beau and sweetheart right now."

"Oh c'mon, Claire. That's why you're mad? No one else had a chance. Mark and Jill have gone out forever, and they're so sweet together, it could put you in a diabetic coma."

Claire said nothing and stormed off the field.

It was third quarter, downtime for the band. Charlie was sitting in the stands with his head tilted to the side, staring off into space. He was concentrating on a conversation in the distance; he didn't like what he heard.

"Yoo-hoo, Earth to Charlie," Lilly said, waving her hand in front of his eyes. She sat down on the bleachers next to him.

He blinked and turned toward her. "Oh, Liliana. Where have you been? I've been waiting for you." He handed her a Diet Coke.

"Thanks. I've been talking to Claire. She's bummed that she didn't win band sweetheart."

"So she's really upset she didn't win?" Charlie asked, confused.

"Believe it or not, yeah. Her senior year isn't going the way she expected. She still hasn't accepted the fact that Matt broke up with her. I know she's going to homecoming with Dan just so she has a date, and I'm sure Dan is going with her to rub it in Matt's face."

"Liliana, Claire's your friend. You must tell her not to go out with Dan. His intentions—they aren't good."

Charlie didn't need to warn Lilly. She'd never cared for Dan, and it wasn't just his "any girl would be lucky to have me" attitude, although that was part of it. There was something cruel in his eyes as he stared you up and down. He seemed like the kind of guy to go home and kick his dog. "I don't like him either; he gives me the creeps." Lilly shivered. "I've already tried to tell her. But Claire's hardheaded." Lilly noticed something just then. "Charlie, I don't know how you do it."

"Do what?" Charlie asked.

The rest of us come back from half time with sticky hat hair. You take your hat off, and your hair is perfect. It's like you don't sweat or something."

"Yeah, or something," Charlie laughed nervously.

After the game they were standing near Lilly's Jeep saying their goodbyes. Charlie gave Lilly a kiss on the cheek. "I'll see you tomorrow," he told her and reluctantly pulled away.

Ian was already trying to hurry Lilly up so that they could go to Bennigan's. Ian and Beth had surprised everyone a few days earlier by announcing that they were going to homecoming together. They made it clear that they were only going as friends, but Lilly thought there was more to it than that. Maybe relegating Ian to the backseat had not been such a bad idea after all.

Charlie walked in the house and was disappointed that his father was still up. He was hoping to avoid his parents tonight and go straight to bed. But no, Louis called him into the living room to talk.

"How was the game?" Louis asked. "Did your team win?"

"No. They never win," Charlie said. "Um, as long as you're up, I was wondering if you would mind if I went on a field trip with the astronomy club tomorrow night." He didn't enjoy always lying to his father, but on the other hand, the lie was more credible than the truth.

"You sure don't have much free time these days, Charlie. I hardly get to see you," his father noted.

"I know, but marching band will be over in another month. Then I'll be home more."

Louis seemed satisfied with that answer. "Just don't stay out too late. We have church the following morning.

"Yes, Father." Charlie excused himself and went upstairs to go to bed.

Saturday morning Lilly went to Jasmine's to pick up her dress. After returning home, she laid it out on her bed, still in its plastic wrapping. Lilly thought it was the prettiest dress she had ever owned. She hoped Charlie would like it, too. Lilly took a long hot shower and washed her hair. Then she set her hair in hot rollers and sat down on the bed with a fashion magazine. Ordinarily she preferred a book, but she felt she needed the advice on hair and makeup. She turned on the radio and listened to Depeche Mode until it was time to get ready.

Charlie kissed his mom on the cheek and then headed out the door. In the garage, he quickly changed into a suit and tie. When he rang the doorbell at Lilly's house, Michelle answered. "Come in," she said. She was holding a camera in one hand and motioning him to come in with the other. Lilly was standing in front of the fireplace. Her hair was pulled up with ringlet curls all around, and she was wearing dangling, teardrop-shaped earrings. Her navy-blue gown flared out at the waist and flowed down to her ankles. Charlie had never seen her in a formal dress and with her hair pinned up. She looked different, but in a good way.

Lilly thought she looked pretty, and she hoped Charlie would notice. She thought he *had* noticed. He had certainly looked her up and down when he came in the door; however, he didn't say anything. She hated to admit it, but she was a little disappointed.

Charlie put a corsage on Lilly's left wrist. Michelle snapped a picture. "Now you two stand closer together," Michelle directed. "C'mon, Charlie, put your arm around her; pretend that you like her. OK. One, two, three." The camera clicked. "Great. Now just a few more," Michelle said.

Finally Lilly complained, "Mom, we really need to go."

"OK, OK," Michelle said. "Have a good time."

Charlie opened the door for Lilly. "I thought Steak and Ale tonight. What do you think?"

"Oh, darn. I was hoping for McDonald's," Lilly said.

After dinner they headed over to the high school. Charlie opened the door for her, and Lilly took his arm as they walked from the parking lot to the gym doors. As soon as they entered, Charlie asked, "Would you like to dance?" Lilly didn't hesitate. She grabbed his hand and dragged him onto the dance floor. Lilly was a terrific dancer, and Charlie was keeping up pretty well. His Arthur Murray practice sessions had paid off.

A slow song came on next. This was Charlie's kind of dancing. He pulled Lilly close to him, and she rested her head on his shoulder. This is much better, he thought. Lilly was smiling dreamily. It was almost too good to be true. Here she was, Lilly Garcia, dancing with her boyfriend at the homecoming dance.

After a few more fast songs, Charlie suggested they take a break. Lilly agreed. She sat at one of the tables near the dance floor, while Charlie went to get her a drink. She looked around and spotted Ian and Beth. They waved at her excitedly. Ian looked quite dashing in a burgundy shirt with a black jacket and tie. Beth was still sporting a Goth style, but her hair was pinned up and she looked Gothic-elegant.

Lilly turned her attention to the other side of the dance floor. Dan walked in with Claire on his arm. They made their way to the dance floor and planted themselves right next to Matt and Jennifer.

"That's disgusting," Lilly said.

"What's disgusting?" Charlie asked, putting her drink on the table.

"Look," Lilly motioned to the dance floor. It was obvious to everyone that Dan was trying to annoy Matt and his date. Lilly wanted to slap the smirk right off his face. Matt and Jennifer finally had to leave the dance floor to avoid them. Claire looked upset.

That's got to be awkward," Beth commented. She and Ian had walked over to Lilly and Charlie's table.

Claire had dressed to impress, but Dan was not the person she had made the effort for. She hoped that Matt would see her with Dan and beg her to come back to him. That plan had backfired royally.

"What nerve," Lilly said. She felt bad for Matt and his date. She didn't know who she was more upset with: Claire, who knew better, or Dan, who was a rude jerk.

"I wouldn't expect any better from Claire," Ian said.

"Or Dan," Beth added.

They finished their drinks and headed back to the dance floor. Lilly forgot all about Claire and Dan. She was too busy having fun dancing with Charlie. To Lilly, every song the DJ played was so good, she didn't want to stop.

Lilly felt a tap on her shoulder. She turned to find Jana, a flute player and wannabe friend of Claire. "Sorry to interrupt, but Claire's in the bathroom, crying. She's asking for you."

Not again, Lilly thought. "I'm sorry, but I'd better go check on her," Lilly told Charlie.

"It's OK. I'll walk over with you," Charlie said. Ian and Beth came along, too.

When Lilly and Beth entered the bathroom, Claire was crying so hard her mascara had run all over her face. Lilly knelt beside her friend and pulled her messed up hair out of her face.

"What happened?" she asked, resting a hand on Claire's shoulder.

In a halting voice, Claire began to speak. "Matt was standing outside of the gym in the parking lot with *that* girl he brought here. Dan said, 'Let's make Matt jealous.' He started kissing me. I didn't want him to. Matt walked off, but Dan didn't stop. I tried to get away from him, and he just held me tighter and shoved me against his car." She shuddered. "I told him to stop it, and he said, 'It's OK. Relax.' Finally I screamed, and he let me go. It was awful; his lips are so gross."

Beth brought Claire a glass of water. Lilly wet a paper towel and tried to clean her up as best as she could. Once Claire had calmed down, she looked up at Lilly. "I want Matt. I need to talk to Matt."

"I don't know if that's such a good idea," Lilly told her.

Claire was insistent. "Please, Lilly, go find him. I know he'll be furious at Dan."

Yes, he definitely would be furious, and he could very well be mad at Dan. But he might be angry at Claire for being stupid enough to go out with Dan in the first place, or possibly at Lilly for interrupting his date. "OK," Lilly said. "I'll try to find him." Beth took one of Claire's arms and Lilly the other. They walked her out of the bathroom and sat her on a bench next to Charlie and Ian. "Keep an eye on her," she whispered to Charlie. "I'll be back."

Lilly spotted Matt and Jennifer on the dance floor. She got his attention and motioned for him to come over.

"What's up?" he asked.

"It's Claire. She wants to talk."

Matt didn't let her finish. "Lilly, can't you see I'm on a date here? Tell Claire I'm not going to ruin my evening to talk to my ex-girlfriend."

"It's not what you think," Lilly said. "Dan got a little rough with her. She's OK, but she's pretty upset. She really wants to talk to you."

Matt turned to his date. "Go ahead," she said. "I'll go get something to drink." Lilly thought Jennifer was pretty understanding about the whole thing. Matt seemed mad, but at least he followed her back to where Claire was sitting.

Claire jumped up when she saw Matt. She tried to put her arms around him. "Oh Matt, it was awful." Matt didn't let her hug him. Instead he held her at arm's length. Claire started sobbing again. His voice grew soft. "Did he hurt you?"

"No. Not that way. But he wouldn't let me go. I screamed, and he got really mad. It scared me. I thought he was going to hit me or something."

"Where is he now?" Matt asked, looking around.

"He stayed out in the parking lot. Some of his friends were out there, I think," Claire said. She was still upset but calmer now. "He told me I was OK for a good time but not good enough to be his girlfriend. Then he told me to find my own way home."

Matt turned and started walking toward the front door.

"Where are you going?" Claire asked.

"To find Dan. Charlie, Ian, would you mind coming along? I'm not looking for a fight, but a little backup never hurts."

"Sure," Charlie agreed.

The boys took their jackets off and handed them to the girls. Then they went outside to look for Dan. Lilly wanted to follow them, but Beth thought that was a bad idea. "Let the guys handle this. Matt and Charlie are pretty cool-headed. They aren't going to let this get out of hand." Lilly knew Beth was right. Thinking back to the Sprite incident, she knew Charlie wasn't the confrontational type.

Dan was standing by his car, sneaking beers with some guys Charlie didn't know. They were joking and laughing. Charlie overheard Dan say a few crass things about Claire. His already low opinion of Dan dropped even lower. Charlie, Matt, and Ian approached Dan and his pathetic band of losers.

"Well, Matt, what brings you out here?" Dan asked, his eyes glassy. "Did you get tired of hanging out with the cool crowd?"

Matt didn't mince words. "I'm going to say this one time, Dan. You keep your hands off Claire. When she says no, she means it."

"Whoa, dude, I didn't think you cared." Dan handed his beer to one of his friends and walked over to where Matt was standing. "It doesn't matter, anyway. I got what I wanted, and I'm done with her," he smiled at his friends.

Matt shoved Dan up against his car. "No. She's done with *you*. And if I ever hear you or your loser friends talking trash about her, I'll rearrange your face." Dan still had a smirk on his face, but he didn't smart off, likely due to the fact that he was a lot smaller than Matt.

Matt turned to Charlie and Ian. "C'mon, let's go."

Just as the guys had reached the gym door, Charlie turned and ran back toward the parking lot. "Hey Charlie, where are you going?" Ian called out. Matt and Ian ran after him.

When they caught up with him, Matt thought he was going to have to break up a fight. Charlie had pinned Dan to his car and stood over him with his fist raised.

"Whoa, wait, Charlie. The second you throw a punch, you're going to have every teacher and assistant principal in the school out here. He's not worth suspension, man," Matt said.

He tried to pull Charlie away from Dan. He was surprised how difficult it was. For a little guy, Charlie was *very* strong. When that didn't work, Matt tried to extricate Dan from Charlie's hold. As soon as Dan was free, he took the opportunity to punch Charlie in the mouth. Matt was afraid that Charlie would go after him again, but by then Charlie had calmed down some.

"What happened?" Ian asked.

Charlie wiped some blood off his lip. "He was telling lies about Liliana, trying to ruin her reputation."

"You heard that from across the parking lot?" one of Dan's friends asked.

"Dude, shut up," Dan told him.

"No. I want to know," Matt said. "What did you say?" Dan said nothing. He just stood there, glaring.

"Start talking, or I'll let him at you again."

"No. Don't," Charlie said. "It was vile; it doesn't bear repeating."

Matt, Ian, and Charlie walked back over to the gym. Dan yelled out, "This isn't over, Gray. I'm talking to you, shrimp." Charlie ignored him and opened the door to the school.

Lilly ran over as soon as she saw the guys come in. "It's taken care of," Matt announced to Claire and the girls.

Lilly was shocked to see Charlie's bloody and swollen lip. "What happened to you?"

"It's nothing," Charlie said.

"It doesn't look like nothing," Lilly said, dabbing his lower lip with a tissue. She turned to Ian. "Would someone mind telling me what's going on?"

"After Matt finished putting Dan in his place about Claire, the moron starts talking trash about you. Charlie got that busted lip defending your honor," Ian told her.

"What was it? What did he say?"

Charlie shook his head. "You don't need to hear it."

"I'd like to be the judge of that," Lilly said, pulling him aside.

Charlie didn't know how to put what Dan said in eighties terms without being utterly offensive, so he used an expression he had often heard in the fifties. "He said you weren't a *nice* girl. I couldn't let him talk about you that way."

She wasn't even upset about the lies Dan was spreading about her. Charlie had stood up for her to another guy; that was what mattered. It was so cool, she had to smile. She looked down so Charlie wouldn't see and continued to dab his lip.

Ian was regaling Beth with tales of their heroism. When he finished telling her all about their run in with Dan, he said, "Yeah. If Charlie hadn't stepped in when he did, I probably would have kicked Dan's ass anyway. No one talks about my mom that way."

Lilly was so preoccupied with Charlie's split lip that she hadn't noticed the exchange going on between Matt and Claire. "Oh Matt, I'm so glad you're OK. I was worried sick. Thank you for sticking up for me." Claire tried to put her arms around Matt, but he gently pushed her back.

"Claire, stop," he said firmly.

"But I thought…"

"Nothing's changed. Look, I've got to get back to Jennifer." Matt put his suit jacket on and walked off. Claire's shoulders slumped. This was the moment when she finally understood it was over. Up until now she had been clinging to some desperate hope that Matt would want her back.

Lilly didn't want to leave Charlie's side, but she knew Claire needed her. She stroked Claire's hair softly, "Is there anything I can do?" Claire was shaking; she was about to lose it.

"Take me home. Now," she said.

"I'll get the car," Charlie volunteered.

After dropping off Claire, it was too late to return to the dance and too early to go home, so they ended up going to the diner. Lilly was stirring her Cherry Coke with her straw. "What a crazy evening," she said. "I'm sorry we had to leave so early."

"Liliana, I really don't care what we do, as long as I'm with you," Charlie said.

"You know, I never thanked you for the way you stood up for me with Dan. You're like my own personal superhero," Lilly said.

"It was nothing." He looked down and cleared his throat. "And uh, thank you for taking care of my lip."

"Sure," she said.

"Look, let's not talk about such unpleasant things," Charlie told her. "We only have a short time before we have to go home."

"OK," agreed Lilly. "So tell me. Where did you learn to dance like that? Charlie, you're fantastic…"

At 12:55 Charlie pulled into Lilly's driveway. "Lips Like Sugar" was playing on the radio. Charlie took her hands in his and slowly leaned over until he was so close she could feel his breath on her cheeks. She leaned in then, too. That was all the encouragement he needed. Very slowly, very softly he kissed her on the lips. He pulled away to gauge Lilly's expression. Her eyes were closed, and she was smiling. The kiss had been a good move on his part. They just sat there, not speaking, until the song ended. Charlie opened the car door for Lilly and walked her to the front door.

Tomorrow was Sunday, family day at the Gray household. "If I'm able, I'll call you tomorrow," Charlie said. Lilly nodded.

"Good night, Charlie," Lilly told him. She was still walking on air after the goodnight kiss.

"Good night, Liliana," On the way home, Charlie found himself humming "Lips Like Sugar."

The next morning at breakfast, his parents were asking about the field trip with the astronomy club when Louis noticed Charlie's swollen lip. "What happened to you?" he asked.

"Uh, the guy next to me tripped, knocking me over in the process. My bottom lip connected with the metal edge of my telescope," Charlie lied.

"Does it hurt? Did you put some ice on it?" Helen asked, going into full mother mode.

"It's fine, Mom," Charlie said.

"Earthans," Louis said. "They are so clumsy."

Lilly woke up Sunday morning to find Michelle had already left for work. She made a decision. Charlie went to church every Sunday; she might as well go, too. She grabbed Abuela's rosary off the bedside table where it lay next to the statue of the Virgin.

After Mass, she made a grilled cheese sandwich and sat out by the pool with a book. This was Lilly's favorite time of year. The weather was great—warm enough, but not too hot.

Lilly heard Michelle's car pull into the driveway. "What are you doing home?" she asked as Michelle walked into the gate.

She walked over to the pool area. "It was slow, so I came home. Now, I want to hear all about the dance." Michelle pulled up a lawn chair next to Lilly's and propped her feet up. "So start at the beginning and tell me *everything*."

Lilly started with dinner and went through the evening. She edited out the part about the fight in the parking lot and ended with the ride home.

"So did Charlie try a lip lock on you?" Michelle asked with a smile.

"Mom," Lilly complained.

"C'mon, Lil," Michelle begged.

"Oh, all right," Lilly said and put down her book. "There was a kiss. It was very nice."

"Mi hija, homemade apple pie is very nice. C'mon, you can do better than that," Michelle scolded.

Lilly hit her mom with one of the lawn chair cushions. "That's all I'm going to say on the subject. Quit trying to live vicariously through my love life."

"OK, OK," Michelle grumbled as she got up. "I won't pry anymore. I'm going to go watch TV, you know, in case you want to call Charlie or something. Pretend I'm not here."

Lilly rolled her eyes and started to pick up her book up again. Then she remembered something. She looked at her watch. It was two o'clock. Last week Charlie had called at four thirty. She hoped he would call today, too.

Much later he did call. He was whispering and Lilly assumed he must be calling from home. "I can't talk for long, but I just wanted to tell you I've been thinking about you all day."

"Me, too. Last night was wonderful," Lilly said. She rolled her eyes at her own trite words. "Last night was wonderful" sounded so cliche, like something out of a made-for-TV movie, but she couldn't think of anything else to say that wouldn't come out even cornier. Charlie told her good night and said he couldn't wait to see her tomorrow. Lilly told him the same and hung up the phone. She lay down on her bed, replaying the kiss in her mind. Despite all the theatrics with Claire, it was still the best night of her life.

COFFEE AND PUMPKIN BREAD

On Monday morning, Beth caught up with Charlie after third period. "I don't know if you're aware of this, but Lilly's birthday is October twenty-second."

Charlie liked Beth. She was very straight forward and just spoke whatever was on her mind. "October twenty-second? That's this Thursday."

"I know. You need to start thinking about what you're going to do for her," Beth said.

"Do you have any suggestions?" Charlie asked. He had no idea what to do for a birthday. Birthdays weren't celebrated on Sentria.

"I don't know what your finances are like, but you two seem pretty serious."

Pretty serious, yes, Charlie thought. Beth was so perceptive, or maybe it was just blatantly obvious how he felt. Charlie nodded. "Um, so what do you think she'd like?"

"She loves silver. Maybe a piece of jewelry? And she likes dark chocolate. Just don't get her flowers. She can't stand them." Beth recommended a jewelry store that sold lots of silver charms and bracelets.

"OK," Charlie said. "I'll go tonight." Beth cocked her head and looked at him. She was studying Charlie, wondering about him.

Charlie felt self-conscious in a kind of paranoid way. "What?" he finally asked.

"You don't have an accent."

"Well, I'm not from Texas," Charlie said.

"No, I mean you don't have an accent from anywhere. You don't sound like you're from the West Coast, the East Coast, the North or the Midwest."

Charlie shrugged. He had to think of a lie quickly. "My mom made me speak clearly and enunciate every word when I was a little kid. I guess I learned to pronounce words in a textbook sort of way."

Beth looked at him skeptically, and Charlie didn't know if she accepted his answer or not. She picked up her book bag and turned to leave. "Just don't forget about the birthday present."

"I won't," Charlie said.

Everyone at the band table leaned over to listen to Lilly. Thanks to Ian, they all knew what happened at homecoming and wanted to know how Claire was doing.

"Well," Lilly began, "I was worried. I hadn't heard from her, so I called her last night. But she wasn't home. Her mom told me she was on a date with a guy from another school, so she can't be doing too bad." Lilly shrugged her shoulders. Claire was doing what she had always done, jumping right into a new relationship.

That afternoon Lilly and Charlie were sitting in Lilly's Jeep. Charlie was sipping his coffee. "Have you ever even *tried* coffee?"

"Uh, no. I don't have to try coffee to know I don't like it. I've never had a broken leg, but I know I don't want one," she told him.

"Not the same thing, Liliana."

"It's supposed to be cold this week." Lilly looked out the window. "Maybe I'll make some pumpkin bread. You want to come over Saturday, and we can bake some?"

"Pumpkin bread?" Charlie asked. "You actually make bread out of that orange squash?" He wrinkled his nose.

"Don't start, Charlie. Pumpkin bread is delicious."

"OK, I'll make a deal with you. I'll try your pumpkin bread, if you try my coffee."

Grudgingly, Lilly agreed. "OK, just don't make it too strong."

"I won't. We'll start you out slow," Charlie assured her.

As soon as he finished his dinner, Charlie asked to be excused. "I need to go to the library. I have a research paper due soon."

"That's fine. We'll see you later," Louis told him. Anything having to do with studying was all right with his father.

Charlie hopped in his car and headed to the jewelry store Beth had told him about. He wished he had asked for more specifics. Should he buy her earrings, a pin, a charm, what? He decided to just look around until he found something that he thought would appeal to her. In a display case on the far side of the store, he found a silver circle-shaped charm. He paused for a moment to inspect it more closely.

For Sentrians, giving a female a circle charm indicated a very serious commitment. A circle, with no beginning and no end, was the perfect symbol of Sentrian love. He probably should get something else. This relationship could never go anywhere. He looked around some more but then ended up back at the same display case.

Why not? he asked himself.

"I can think of lots of reasons why not," the voice in his head said. Before he had time to respond, a sales clerk approached him.

"Can I help you?"

"Yes, I'd like to get this charm, and I'll need to get a chain for it, also."

"Is this a gift? Would you like it gift-wrapped?"

"Yes, please," Charlie said. To his Liliana, it would simply be a nice piece of jewelry, and for that, he was glad. He didn't want to scare her off. Now the voice in his head was screaming at him. He told it to be quiet.

On Thursday Charlie and Beth arranged a small celebration for Lilly after band practice. Beth brought the paper plates and napkins. They insisted on singing "Happy Birthday" to her, and Lilly endured it. After their ritual trip to McDonald's, Charlie dropped Ian and Beth home. Beth gave Charlie a look. "See you guys tomorrow," she said.

"OK, bye, Beth," Lilly told her.

When they returned to the band-hall parking lot, Charlie turned to face Lilly. "I'd like to give you my gift now, if that's OK."

"Charlie, you didn't have to get me anything," Lilly said.

"Nonsense," Charlie said. "Eighteen is a milestone birthday here on Earth."

"Here on Earth?" Lilly asked.

"What I mean, is that, uh, eighteen is a milestone birthday everywhere," Charlie stumbled, trying to cover his mistake. "Here," he said, handing her the small package.

Lilly recognized the wrapping immediately. It was from her favorite jewelry store. She tore open the paper and opened the box. "Charlie, it's beautiful," she said. She picked it up to admire it. A perfect silver circle. "So unique, I love it." Lilly threw her arms around Charlie.

"So, will you wear it?" he asked.

"Always," she said. She lifted up her hair, and he slid it over her head and fastened the clasp. This time it was Lilly's turn to initiate a kiss.

It was cold on Saturday, as predicted. Charlie drove up to Lilly's house early. He was surprised to find her alone. Michelle had to work and would be gone most of the day. That made Charlie kind of happy and kind of nervous.

"Are you sure it's OK with your mom that I'm here?"

"Uh-huh. I told her you were coming over."

"And she doesn't mind?" Charlie asked incredulously.

"Charlie, Michelle adores you, and she trusts me. Why are you so worried? You're not going to try anything, are you?"

"I uh, I mean, no," Charlie said.

"Relax, I was just kidding. C'mon." She grabbed his hand and led him into the kitchen. The mixing bowls were in the sink, and the pumpkin bread was already in the oven. Charlie had to admit it smelled good.

While she checked the oven, Charlie went over to Michelle's coffeepot and started brewing. He looked out the kitchen window into the Garcia's backyard. They had a very nice swimming pool. Even with the cool weather and the leaves on the ground, it looked inviting. He could hear the lapping of the water against the side of the pool, beckoning him, enticing him…

"That smells awfully strong," Lilly commented, startling Charlie out of his reverie.

"Don't worry, that's for me. I have something different in mind for you." He pulled a small metal box of General Food's International coffee out of his jacket pocket—Suisse Mocha.

Lilly came over to inspect. "So we can celebrate the moments of our life," she joked.

"What?" Charlie asked, not catching the reference.

"You know. From the commercial." She sang a little bit of it. Charlie didn't get it. "Oh, never mind," Lilly said.

Charlie took out a teakettle and heated up some water. "I promised I'd start you out slow. This is coffee with training wheels."

While the pumpkin bread was baking, Charlie prepared Lilly's coffee. He poured some into a mug and poured himself a mug from the coffeepot. They sat down at the kitchen bar. Charlie watched her closely as she took a sip.

"Not bad," she admitted. "But I know this is like, pseudocoffee. The real thing is kind of strong and bitter."

"For some, it *is* an acquired taste," he agreed.

"Why is it so important that I drink coffee?" Lilly asked.

"Coffee is much more than a beverage. It's an experience."

"You know, Charlie, you could write your own commercial for the coffee industry. You're coffee's biggest fan." The buzzer went off on the oven. Lilly jumped up to take out the loaves. While the bread cooled, Charlie made Lilly another half a cup and refilled his mug.

"OK, your turn," Lilly said, bringing over a slice of pumpkin bread on a plate.

Charlie took a small bite to taste. He was pleasantly surprised. He couldn't believe how good orange-squash bread could taste. "You were right. This is really good." The only thing that would make it better was if he had picante sauce to dip it in.

"Told ya," Lilly said smugly.

After they finished their bread, Lilly started clearing the table. "Here, let me help," offered Charlie. Lilly filled the sink with water and soap and began scrubbing the mixing bowls. Charlie brought over their mugs and silverware. He came up behind Lilly and kissed her on the cheek as she continued washing. He took a towel out of the drawer and began drying.

"You really like your necklace?" he asked.

"I never take it off," she said. She rolled the charm between her fingers. After the dishes were done, they went into the den.

"So what do you want to do today?" Lilly asked. "Take a walk, rent a movie?"

"No. No TV," Charlie said. He pulled out a CD from his jacket pocket and loaded it into the CD player. He took off his jacket and put it on the chair. Then he closed the blinds and turned on the lamp, creating a cozy atmosphere. "Unchained Melody" began to play. He grabbed Lilly's hand and pulled her close to slow dance.

"Is this OK?" he asked her. She nodded. After it ended, "I Can't Help Falling in Love with You" began to play.

"Is this a CD of the oldies?" Lilly asked.

Charlie nodded. "These are some of my favorites from the fifties and sixties. Do you like them?"

"Umm," Lilly said as she snuggled her head into his chest. The music was soft, and in the quiet of her living room, she could hear his heartbeat. She jerked her head up. Something was wrong. It was pounding too fast. She was no doctor, but she knew no one should have such a rapid heartbeat. "Charlie, are you feeling OK?"

"Perfect, why do you ask?"

"Your heart rate is so fast. Are you ill?"

Charlie laughed, "No, I'm fine. I just have a very rapid heartbeat." So did all his people.

"Maybe we should sit down," Lilly said. "You need to have that checked out. It's not normal." She sat down on the couch and motioned for him to sit down, too.

"For me, it is. Trust me. I am completely healthy." He put his arm around her.

"Maybe at least chill out on the coffee. All that caffeine can't be good for your heart."

"Caffeine has no effect on us. I mean me. I mean, it doesn't affect me like it does some people." He grabbed her chin and turned her face toward his. Enough of the talk, especially when mouths could be used for other things. He put his hand behind her head and moved closer to her. She put her arms around his shoulders and drew near him. They kissed. Previously, their kisses had been short, innocent pecks. This time Charlie took his time and kissed her deeply. Lilly returned the kiss with equal intensity. Charlie pulled Lilly so close to him, he could feel her ribs through his shirt. She snuggled into his shoulder, and he held her tightly.

Lilly turned her head and looked into his eyes. "Charlie, I think I'm in love with you." Charlie's breath caught; he was shocked and didn't know what to do. Finally, he leaned over and kissed her forehead. He took her hand and traced a circle on her palm.

The voice in Charlie's head spoke up. "Now look what you've done." Charlie told the voice to shut up.

Charlie went straight to his room. It was rather late, but his parents were still not home. He got ready for bed. He took off his outer shirt and realized that he could smell a trace of her perspiration on it where Lilly had curled up next to him. Although sweating was a filthy Earthan trait, Charlie was not repulsed. He inhaled deeply. It smelled like Liliana, and that made it OK. Charlie sighed. She had told him she loved him. It was both endearing and troubling at the same time. Maybe he had discouraged her by not saying anything back. That was probably a good thing, but he still felt bad. He decided not to think about that tonight. He was content to keep the status quo for as long as possible.

Lilly was lying awake in her room, tossing and turning. She worried she had done something wrong. The moment seemed right, so she had just told him the truth. She did love him, but maybe she shouldn't have said it. Obviously, he did not feel the same way.

Lilly sighed. For once she wished she could ask Claire what to do. This whole boyfriend/romance thing was uncharted waters for her. Tomorrow she would do the only thing she could do. She would act as if she had said nothing at all.

THANKSGIVING

Conversation among the seniors the next day at lunch turned to college and entrance exams. When Lilly found out Charlie had not taken the SAT or picked a college, she couldn't believe it.

"What are you waiting for?"

"I'm not sure what's going to happen next year. My father's job is very unpredictable." That was definitely true.

"You mean you can't even pick a college if it isn't part of your dad's plan?" Lilly asked. His silence told her all she needed to know. "Look, you can at least take the SAT," Lilly told him. She convinced him to sign up for the next available test.

"Charlie, just think. Wouldn't it be great if we could go to the same school?" Lilly said excitedly.

"Yes," Charlie agreed.

"Have you at least thought about where you'd like to go?" Lilly asked. Charlie shook his head no. "Well, I'm thinking of Texas A&M or UT. Does either of those schools interest you?"

"I think either one of those schools would be great." He knew nothing about those two schools. To him, A&M sounded like an Earthan candy.

"Well, let's apply to both, and we'll see what happens. Charlie, you're a genius. You could get in anywhere."

That amused Charlie. He had been an excellent student on Sentria but his Earthan high school transcript was completely fabricated. Still, his fabricated grades were very good.

Lilly spotted Susan, the oboe player, standing in line on the other side of the cafeteria. This past summer Claire and Lilly had made plans to room together next year for college, but that was before the huge homecoming disaster. Lilly hadn't spoken to her in weeks. Lilly thought maybe she should try to find someone else to room with. "I'll be right back, I'm going to talk to Susan."

While she was gone, he thought about next year. If only her vision of the future could come true. Even if the Sentrian elders extended his father's job for a few more years, which was unlikely, he would probably not be allowed to stay and attend college. More likely, they would send him back to Sentria to go to work and hopefully find his One.

The trouble was, he didn't want someone else. This was not good. How could he ever find his One when his feelings were so strong for Liliana? He glanced over to where she was standing. She was talking and laughing, not a care in the world. He envied her.

Lilly ran back. "Charlie, guess what."

"You and Susan might room together next year," Charlie said without thinking.

Lilly was shocked. "How did you know?"

"Lucky guess," Charlie suggested. Lilly just stared at him. How did he know that? She had never brought it up before.

Louis Gray was in a foul mood the next day. Charlie's parents had been at an all-day meeting with the other Sentrian adults and the elders. The Earthans had found out some secret information that could potentially threaten their mission. They would have to double their efforts to hide their existence. That meant very long hours for Louis; even Helen would have to go to work. Data would have to go missing, disinformation spread. Research would need to be altered, whatever was necessary to keep the Earthans in the dark. While this was a difficult thing for his parents, it made it easier for Charlie to see Lilly.

He took full advantage of the situation. On Saturdays, he and Lilly would get in his car and just drive. One weekend they went to Spring, another they went to Lake Jackson, and another they went to Brenham. Soon he was attending Mass with Lilly. On Sunday afternoons they would stay in and watch movies. "Do you like *Back to the Future*?" Lilly asked one afternoon.

"Uh, I've never heard of it," Charlie answered. He should have just said, "Sure, I like it," but he was thinking of something else: Liliana standing beside a waterfall with her wet hair blowing in the wind.

"You've never heard of *Back to the Future*?" Lilly was surprised. "What? Are you from another planet or something?"

His eyes grew wide. "What makes you say that?" Charlie asked a little too harshly.

"I was just kidding. It's just a movie I thought you would really get into because part of it is set in the fifties, but we don't have to watch it."

"Oh," Charlie said, relieved. "Of course I want to see it." Lilly popped the movie into the VCR and pushed play. She was right. He did like it, even though the time travel aspect was ridiculous. Everyone knew that a DeLorean could never be turned into a time machine.

Michelle and Lilly invited Charlie over for Thanksgiving. His parents were working through the holiday and would not be home until Friday, so he eagerly accepted. Thanksgiving was an Earthan custom that Charlie was unfamiliar with. He knew it involved saying thanks for your blessings and eating turkey, but that was about all he knew.

When Charlie arrived for dinner, Lilly was pulling a pumpkin pie out of the oven. Charlie wrinkled his nose.

"Don't start with me, Charlie," Lilly complained. "You thought you wouldn't like my pumpkin bread, and now you love it."

"True," Charlie agreed. "Is there anything I can do?"

"Well, you can make the coffee if you want. But that's it. You sit down. You are the guest."

Charlie was happy to make the coffee. He had a cup of Mrs. Garcia's before, and it was terrible. "Where is your mom, anyway?"

"She's just leaving work. She'll be here soon," Lilly said.

Charlie started the coffeepot, then sat down at the bar. Michelle walked in a few minutes later and took off her coat. "It smells great, Lil. What can I do?"

"You can set the table and fill the glasses. Otherwise we're all set."

Charlie was impressed. For the first time since he had been having dinner with Lilly and her mom, they actually said grace. He was surprised when Lilly and her mom poured gravy over the turkey and potatoes, but completely left it off the cranberry sauce. *When in Rome,* Charlie thought and did the same. The food was all so good, and just like the Earthans, he ate way too much.

After dinner they went to the den to watch TV. Charlie poured the coffee, and Lilly sliced the pumpkin pie. Lilly was excited because *Rudolph, the Red-Nosed Reindeer* was coming on next.

"Don't you love it? I watch it every year. I have since I was a little girl."

"You mean like the song?" Charlie had heard the song. Lilly nodded. Charlie didn't know they had made a movie of it. He thought that was kind of strange. The song wasn't even that long. How much plot could this movie have?

"Yes, of course. Don't tell me you've never seen it."

Charlie didn't want to admit he hadn't seen it, like with *Back to the Future*. Instead, he said, "It's been a while."

"C'mon then," Lilly said. They sat on the couch and Lilly looped her arm through his and leaned against his shoulder. However bad this *Rudolph* movie was bound to be, it would be worth it just to have Lilly's warm cheek against his arm. Charlie was only halfway paying attention, when

Lilly sat up and said, "Next is my favorite part: the Island of Misfit Toys. Remember? They had a Charlie-In-The-Box. Just like you. Gosh, when I was a kid I always thought that was so funny." Lilly laughed just thinking about it.

Charlie thought it best if he laughed, too. So he did. Luckily, there was a commercial break. Charlie excused himself and ran to the bathroom. He whipped out his PCD and quickly typed in: Who is Charlie-In-The-Box and what about him is funny?

A response popped up on the screen.

CHARLIE-IN-THE-BOX IS A CHARACTER FROM THE 1964 CHRISTMAS-THEMED MOVIE *RUDOLPH, THE RED-NOSED REINDEER*. HE RESIDES ON THE ISLAND OF MISFIT TOYS AND HIS OFFICIAL CAPACITY IS SENTRY OF THE ISLAND. THE HUMOR OF HIS NAME LIES IN THE FACT THAT THE EARTHAN TOY THE CHARACTER IS BASED ON IS ALWAYS CALLED A JACK-IN-THE-BOX; THUS BY HAVING THE NAME CHARLIE, HE IS A MISFIT TOY.

He returned to the couch and sat down next to Lilly. This time he boldly put his arm around her. They watched the segment about the Island of Misfit Toys, and Charlie laughed in all the appropriate places. It did make him think, though. He was the Sentrian equivalent of a Charlie-In-The-Box. Getting involved with an Earthan—who ever heard of that? If the Sentrian government ever decided to designate an island for its anomalous and deviant citizens, Charlie would be the first to go.

Predictably, Michelle fell asleep in the recliner halfway through the movie. After it was over, Charlie said, "Thanks for having me over. I really did like the pumpkin pie."

"Thanks for coming," Lilly said, grabbing his hand. "Let me walk you out."

"No, Liliana. It's much too cold. Stay in here where it's warm."

"If you insist," Lilly said. She tilted her head back, closed her eyes, and puckered up. Charlie kissed her on the cheek. "Your mom's awake now," he whispered in her ear. Lilly turned to look, and Michelle waved at her. Sometimes having a mother could be so inconvenient.

When Charlie got home he was tired but happy. The food was good, but the company was even better. He thought Sentrians were immune to the effects of tryptophan but maybe not. All he wanted was to crawl in bed and sleep.

Charlie awoke to the sounds of whispering. It was dark outside, and Charlie wondered if his parents were just getting in or just getting up. He looked at the clock. It was five in the morning.

"I wouldn't mind the long hours, if I thought it would do any good, but I'm still not convinced it will," Helen said.

"I wouldn't mind the long hours, but it's giving up the worship days I mind," Louis said. "One day they tell us they respect our right to worship and have a day of rest, then the next day it's 'No, you can't go to services today. You must come to work.' Do they think we are total fools? That we don't know the Sentrian code of law? Or maybe they know we're too scared of them to complain."

"I think the latter. Just don't say that around the others. We don't need to get on Mr. Conner's bad side," Helen warned.

"I wouldn't dare," Louis said.

"Do you think we should tell Charlie?" Helen asked.

"Only as much as we have to. We don't need to burden him with this. Besides, there's nothing he can do about it. And I don't want you worrying about it either, dear. It will be fine."

Charlie got up then and went downstairs to the kitchen. "What's going on?" he asked. "Did you just get home?"

"No dear, we got home a few hours ago. Unfortunately we have to go back soon. You'll be on your own for a while. We're going to be working a lot," Helen said.

"For how long?" Charlie asked.

"Until we return to Sentria for Christmas break." All the families on the mission would return to Sentria for the extended holiday.

"Why? What's going on?" Charlie asked.

"Mr. Conner is not pleased with the way things are going. It turns out the information breach is much larger than they first thought," Louis said.

"I can't think about it anymore," Helen said. She hurried into her bedroom and shut the door. In many ways she was like a child. When things got too stressful, she preferred to hide in her room.

Louis watched her go and sighed. When she was out of earshot, Louis told Charlie, "All you need to know is that your mother and I are going to be keeping very late hours." Louis handed him a roll of cash. "For food and whatever else you need for the week."

Although Charlie was concerned for his parents, this couldn't have been better news for him. He waved good-bye when they left for work. Then he ran up the stairs, raced to the phone, and called Liliana.

"Hello," Lilly answered the phone groggily. It was then that Charlie looked at the clock. It was only five thirty; he should have waited to call.

"Did I wake you?" Charlie asked.

"That's OK. I was going to get up soon anyway. What's going on?"

"Well, I wanted to see if you had plans today."

"Not really, but aren't your parents home? I thought you said you had things to do with them today."

"Now they have to work. My schedule is wide open for the foreseeable future."

The following Friday the school held a pep rally for the last football game of the year. The band stood on the floor of the gym and played the fight song. All the classes stood up in the bleachers and clapped while it was being played. Then the coaches started talking about the team and how wonderfully they were doing. (They had lost every game except for two.) Next the cheerleaders came out and motioned for everyone to get up. The students stood up and started stomping their feet and clapping.

Amid the ruckus, Charlie heard a sound that got his attention. It was the sound of stressed metal, and it sounded as if it was on the verge of shearing. Charlie tilted his head to ascertain where the sound was coming from. It was the freshman section of the bleachers. They were still shouting and stomping, completely oblivious to the imminent danger.

Charlie thrust his trumpet into Matt's empty hand and ran toward the bleachers. "Get off of the bleachers," Charlie yelled. "They're going to fall." Most of the freshmen continued to shout and clap, not hearing Charlie. Others simply ignored him. The left side started to buckle. A freshman girl at the top of the bleachers lost her balance and fell. Charlie ran over and caught the girl before she hit the ground.

"It's OK. You're all right," Charlie said, as he set her down lightly. The girl stared wide-eyed at Charlie, then took off.

Lilly ran over to Charlie. "What's happening?"

"Not now, Liliana," Charlie said. At that moment the rest of the section began crashing down. Students were falling on top of each other. Charlie and Lilly ran over to help. Staff and students joined them to help the freshmen off the now collapsed bleachers. Fortunately, a broken ankle was the worst of the injuries. No one noticed what Charlie had done except the freshman girl and Lilly. Charlie knew the freshman girl wouldn't tell anyone. He had seen the fear in her eyes.

After learning everyone was safe, Lilly approached Charlie. "How did you know the bleachers were about to collapse?"

"I didn't know. I saw them shifting, and I ran over."

Except Lilly knew that wasn't true. She had been watching him and knew that his back was to the bleachers. "No. You weren't even looking in the right direction." Did he really expect her to believe that he could see something from that distance when no one else did? Lilly had gone with him to the eye doctor. She knew better than anyone that even with thick glasses his vision wasn't great, and yet, he was the first person to notice something was wrong. "So how did you know?" she asked him.

Charlie started to make up a lie, when Lilly followed with another question. "And how did you get to that girl so quickly?"

Charlie was losing his temper. "Why do you have to be so inquisitive? Do you really have to know everything about everything? Can't you, just for once, drop it?"

Lilly flinched. Charlie had never used such a harsh tone with her before, and it hurt her feelings. She turned to walk away. "Liliana, wait," he said. "I'm sorry."

"Whatever, Charlie." She headed for the band hall. Lilly sighed. Maybe her eyes were playing tricks on her. That had to be it.

REVELATIONS

Charlie awoke earlier than he intended. The voice in his head was arguing with him. "You need to end this. You've taken things too far."

"I've got it under control," Charlie told the voice defensively.

"It doesn't look that way to me." The voice had a point. Besides, it was getting harder and harder to keep it a secret. "What about when we return to Sentria?"

"I haven't figured that out yet," Charlie said.

"Well, you better figure it out. We're not going to stay here on Earth indefinitely."

"I know, I know," Charlie said.

"I still don't think continuing this relationship is a good idea. Are you sure you know what you're doing?"

Charlie put his pillow over his ears and tried to silence the voice. Unfortunately, he had to admit, the voice was correct. The more time Charlie spent with Liliana, the more time he wanted to spend with her, but reality was rearing its ugly head. At the end of the month, he would have to return to Sentria for two weeks. How would he explain his absence and that he wouldn't be able to contact her during that time?

That wasn't the only reality Charlie had to deal with. Lilly was not stupid, and she was starting to notice things about him, the recent pep rally being the most obvious. But there were other things. Things he could not easily explain away. The rapid heart rate was one. Also his extraordinary hearing and that no matter how hot it was, he didn't sweat. He couldn't even think about the numerous verbal slips. The charade was a burden, but what choice did he have? No other choice, if he wanted to keep seeing Lilly. Charlie sighed. Just thinking about it had put him in a really lousy mood.

Charlie was right about one thing—Lilly had noticed his strange behavior of late. He had always had his idiosyncrasies, but now it was like he was undergoing a personality change. When they first started dating, Charlie had been so easygoing, but now he was moody. It reminded Lilly of how he was at the beginning of the school year. Sometimes she wondered if he even wanted to be around her. Lilly hoped it wasn't the beginning of the end for them.

At the end of the school day, Lilly met up with Charlie. "So, you want to go to the diner this afternoon?"

Charlie shrugged.

"It's a simple question. Do you want to go or not?"

Charlie blew out his breath. "I guess so. I'll meet you at your house in an hour." He walked off before she had a chance to say good-bye.

By the time Charlie got to her house, it was thundering and lightning. They decided to wait out the storm. Lilly tried to engage him in conversation but he didn't say much. She finally gave up and started her homework.

The severe rainstorm left the road wet and slick, with tree limbs and leaves all over it. Lilly volunteered to drive to the diner and to her surprise, Charlie didn't even put up a fight. He was preoccupied and climbed into the passenger side of the Jeep without a word.

Lilly was playing her Depeche Mode tape and singing along. She had a nice voice, and normally he enjoyed her singing, but not today. Lilly tried to engage him in conversation. "So, do you think my mom will really get me a new car stereo for Christmas?" Charlie didn't answer but stared straight ahead.

This is great, Lilly thought. They had only been in the car for five minutes, and he was already sulking. "It would be so cool to actually have a CD player instead of this old tape player." No response from the copilot seat. Now Lilly was starting to get annoyed. "So Sunday, do you want to help my mom and me put up the Christmas tree? Silence. "My, you are in such a loquacious mood. I can barely get a word in edgewise," Lilly said.

"Stop," Charlie said.

"What?"

"Stop!" Charlie shouted. There was a fallen oak tree in the middle of the road just a few feet ahead of them. Charlie grabbed the wheel and steered them to the shoulder, while Lilly applied the brake. The Jeep skidded on the wet pavement, but Charlie managed to navigate them safely to the side of the road.

"Whoa. That was close," Lilly said. She should have been paying more attention. She looked over to see if Charlie was OK. "Hey, Charlie, what's wrong?"

He was staring straight ahead, and the expression on his face kind of worried her. He seemed *annoyed* with her. "Nothing," he said tersely.

"I don't buy it. You haven't said two words to me all day. And you've been so angry lately, like I'm getting on your nerves. Do you want to break up or something?"

Charlie turned and looked at her. He sighed. "No, that's not it at all," he said simply. He got out of the Jeep and started walking around it, checking the tires.

Lilly followed him. "Look, I've been really happy these last few months, but if this isn't what you want, then please, spare us both the pretense, and let's end this now."

"I told you. That's not what I want," Charlie said as he leaned over her right front tire. His tone wasn't harsh, but it was cold.

"Then what exactly is it that you *do* want?" Lilly asked.

"Never mind," he said.

"Forget it. Never mind. Just drop it. Is that all you know how to say?"

Charlie didn't say anything in response.

"You know what," Lilly said. "How about you never mind? How about you forget it? I am *so* out of here." He had turned away from her, and that made her even angrier. She flung the car keys, hitting him in the back. That got his attention.

"What's this?" he asked, stooping to pick up the keys.

"Drive yourself home. I'm walking."

"Don't be ridiculous," Charlie told her. She ignored him and headed down the road. "Liliana, you can't walk home. It's at least ten miles. C'mon, be reasonable," he said. She continued walking. "Come back," he said. "Don't run away. Talk to me."

She turned around then but didn't come any closer. "Oh, so now you want to talk. Too little, too late," she yelled at him. She turned back around and stormed off.

Charlie sighed. Why wouldn't she listen to him? Now he was angry, too. Charlie could hear Liliana griping about him, but he filtered her voice out. It would be better if he didn't hear what she was saying. They were both angry, and he didn't want to overhear something from her that he might be tempted to throw back in her face later.

After a few minutes of rapid walking, Lilly started to calm down. Charlie was right. It would be stupid to try to walk home just to prove a point. She would have to get back in the Jeep with him, whether she wanted to or not.

She muttered to herself. "So now you want to talk. Well, great. I'm not really in the mood. Just because I have to ride back in the car with you doesn't mean I have to talk to you. You're not the only one who knows how to give the silent treatment. I'm not going to say a thing to you. I can do it, too. Watch me. Just who do you think you are? Acting all miserable and not talking to me. But then you say you don't want to break up. Well, which is it? Maybe it's not up to you anymore. Maybe I want to break up with you. You've got a lot of nerve telling me never mind. You like not talking to me? Fine, then don't. The next thing that comes out of your mouth better be a big fat apology. Some groveling wouldn't hurt either," she said, as she made her way back through the woods to the highway. Oh, who was she kidding? Angry or not, she wanted to try to work things out. If he apologized and suggested they go to the diner, she would say yes in a heartbeat. She started running then, to get to him faster.

Charlie kicked a large rock that was in his way. It went flying into the woods. Why did she have to be so stubborn? In another half hour, it would be dark. If she didn't come back soon, he would have to go after her. He picked up the tree next and threw it as far as he could. It landed deep in the woods. Charlie looked up then. Lilly was standing across the road, staring at him in disbelief. Charlie froze. It was a very conspicuous show of strength. No Earthan could have moved it.

Lilly ran up to him. "Charlie, how did you do that?" He started to walk away but she ran and stood in front of him, blocking his way. "Tell me," she demanded.

"I don't think you want to know," he finally said.

His tone was so serious. Was he trying to frighten her? Well, it wouldn't work. "Yes, I do want to know what's going on with you. One minute you're happy; the next you won't speak to me. You tell me you don't want to break up, but when I ask you what you do want, you get angry. You say things that are odd. You know things you shouldn't know. You are able to do the impossible. Like throwing that tree…Shall I go on?"

He was silent for a moment, gathering his thoughts. "If I tell you, it might change things. How you feel about me. In fact, it probably will."

"That's not possible, Charlie," Lilly said. She cupped his cheek with the palm of her hand.

He grabbed her hand and put it down at her side. Then he stepped a few feet away from her. "OK," he said, taking in a breath. "Liliana, this is going to sound crazy, I know. But I'm not from here. I mean, I'm not from New Mexico. I'm from somewhere very far away."

"How far?" Lilly asked.

"Light-years," Charlie said.

"Be serious," Lilly said, shaking her head. If this was another attempt at evading the question or joking around, then she wasn't amused. She looked at his face. He wasn't kidding. "You're serious?" she asked. He nodded. That would mean…No, it couldn't be. Lilly thought back: his rapid heartbeat, incredible strength, never sweating. There was definitely something different about Charlie.

"Where, exactly?" she asked. She tried to sound calm, but she knew her voice was shaking.

"My planet is called Sentria. It's two galaxies away from the Milky Way. We come here periodically to make sure Earthans don't learn of our existence."

"So you're here to spy on us?" Lilly asked.

"Essentially," Charlie said. "The last time my family was here, some of your people actually found out about us. We had to make it seem like they were crazy conspiracy theorists."

"New Mexico," Lilly said. Of course. "You came from Roswell, didn't you?"

"Yes," Charlie said, "the last time I was here was back in 1958."

"You came from the fifties?" Lilly asked. Charlie nodded. "So you're, like, really old. You're my mom's age." Lilly started backing away from him.

"No," Charlie said calmly. "I'm your age. We can time travel."

Lilly stopped. "Like *Back to the Future*?"

"When it suits our purposes," he said.

Lilly's eyes grew wide. "Those Roswell pictures. That's what you really look like." Lilly shivered and crossed her arms. Just thinking about how many times Charlie had held her in those alien arms gave her the creeps. And she didn't even want to think about those alien lips pressed against hers. It was like kissing ET—so gross. She moved even farther away from him then.

"Liliana," Charlie was laughing at her. "Those were photos my government disseminated. They aren't real. They are just doctored images of some of our old fetal exams. We used them to perpetrate the whole conspiracy theory."

"So this is your real skin?" she said pointing to his body. She stayed at a distance.

"Yes. I'm flesh and blood," Charlie said.

"Just not *our* kind of flesh and blood," Lilly said. "That's why you can move that tree."

"Yes," Charlie said.

Lilly felt weak. She leaned against the bumper of the Jeep.

Charlie observed her pallor. "Are you OK?" He wanted to go over to her, but he knew that was probably not a good idea.

"I'm great," Lilly said. "My boyfriend's not even human. But other than that, everything's cool."

"No, I am human. I'm just not *Earthan*. I was made in God's image, just like you."

Lilly grew quiet then. She had asked for the truth, and he had given it to her, and now she had made the leap from disbelief to acceptance. But it came at a price. He moved toward her, but she looked as if she might run, so he stopped. Her fingers found her necklace, and she began playing with it. Then she realized it was the necklace *he* had given her. She dropped it and began twirling her hair with her fingers. He looked in her eyes. He saw fear there.

"Liliana? Are you OK? Speak!" Charlie commanded.

"This. Can't. Be." Lilly was mumbling very softly. Charlie would be the only one on this planet able to hear her.

"Liliana, I'm sorry. I didn't mean to frighten you. I'm sorry about all of this. I didn't mean for this to happen." Charlie approached her very slowly with his hands raised, showing her he meant her no harm.

Lilly backed away and looked at him. "What? You didn't mean for me to find out about you?"

"No," Charlie said. "I didn't mean to fall in love with you." Lilly said nothing. After what seemed an eternity of silence, Charlie asked, "Would you like me to take you home now?"

Lilly nodded.

―――

This time Charlie drove. They rode along in silence. Lilly sat as close to the passenger-side door as she possibly could. Charlie was afraid she might try to jump out the window. When he pulled into her driveway, she turned to him and finally spoke. "Charlie, I need some time alone, time to think about things."

"I understand if you don't want to see me again." He understood, but he hated the idea.

"No," she said. "I didn't say that. I'm just really confused." Charlie handed her the keys. She got out of the Jeep and ran into the house. Lilly locked the door behind her. She didn't know if it would do any good, but it made her feel better. Charlie sighed. He got into his Mustang and drove off. Lilly peeked out the window to make sure he was really gone.

She threw her purse down on her desk and lay down on her bed. She sat up suddenly. Charlie, her Charlie, was not from this world. In an instant, her reality had gone from normal and sane to bizarre and out of control. Why couldn't she a have a nice *normal* boyfriend? She didn't need a Mr. Rochester or Superman. She didn't want or need the drama that was the hallmark of Claire's love life. But now she was the one living the soap opera. This was not what she had signed up for.

All night she tossed and turned. She sat up suddenly in the bed and looked out her window at the night sky. Somewhere out there was Charlie's home. She shivered. Her feelings for Charlie were so conflicted. Lilly got out of bed and turned on her light. She sat at her desk, opened her notebook, and began a list. It was very short.

Cons	Pros
Charlie is an alien.	I'm in love with Charlie.

She chewed on her pen as she looked at the Pros column. Would that be enough to overcome his one big negative? It was going to be a long, nerve-wracking weekend, and she wasn't even sure what she would say to him come Monday morning.

Charlie went home to his empty house. He lay down on his bed and thought about the events of the day. He wished he could get a do-over. What if Liliana never spoke to him again? He spent a sleepless night. Finally, at about six in the morning, he nodded off. When he awoke, his parents had already left for work. It was a quarter of nine, so he decided to get up and take a shower. Then he went to the kitchen and made a pot of coffee. He couldn't stand it anymore; he had to know, one way or the other. He picked up the phone and called her.

The phone rang once before Lilly picked up. "Hello?"

"It's me. I just wanted to check on you. Are you OK?" he asked.

"I am now. I was kind of hoping you would call."

"Really? I was afraid I had scared you off," Charlie said.

"I don't scare that easy," she said. "Listen, I want to see you today. I have a lot of questions."

"I can be over in twenty minutes. Is that OK?"

"Perfect," Lilly said.

They stopped at McDonald's for coffee and hit the road again. Charlie thought it might be easier to talk if they were driving somewhere. No sooner had they pulled out of the drive-through than Lilly started grilling him. "Yesterday, you said you were made in God's image. You mean *my* God is your God?" Lilly asked.

"Liliana, there is only one Creator. We are your descendants."

"Our descendants?" she asked.

Charlie asked her, "What do you know about the Tower of Babel?"

Lilly thought back to Sunday school when she was a kid. "The people tried to build a tower that reached to heaven. God was upset with them, so He confused their language and scattered the people over the Earth."

"Yes, but there were a few, the masterminds, that God thought were too dangerous to stay on Earth. He relocated them to another planet. My planet—Sentria. This is why my parents can't find out about us. They would never comprehend our relationship. They believe my One is on Sentria, and I just haven't met her yet."

"Your *One*?" Lilly asked.

"The one I'm supposed to marry. Soul mate is a close approximation of the word. My people believe that God has selected one person for each of us, our One. We are created for our One. Our One is the only person to whom we can belong."

"So you bond for life?" Lilly asked.

"More like for eternity," Charlie said.

"One person for eternity? So your people can't fall in love more than once?"

"Not usually. It goes back to the beginning. After the Fall, free will was taken away from the angels who remained in heaven. When God created man, we all had free will, but after my people were sent to Sentria, God limited our free will. For example, Earthans have the ability to reject God, but Sentrians cannot disbelieve. After the exile, God also made my people only able to fall in love with one person—of His choosing—and we can never separate, not that we'd ever want to."

Charlie pulled up to the sea wall at Galveston. They took off their shoes and began walking up the shore. Charlie found the sound of the waves crashing onto the shore soothing. He didn't want to talk about such serious matters. If only he could step back in time, go back to a few weeks ago, before any of this was an issue. He imagined himself carrying Lilly into the sea and…

"But wait." Lilly broke his train of thought. "When I asked you if Sentrians can fall in love with more than one person, you said 'not usually.' What did you mean?"

"Sentrians have a life-span of about forty years. We don't get sick, but occasionally a person may die in an accident. There is a provision for the surviving spouse to take another person as a placekeeper to keep the family intact and be a role model for the children. But it's not the same. You can't truly love the placekeeper the way you love your One, and as soon as you die, you join your One. But as I said, that doesn't happen very often."

She stopped walking, and he turned to face her. "So after you die, you'll meet up with your One in heaven?" Lilly asked.

"Yes. We call it Sonora, but it is the same thing. We are with our One in the afterlife," Charlie said.

"So where does this leave us?" Lilly asked. "If your soul mate is on another planet, I guess I'm just some sort of diversion; someone to hang out with until you return."

"No, Liliana, you are so much more than that." He looked into her eyes. "Maybe there's something wrong with me. I don't know. I can't explain how this happened. It was never *supposed* to happen. But I know I couldn't love someone else. For me, you are my One."

"Oh," Lilly said. That was kind of cool and kind of scary at the same time. Scary in an intense way. She wanted to ask him more about it, but she was kind of afraid of the answers.

She changed the subject. "So why do you only live forty years?" At her age, forty seemed a long way off, but then again, Michelle was thirty-nine. She couldn't imagine her mom dying next year.

"God limited our life span after the Tower of Babel. That's another reason we marry so young. Twenty is middle-aged for us."

"So I guess if all your people believe in God, you all go to Sonora when you die," Lilly said.

"You'd think so, but unfortunately there are some Sentrians who believe there is a God, but don't believe *in* Him, if you know what I mean. Just because we all believe God exists doesn't mean that we all believe we need his love and forgiveness. Our arrogance and our belief in our own abilities is what landed us on Sentria to begin with. Some of my kind have a tendency to make gods of themselves."

Lilly thought of something then. "So I guess Charlie isn't your real name."

"No. It's a name my parents chose when we were in Roswell. They wanted me to have an American-sounding name, kind of like your mom's parents did for her. Back then, there was a commercial for hair oil with a guy named Charlie. 'Use Wildroot Cream-Oil, Charlie.' We all liked the sound of it, and the name stuck."

"You were named after a hairstyling product?" Lilly asked.

"Yes. What about you? How did your mom pick your name?"

"I was named for my grandmother, who died in the car accident. Liliana Elsa."

"Elsa's your middle name? I never knew that."

"Charlie, stay with me," Lilly scolded. "So what *is* your real name?"

"Silas," Charlie said.

"Silas," Lilly repeated. "It suits you, but so does Charlie. I think I prefer Charlie." Lilly put her arm through his as they walked. This was the first time she had initiated any physical contact since she found out who he was. He took it as a positive sign.

"So tell me how you knew about the bleachers. Can you predict the future or something?"

"No. I am what's called a supersonos. Some of my kind have superhearing. I *heard* the sound of the metal bolts breaking."

"Whoa, that's cool," Lilly said.

Charlie shrugged. "Sometimes. Any more questions?"

"Tons. How old were you when you were here before?"

"I was ten when we arrived and fourteen when we left. We stayed for a long time back then."

"So what were you doing on Sentria between then and now?"

"Earning an advanced degree in physics and biotechnology and another in information technology. With our shortened life-spans, we have to get into the work force earlier. Be good little worker bees for the government."

"Then what? It was time to come back to check in on the little Earthlings, so you got into your time machine. How exactly does that work?"

"It's kind of complicated, but look." Charlie picked a stick off the beach and drew a straight line. "This is how Earthans think of time, in a very linear fashion." Then he drew a circle over the line intersecting it in the middle. "We have a more circular view of time. This circle represents a forty-year life-span, our life-span. We can enter your linear timeline at any time within our circle." Charlie drew lines from the circle to the straight line.

"Like spokes on a wheel."

"Kind of," he said. "But we don't have to originate at the center."

"Can you go back in time?"

"Yes, but there's really no point. Our mission is to dispel any theories on extraterrestrial life. We've already accomplished that in the past. My father's been coming to Earth since the forties."

"So what brings you back now?" Lilly asked.

"Your NASA scientists. Your telescopes and satellites are becoming more sophisticated. We want to be sure you aren't getting too much information."

"So you've been spying on us all this time. Would it really be so bad if we found out about you?"

"Our leaders seem to think so. They think you might try to attack us out of fear or ignorance. Then my people would have to decimate you. We don't ever want things to escalate to that point."

"Well, what's going to happen now that I know?"

"Nothing, I hope," Charlie said. "You're not going to run to the *National Enquirer*, are you?"

"I wasn't planning on it," Lilly said.

"Good," Charlie said. "I know I can trust you, and I'm relieved that you know. It was getting harder and harder to come up with explanations for my strange behavior." He turned to face her then. Now he had a question for her. "Liliana, I know you noticed. Why didn't you say something?"

She had noticed, but she'd brushed it aside. She didn't want to borrow trouble. "Yeah, well, I was just so happy; I was trying hard to ignore it."

"Things will be changing in a few weeks for me. For us. My family and I are returning to Sentria for the Christmas break, and I don't know what my parents' work schedule is going to be like when we get back. Liliana, I can't contact you while I'm gone."

"You mean you'll be gone the whole two weeks?" Lilly asked.

"I'm afraid so."

"Oh," Lilly said. For the past few months Lilly had seen Charlie every day, for several hours at a time. Being apart for two weeks seemed like forever.

"C'mon," Charlie said.

"Where are we going?"

"To my house. This might be the only chance I have to show you my room."

Charlie's house looked like it came straight out of a *Leave It to Beaver* episode. The furniture, draperies, and the wall hangings, looked like they were from a different era. Mrs. Gray had a turquoise kitchen, complete with an old white Mixmaster on the counter. When Lilly walked through the Grays' living room, she paused at a photograph. There was a black-and-white picture of a couple and a young boy. The boy was Charlie. The woman wore a short-sleeve cashmere sweater with a small pearl necklace. Her hair was in a bubble flip. The man wore a suit and tie, and Charlie was wearing a button-down plaid shirt. All three wore the same type of dated glasses Charlie used to wear. Lilly briefly wondered if Mrs. Gray wore her necklace and high heels when she vacuumed the house.

"These are your parents?"

"Yes, this was from my first trip to Earth. I was about twelve in that picture."

"You all wear glasses," Lilly noted.

"Sentrians are severely myopic." When she paused at the foot of the stairs, Charlie grabbed her hand. "C'mon, I want to show you something."

Lilly was in awe when she walked into Charlie's room. There were so many electronic devices and other sophisticated pieces of equipment. He had at least three telescopes and two computers. There were so many gadgets. She didn't even know what most of them were for.

Charlie picked up his PCD. "OK, ask me a question. Anything."

Lilly thought for a second. "What is the capital of Texas?"

Charlie punched a few buttons on the device then turned the screen to face her. Austin appeared on the screen along with a summary of facts about the Lone Star State.

Lilly grabbed the PCD out of his hand. "How did you do that? That is so cool." Charlie let Lilly play with it for a while. She read a biography on Charlotte Bronte, searched fashion trends of the fifties, and even played a game of Ms. Pacman.

"Liliana, come here," Charlie called to her. He was at a large desk powering up what looked to her like a supercomputer. Reluctantly, she put the PCD down and joined him.

He pushed a few buttons. Then "You Send Me" began to play.

"Let me try," Lilly said after the song ended. She told him what she wanted and he typed it in. "Shell Shock" by New Order began to play.

"You want to know how I learned to dance so well?" Charlie asked. Lilly nodded. He punched some more buttons, and a screen with Arthur Murray dance lessons appeared. Dina, the friendly holographic dancer, appeared.

"So, who is the better dance partner, her or me?" Lilly asked.

"Definitely you," Charlie answered. The sun had disappeared below the horizon by then, and the stars were twinkling in the sky. Charlie walked her onto the balcony. A very unusual-looking telescope was pointed into the sky.

Charlie looked into the eyepiece, made a few adjustments, and then motioned for Lilly to take a look.

"You see that little star next to the bright star?" he asked.

"Yes," Lilly said.

"That's my galaxy. Sentria's too small to see, but at least you get an idea where it is."

"Tell me about Sentria," Lilly said.

"What do you want to know?"

"Everything. What's it like? What do you do when you're there?"

"Sentria is a small planet, much smaller than Earth. There are three moons that orbit Sentria, and the atmosphere gives a violet cast to the sky instead of blue. The gravitational pull on Sentria is stronger than here on Earth. There is much more resistance to everything we do: walking, lifting things, pushing, pulling. That's why we are so strong. We have to be. It's also warmer. A summer day could be 115 degrees. We have internal thermal controls instead of external like you do. That's why we don't sweat. What do I do there? Well, I just graduated with my dual degrees, as I told you. If I were there now I would start working for the government. On Sentria everyone works for the government, and they assign you a job based on your skill set."

"Really?" Lilly asked. She thought that was interesting. "Where do you live? What are your homes like?"

"I live in a town named Isacar. It's near the capital, New Cairo. We were assigned to live there because of my father's job. Our house there is smaller than our house here on Earth. It's kind of plain, square shaped, and gray. On Sentria, the size of the house you get is based on the number of children you have and your value to the state. Those with important government positions have nicer homes and other privileges."

"Does the government decide how many kids you have, too?" Lilly asked sarcastically. She was stunned when he told her yes.

"When you get engaged, you go to the marriage and procreation office and draw a card," Charlie explained. "It's kind of like a lottery. The cards have the numbers zero, one, two, or three on them, indicating the number of children you're allotted. If you draw the zero card, you're sterilized on the spot."

"Whoa. Your government sounds pretty controlling."

"In certain ways, I guess, but it's for our own good. They do it all to maintain order and peace. I guess that's why I find books like *Atlas Shrugged* and *1984* so fascinating. Rebelling against the government is such a foreign concept to us."

Lilly couldn't understand how he could take it all in stride. "Call me paranoid, but I could never be so trusting of the government. And I am deeply suspicious of any government that claims to be doing things for my own good. Doesn't that ever bother you, the control thing?"

"You make it sound like we don't have any freedoms."

"It doesn't sound like you do. Name one," Lilly challenged.

"The government cannot dictate who our One is," Charlie said.

Lilly shook her head. "That doesn't count. God chooses your One. Try again."

Charlie thought. "We are afforded some privacy in our own homes. We can say anything we want in our own homes without worrying about the government leaders or political police listening in."

"Political police? You *actually* have a political police? How magnanimous of them—letting you speak freely in your own homes," Lilly said sarcastically.

"Look, they don't want our speech to incite a rebellion or something. Earthans have a long history of war, but Sentrians have lived in peace for a thousand years. Our goal in life is to find our One and be happy. We don't live as long as Earthans, so we don't have the luxury of time to fight for rights we don't deem as important."

"So none of this Big Brother stuff bothers you?" Lilly asked.

"Sometimes." Charlie shrugged. "But Sentrians are more interested in their electronic gadgets. As long as a Sentrian has his PCD, he couldn't care less about his so-called freedoms. When the exiles first arrived, Sentria was a type of theocracy. God appointed a king and limited our free will. It was a time of repentance for my people. Over time, certain Sentrians wanted absolute power and control. They became an elite class and infiltrated the government. That's when they started trying to control most aspects of our lives. But our religious law is sacred, and they cannot interfere with it. Besides, as long as you follow the rules, they leave you alone."

"You don't seem to be following the rules. What would happen if they found out about us?" Lilly asked.

"They're not going to find out about us." It came out a little harsher than Charlie intended. "I've given them no reason to be suspicious, and the little spy they have here with me couldn't care less what I do."

"Little spy? What are you talking about?" Lilly asked.

"His name is Henry. Henry Conner. He's the magistrate's son, a sophomore. There are six other Sentrian families here. Each family is put in proximity to another family to keep tabs on one another. My father was worried because the magistrate lives in our neighborhood, and his son is in our school. But the whole semester, he hasn't said one word to me. I hardly even see him.

"I don't think I know him," Lilly said.

"I'm not surprised. He pretty much keeps to himself."

"And you're not worried he'll find out about us? I mean, it's not exactly a secret that we're going out."

"You'd have to know Henry. He's completely oblivious to everything around him. He's sort of weird. He's very asocial and doesn't really fit in with his peer group. His father may be the magistrate, but he's just here like the rest of us, biding his time until it's time to return home."

If Charlie thought Henry was weird, he must be strange indeed. "Who's this magistrate person?" she asked.

"Head elder of the Sentrians. He's the man in charge while we're on our mission here, and when we return to Sentria, he'll go back to his high position in the government." Charlie looked at his watch. It was getting late; best not to take chances. "I think I'd better get you home before my parents come back."

"Can you stay for a little while?" Lilly asked when they got to her house. "I'm starving, and you must be, too. I could make us some crappy pizzas."

"Crappy pizzas? Sounds appetizing," Charlie said.

"It's a name my mom and I came up with for cheap frozen pizzas. OK, so they aren't the best, but they will fill your stomach."

"I am pretty hungry. The cardboard box would taste pretty good right now," Charlie said. Lilly prepared the pizzas, and Charlie brewed the coffee.

Charlie didn't want to leave. He had been very worried this morning, but this day had turned out so much better than he could have hoped for. "I am so happy, you know. It's such a relief," he told her as he spread peanut butter on his pizza.

"This clears up a lot of things for me, too. Now I understand why you do the things you do," she told him, looking down at his plate.

"And this doesn't change the way you feel about me?" he asked.

"I'll admit I was freaked out at first, but I've gotten used to having you around. I think I'll keep you," Lilly told him.

CHRISTMAS BREAK

Michelle had Sunday off, so she joined Lilly and Charlie for Mass. Afterward, Michelle took them all out to lunch.

"Thank you for inviting me," Charlie told Michelle.

"You're welcome. Be sure and eat up. You're going to need your strength to help us with all the Christmas decorations." Michelle really liked having Charlie around. Lilly noticed that she kind of treated him as if he was the man of the house. She even had honey-dos for him. Charlie didn't mind. It made him feel like he belonged.

Over the years Michelle had amassed quite a collection of Christmas decorations from her mom and Abuela. Lilly was relieved to have such a strong guy to help with all the heavy lifting. She sent Charlie into the attic to bring down the boxes. Charlie was small enough to fit easily through the attic door but coordinated enough to carry multiple boxes down at a time.

With his aptitude for electronics, Charlie was the perfect person to put the strings of lights in working order. He replaced the broken bulbs, and Lilly was impressed at how evenly and symmetrically he hung the lights on the tree.

"How does it look?" Charlie asked.

"Like someone with advanced degrees in math and science decorated it."

"Is that bad?" Charlie asked.

"No. Just very precise. And I happen to like precision. Can you help me with the beads now?" Lilly asked. Charlie stood on a step stool, and Lilly tossed him a string of beads.

"You know," Charlie said, "I've noticed that every Christmas tree is different. Why all the variation in Christmas tree decoration? It would seem, if you are all celebrating the same holiday, you would decorate in the same fashion."

"Well, a lot of it is about tradition. For example," Lilly said, picking up an ornament, "we treasure this ornament because Abuela made it herself. In our family, either white or multicolored lights are fine, but no blinky lights—too Las Vegas. And tinsel is so messy. We prefer beads. It is also our tradition to have a star as a tree topper instead of an angel." Lilly thought about it for a second. "Charlie, don't your people celebrate Christmas?"

"Yes, we celebrate the coming of the Savior. The star that went supernova and led the wise men to the Christ child was closer to my solar system than yours. But we have a feast day, not a Christmas tree, and we celebrate it at a different time of year. When I return to Sentria, we will celebrate a different holiday."

"What holiday is that?"

"It's called the Holy Day of Reconciliation. It is to commemorate God bringing us to Sentria and making peace with us again."

Lilly wanted to ask more about it but Charlie grew quiet, and a moment later Lilly realized her mom was coming down the hall. Michelle had been hanging the stockings and putting out her snowman collection in the den. She came into the living room to help with the tree. The three of them put the finishing touches on it then sat on the couch to admire their work.

"You guys did a great job. The tree looks fantastic," Michelle said.

"You say that every year, Mom."

"Well, I mean it every year. Hey, Charlie, if you aren't doing anything for Christmas Eve, we always have tamales and go to Midnight Mass. You should come over."

"Mom, Charlie's going out of town for Christmas break."

"Are you visiting family?" Michelle asked.

"Yes," Charlie said simply.

"I wish you could be here, but I know it'll be nice for you to see them at Christmas. You have a safe trip. And don't worry, I'll try to keep Lilly entertained while you're gone." Michelle yawned. "I think I'll go watch TV, if I can stay awake."

"Can I make you some coffee?" Charlie asked.

"That would be great," Michelle said.

Charlie went into the kitchen to make the coffee, leaving Lilly to her thoughts. She normally loved this time of year, but this year she felt kind of empty inside. A few minutes later Charlie returned with two mugs of steaming coffee in his hands.

"Here. I thought this might keep you warm," he said, handing her a mug.

"Thanks," Lilly said.

"What's wrong?" he asked.

"It's nothing; I'm just being selfish."

"How do you mean?" Charlie asked.

"I wish you weren't leaving. I don't want you to go."

"I know," Charlie said. "Me neither." Even though Sentria was his home, and it would be good to see some of his friends, he really didn't want to leave Lilly. "Let's just enjoy tonight. We still have two weeks until I leave."

Lilly rested her head on Charlie's shoulder, and they gazed at the Christmas tree. A few minutes later, they heard Michelle snoring in the recliner.

Finals were scheduled the week before Christmas break, and Charlie came over every afternoon to study with Lilly. She worked very hard and made all As. Charlie aced his finals without much effort.

There was only one day left of school before Christmas break. Charlie planned a special evening for their last night together. He drove Lilly around to look at Christmas lights, and then he took her to the diner for dinner. The Christmas lights were pretty, and Lilly appreciated the effort, but her mind kept drifting back to the fact that Charlie would be leaving soon.

They returned to Lilly's house to exchange gifts. "Here, open mine first," Charlie said.

She opened the package and saw that it was full of CDs. "I created them from my computer files. All of our favorite music." Charlie had been introducing Lilly to music from the fifties and sixties, and Lilly had turned him on to Depeche Mode and New Order.

Lilly hugged him. "This is perfect. I can listen to these, and it will remind me of you." She pulled out a large gift bag. "My turn."

He opened the bag and peered inside. "New clothes?"

"You are in desperate need of a fashion update. It's from Michelle, too." He pulled out a polo shirt, new jeans, and a pair of dark blue tennis shoes.

"Thanks. I feel so eighties." He leaned over and kissed her cheek.

"There's more," she said. "Check the bottom of the bag."

He pulled out a framed picture. It was one of the homecoming pictures Michelle had taken of the two of them. Charlie smiled. That was such a happy time for them. This was the first and only picture he had of Lilly. "The clothes are great, but this is the best."

Charlie got home a little before nine. He took the homecoming picture out of its frame and carefully packed it in his duffel bag. There was no way he was leaving that picture behind. The next day Charlie barely saw Lilly. They sat together at lunch and talked about what they would do when Charlie returned. Of course, that all depended on his parents' work schedule. After last period he gave Lilly a hug good-bye, and that was the last time they saw each other. Lilly's stomach was in a knot, but it wasn't just because she would miss Charlie. She wasn't as perceptive as Beth, but she had a bad feeling about Charlie leaving.

It was very late that night when the Grays traveled to the vacant field. They needed the cloak of darkness in order to make the trip without drawing attention to themselves. As soon as they arrived, Louis punched in a pass code that opened the gate. They waited with the other families until it was time to leave. They were all wearing their travel uniforms.

Mr. Conner ordered the families to line up. "The ship has docked. Begin the loading protocol."

They gathered their belongings and lined up in an orderly fashion. Out of the darkness a large ship gradually materialized. The families began boarding.

The inside of the ship was divided into two compartments with a hallway between them. Each department was subdivided into individual pods, one pod for each family. The Grays went straight to their respective pod.

Louis Gray opened the storage compartment, and Charlie helped him put in their belongings. The pods were very sparse. They were designed for only two purposes: to store their things and to hold the sleeping chambers, which were nothing more than built-in cots with a clear cover over them. The covers opened, and the Grays climbed in. As soon as they were safely in place, the covers closed. The entire loading protocol took less than ten minutes.

Charlie closed his eyes and waited for the sleeping vapor to engulf him. The last sound he heard was the quiet hum of the engines. He hoped he would have pleasant dreams of Earth.

Michelle was scheduled to work the entire weekend before Christmas. Lilly was relieved. If her mom was home, she would insist on dragging her to a movie or to a restaurant.

She took advantage of the school break to sleep in. When she finally got up, she made a pot of coffee and grabbed a book. Catching up on her leisure reading over the holiday was usually a priority for Lilly, but her mind kept wandering. After five minutes of reading the same paragraph over and over, she decided to go for a walk. She put one of the CDs Charlie had made for her in her Discman and headed out the door. For the first time she could remember, Lilly could not wait for Christmas break to end.

Charlie awoke to the familiar sight of a violet horizon. The journey had taken almost two days. It would be Sunday night on Earth. He jumped out of the sleeping chamber as soon as the cover opened. He took his duffel bag out of the storage compartment and debarked. It took some effort to walk out of the ship. He had grown used to the lighter gravitational pull on Earth. Now that he was on Sentria, it felt as if he was walking through waist-high water.

A small group of friends and family members had gathered to welcome the travelers home. There were a couple of acquaintances of his parents and some former students from the learning center Charlie had attended, but most of the people he did not recognize. He was surprised to see Eve among the group. She nodded, and he gave her the Sentrian wave. He wondered who she knew who was returning from the mission. As soon as Louis and Helen were ready, they headed home.

Sentrians did not have individual cars like on Earth. Instead they traveled by a very sophisticated rail system. Its branches ran throughout all the major cities and many of its smaller towns. Charlie and his parents climbed into an empty car. Louis punched in the coordinates, and the car flew down the tracks to its programmed destination.

It only took ten minutes to get home. Charlie's house was on a street with nine other houses. They were virtually identical. The only difference was that each was painted a different color. The car pulled up in front of a gray home on Vespa Street. Charlie climbed out of the car and walked up the steps to 396A J1.

As soon as Charlie unpacked his bag, he went straight to the electronic note board in his room. A few of his friends had left messages for him. Charlie retrieved the first message. It was his friend Daniel. "Silas, I'm glad you're back. We have a lot to catch up on. Quite a lot has happened since you've been gone. Contact me when you're able."

Daniel was the one person he really wanted to see tonight. Charlie quickly scanned through the other messages. Most were from former classmates welcoming him home. One was from Eve, the girl he saw earlier greeting the returning ship. Charlie had briefly dated her the former spring season, but he quickly realized she was not the One. They both agreed it was best to go their separate ways. He thought it odd that she would leave him a message. Charlie closed the note board without retrieving it. Tonight there would be a festival for the Sentrian Holy Day of Reconciliation to commemorate God forgiving his people after their exile from Earth. He lay down on his bed, intending to rest, but after a few minutes he got up and took the picture of Liliana out of his bag. He wondered what she was doing.

As soon as Charlie arrived at the festival hall, he searched the crowd for Daniel. He was curious about the message Daniel left him. He finally found him standing by the refreshment table.

"Silas," Daniel said, waving his second and third fingers in Sentrian greeting. "So, how is Earth in 1988? It can't be as good as the fifties."

"Actually, it's pretty great," Silas/Charlie said. He poured himself a cup of pentab, an inferior facsimile of coffee. He grimaced as he swallowed it.

"C'mon, it's not that bad," Daniel said.

"Yes, it is."

"You're just spoiled by the real thing."

"I suppose. I saw your message. So tell me, what's been happening since I've been away?"

"Not here," Daniel said, glancing over at the magistrate and his family. "Let's go outside." When they were out of the sight of the prying cameras, Daniel said, "I don't know how much your parents have told you, or how much they even know, but the mission was very nearly imperiled while you were down there."

Silas only knew that his parents had been working themselves to death over some near catastrophe. "Not much," Silas told him.

"You know Jude's family, don't you? His father?" Daniel asked.

"Sort of." Jude's father worked in a different department than Louis. "My father hasn't said anything about him."

"That's because they put him in isolation until the ship returned. He's in deep trouble. Evidently he became too friendly with some of the Earthans and let some secrets slip. The magistrate and the elders had to scramble to cover it up. The adults have been doing everything in their power to prevent the Earthans from finding out the truth."

"This is a really big deal."

"Yes, it is a big deal," Daniel said. "I heard they're going to initiate new rules for those returning to Earth. Sorry, friend, but they are going to put all of you under the microscope. They'll be watching everyone more closely."

Charlie's mood darkened. This was not good. It would necessarily affect his ability to see Lilly. "What's going to happen to Jude's father?"

"He's already been sentenced. He'll be locked up for the next five years. If he doesn't get into any trouble in prison, they will release him for the last year of his life."

"That's harsh," Charlie said. With only a forty-year life-span, a five-year sentence was brutal.

"They mean business. You watch yourself down there. Hey, did you hear about your old girlfriend?"

"Eve was *not* my girlfriend. We just dated a few times."

"OK, OK, your *almost* girlfriend. She's getting married to the magistrate's son."

"Henry? I mean Hosea?" Silas nearly choked on his pentab. "But he's been down on Earth with me."

"I know, but they evidently bonded through electronic communications."

Charlie processed this information. Henry/Hosea did not seem Eve's type, but then who was he to judge who someone's soul mate should be? Hosea was an introvert, a loner. Eve was outgoing and social. She was also quite attractive. She had platinum-blonde hair and violet eyes, an exotic Sentrian trait. From his brief time with her, he knew Eve was very ambitious and had lofty political aspirations. Marrying the magistrate's son would certainly go a long way toward attaining those goals. It appeared this arrangement was mutually beneficial.

"Eve's mother and the magistrate's wife have been busy making the preparations. The wedding is this Friday."

"So soon?"

"Yes. The magistrate is taking Eve back with them to Earth."

"That's crazy. Why wouldn't they stay here?"

"I don't know," Daniel said. "It seems strange to me, too." His wife, Elizabeth, walked up to them with their daughter. "It's good to see you, Silas."

"It's wonderful to see you, too, Elizabeth. Hannah is getting so big."

"Yes, she's growing like a J-aphthenia plant. I hope you'll make time during your visit to come to our house for dinner."

"I wouldn't miss it. Name the date."

"How about Wednesday?"

"I'll be there," Silas said.

The secretary to the magistrate walked up to the podium then. He motioned for silence. "We will now assemble in the temple for our service before the feast."

Charlie joined his parents for the service, but he made a mental note to ask them later what they knew about the scandal involving Jude's father.

The mood was light in the banquet hall during the feast. It wasn't just a celebratory dinner; for many it was a family reunion with those who had been on the mission. As much as he disliked being separated from Liliana, Charlie had to admit it was good to see everyone. As the meal was ending, the magistrate walked to the front of the banquet hall to speak. Everyone grew quiet and turned their attention to him.

"It is a pleasure, my friends, to be with you; to have fellowship with you and break bread during this Holy Day of Reconciliation. I want to thank you all for the warm welcome you have given my family and all the families who have returned for a short respite before resuming their mission on Earth. Before we retire for the evening, I would like to extend an invitation to all of you for the wedding of my son Hosea to his lovely bride, Eve. As you are likely aware, the ceremony is this Friday. They make me very proud."

The magistrate motioned for the couple to stand. Eve was on her feet immediately, and Hosea reluctantly stood with her. The hall erupted in applause. Hosea looked like he would prefer to sit under the table than to be the center of attention. After the applause died down and the couple took their seats, the priest walked up to the front of the hall and performed the benediction. Then he closed the services. "Go in peace. Serve the Lord."

"Thanks be to God," the people responded.

The magistrate's family, including his soon-to-be daughter-in-law, exited the hall first. The elders' families and other government officials were next to leave, and finally the commoner families filed out. Silas knew that, although it was worded as an invitation, it wasn't optional. Attendance at Hosea and Eve's wedding was mandatory.

"Good morning," Silas told his parents as he sat down at the breakfast table. Louis was reading the Sentrian news on his PCD.

"Good morning, Charlie, I mean Silas," his mother said. "Do you want a cup of pentab?"

"No thanks, Mom. But you can call me Charlie. I don't mind."

"That's a good idea, son. I think it best if we all call each other by our Earthan names so we don't slip up when we return," Louis said.

"Father?"

"Yes?" Louis did not look up from his PCD.

"What really happened on Earth this past month? Daniel was telling me Jude's father is in a lot of trouble."

Louis sighed and put his PCD down. "I suppose you might as well know. Mr. Lassiter made a foolish mistake. He thought he could help the Earthans by sharing some of our technology and formulas with them. Even worse, he trusted them to keep quiet about it. Well, they didn't. Instead, they went to Mr. Jones and asked him if he thought this technology was possible. Being the pond slooth that he is, Jones ran straight to the elders with the information. We all worked overtime to discredit the Earthans and cover up Mr. Lassiter's mistake. Unfortunately, a few Earthans lost their jobs, and Mr. Lassiter, of course, will be incarcerated for a very long time. Tragic, really."

"I'm just glad you weren't working in Mr. Lassiter's department. You never would have turned him in, and then they would have found some way to blame you for the security breach," Helen said.

Louis nodded and turned his attention back to his PCD. Charlie thought back to his electronic note pad and the message from Eve. Now that he knew she was planning to come to Earth with Henry, he was suddenly quite interested in what she had to say. He shut the door to his room and took the note pad to his bed. Eve appeared on the screen, beautiful as always. Her voice was alluring, seductive. Charlie could certainly understand why any male would be attracted to her.

"I hope this message finds you well and happy. We all look forward to your return for the Holy Day celebration. Because of our history together, I wanted you to hear this from me first. Silas, I've found my One. It's Hosea. We are getting married soon after you return. I hope you will be able to attend. I haven't given up on you, though. There's still time for you to find your One, and then you will be just as happy as I am."

Charlie rolled his eyes.

"I hope we can be cordial to each other. I will be returning with Hosea to Earth and will be attending school with both of you. I'm even planning on joining the band, just like you. The magistrate has given me an important role in the supervision of the younger generation while the parents are working hard for the good of Sentria. You might as well start referring to me as Evelyn, my Earthan name. Good-bye for now, Silas." Eve/Evelyn's image faded from the screen and the message ended.

So Eve would be coming to Earth in an official capacity as supervisor of the youth. There was something that bothered Silas. Why was she joining the band? He wished she would pick a different activity. Charlie leaned back in his chair and chuckled to himself. He had to admit he was partially amused and partially dismayed by her message. Amused that she thought he'd be crushed by the announcement of her pending nuptials. Dismayed that his power-hungry ex-girlfriend was returning with him to Earth in a position of authority.

With far fewer distractions than Charlie had, time was passing very slowly for Lilly. She thought it was pitiful that she couldn't even think of anything to do for the two weeks Charlie was gone. What had she done before she met Charlie? It was only Tuesday afternoon, and she found herself in front of the TV, only minimally cognizant of what was happening on the screen. About twenty minutes into the program, she switched it off.

It wasn't that cold. She could take a walk around the neighborhood, but she was lonely and wanted to be around other people. She grabbed her jacket and headed for the mall. There, she could at least walk around and people-watch. Even hanging out at the food court sounded better than sitting alone in an empty house.

She walked around the first floor of the mall and was about to hop on the escalator when she felt someone tug on her arm. "Beth, what are you doing here?" Beth was definitely not the "hang out at the mall" type.

"Ian just *had* to get a CD. Some wretched sellout band he likes. So pathetic." Beth rolled her eyes. Now that Ian had a driver's license, they no longer bummed rides from Lilly. "So what are you doing here?" Beth asked.

Lilly shrugged. "I was kind of bored at home and decided I'd get out of the house for a bit."

"Gee, Lil. You're really lost without Charlie."

Gee, Beth. Thanks for noticing, Lilly thought. She blew out her breath. "Is it that obvious?" Beth nodded. "Man, I'm even more pathetic than Ian."

"Please, Lil, no one's *that* pathetic. C'mon," Beth said. "You're joining us for a slice of pizza at the food court."

"Oh no. I don't want to tag along. You two have a good time," Lilly said.

"I insist that you come. You won't be a drag; I won't let you."

"Mom," Ian said as he walked up to them. "What are you doing here?"

"She's joining us for pizza," Beth said.

"Cool."

Silas arrived early at Daniel and Elizabeth's house for dinner. He wanted to know if Daniel had found out anything new about Eve and her position on the mission.

"Silas," Elizabeth greeted him warmly. "Daniel's in the basement tinkering with the comfort controls in the house. Maybe you can give him a hand. They haven't worked correctly since we moved in. Oh, and tell my dearest that dinner is almost ready."

"Will do," Silas said and walked down the stairs.

"Welcome, Silas," Daniel said.

"Elizabeth sent me down to help."

"I'm glad. If I don't get these comfort controls working properly, my darling bride will end my life prematurely. She hasn't been able to make a cup of hot pentab all week. Here," Daniel said handing Silas a tool that vaguely resembled an Earthan wrench.

"Have you heard anything new about Eve coming to Earth?" Silas asked.

"Why the interest? I thought you two didn't click." Daniel naturally assumed Silas was jealous.

"We *didn't* click," Silas emphasized. "She sent me a message a few weeks ago. I finally watched it after the celebration. She had some very interesting things to say."

"All I know is what I told you the night of the feast, but I did hear that the magistrate's going to make a big announcement before the mission group returns to Earth. So tell me, what kind of interesting things did she have to say?"

"Well, according to her message, she's coming to Earth in some kind of leadership role. She's going to be in charge of the youth while the adults are working."

"Your ex is going to be your supervisor?" Daniel asked. "I hope she doesn't hold a grudge."

"Me, too." Silas didn't really think she would. After all, she was about to get married. He was more concerned about how much control she would have over him and his peers when he returned.

"Daniel? Dinner's ready," Elizabeth called down. They put down their tools and went upstairs.

After saying a blessing, the guys knelt down to eat. They reclined at the table while Elizabeth was in the kitchen preparing Hannah's meal. "Silas, I have someone I want you to meet," she said.

Oh no, here we go again, Silas thought. It was always the same. If his friends and family weren't trying to set him up with someone, they were reassuring him that he wasn't too old to find his One. Why couldn't they let God handle that part and leave him alone?

"She's seventeen. She's from the Coral province and she…"

"Thanks, Elizabeth," Silas interrupted. "But I really don't have time right now. Maybe when I return from the mission."

"Oh sure, Silas. Just let me know." Charlie could tell by her expression she was a little disappointed.

After working a double shift on Christmas day, Michelle took the next day off and insisted on blowing all her holiday double-time pay on post-Christmas sales with Lilly. Her mom had bought her a new stereo with a CD player for the Jeep. She had given it to Lilly before Charlie left so that he could install it for her. Now, they were listening to one of the oldies CDs Charlie had given to Lilly as they were driving to the mall.

"So do you have plans for New Year's?" Michelle asked.

"No, not really." Beth and Ian had invited her over to Beth's house to pop fireworks, but Lilly didn't enjoy fireworks and really didn't want to go.

"Jeannie and Bill invited us over for a New Year's party. You want to go?" Jeannie was a nurse who worked with Michelle. They had a really nice house in River Oaks, and their parties were always extravagant affairs.

"Actually, Mom, I just thought I'd stay home. There's a *Twilight Zone* marathon on, but you go ahead."

"Nah. I don't want to go without you. Besides, *Twilight Zone* sounds like more fun."

"Mom, you should go. You love their parties. I'll be fine."

"I don't know," Michelle said. "I told Charlie I'd keep you company while he was gone, but you're not making it very easy."

"Mom, c'mon," Lilly said.

"All right, all right. I'll go."

Eve and Hosea's wedding took place a few days before the Earthan New Year. When Silas and his family arrived, they were amazed at the decor. Silas could not remember a more elegant ceremony.

Sentrian weddings were traditionally somber affairs reflecting the seriousness of the occasion. They were first and foremost worship services to the Lord. The bride and groom were giving thanks to the Lord for sending them their One.

Eve was dressed in a flowing white silk gown. In Sentrian custom, the bride wore the couple's personal color for the sash and jewelry. Silas was not surprised that Eve's color was blood red. She wore red satin sashes around her sleeves and waist and rubies in her chain maille jewelry. The ten bridesmaids all carried glowing vermilion lamps. Rather than exchange rings, the couple gave each other ornate circle charms to replace the simpler engagement charms they wore around their necks. The priest ended the ceremony by wrapping their hands together using one of the sashes flowing off Eve's sleeves to show they were now bonded together forever.

As soon as the newlyweds left the wedding hall and were on the way to their honeymoon, a lavish reception ensued. Decadent appetizers and traditional Sentrian dishes were served. There was roasted lamb with caramel sauce and celery dumplings, and deep-fried red onion coated in cocoa powder. Hot sparkling waters and a myriad of flavored beverages flowed from large fountains in the middle of the hall. And of course, pentab. The reception lasted well into the night, with traditional Sentrian music and dancing.

Silas watched as his parents and all the other married couples headed for the dance floor. He reflected back to the homecoming dance with

Liliana and wished she were here with him. Why had he fallen in love with an Earthan? Or why couldn't Liliana be Sentrian? If he met her here, she could be his wife. He shook his head. There was no use thinking about what could never be.

Lilly was popping popcorn. She could hear the *Twilight Zone* theme music from the kitchen. Michelle had left for her party, and Lilly had the house to herself. She was in full countdown mode, but not for the New Year. In forty-eight hours, Charlie would be back.

Mr. Conner and the elders convened a meeting prior to the departure. Eve/Evelyn and Henry had returned from their honeymoon and were in attendance. Due to the circumstances with Mr. Lassiter, Mr. Conner had decided that assimilating with the Earthans was no longer the goal. He and the elders thought a more distant approach was better.

As a formality, Mr. Conner opened the meeting up to questions, but the people's input really didn't matter. The magistrate and elders had already decided on the new rules.

"But won't the Earthans be suspicious if we suddenly close up and stop socializing?" Mrs. Hampton asked.

"You don't need to completely close yourselves off, but you do need to practice discretion in what kind of contact you have with them," a fat elder named Bob said.

"But I'm president of the book club. Do I have to give that up?" a man asked.

"And my son plays baseball. They'll probably go to the playoffs," said another woman. The families all began talking at once.

"Silence," the magistrate commanded. "Enough." The group quieted down immediately. "You may remain in your social activities as long as you follow the rules. Casual socializing is still a good way to find out exactly what they know. But be careful of what you say, and do not become overly friendly with them. That is the new directive. Bill will be in charge of monitoring the adults, and I've made my daughter-in-law, Evelyn, overseer of the youth. They report directly to me, so I expect all of you to cooperate with them and do whatever they say. Remember, we will be watching you."

Charlie swallowed hard.

"The meeting is adjourned," Bob said. The families went back to their respective homes to pack for the trip back to Earth.

STRAINED REUNION

Lilly woke up early the first day of school following Christmas break. She wanted to look extra special for Charlie's first day back. She wore Charlie's favorite sapphire-blue blouse and even curled her hair.

He hadn't called her last night when he should have been home, and Lilly assumed he wasn't able. But now, while sitting in the band hall waiting for him, she began to worry. What if something happened, and he was delayed? What if his government decided not to return at all?

Two minutes before the bell rang, Charlie rushed into the band hall. Lilly jumped up when she saw him, but he wasn't paying attention to her. His eyes were darting all over the room as if he was looking for something or someone. Lilly ran over to him and tried to put her arms around him, but he moved away. She was shocked, hurt. He looked at her and softly but firmly told her, "Don't." Lilly picked up her horn and walked to her seat.

Evelyn, who had just finished her audition for the band watched the entire exchange. She saw the Earthan female jump up and greet him enthusiastically. Charlie had done everything correctly. He had stepped back when she approached and maintained a distance from her. Evelyn was prepared to chalk the whole thing up to an excitable Earthan youth greeting a returning band mate after a long holiday, except for one thing: she saw the look on Charlie's face. It was a look she had expected to see on his face when she and Charlie were dating but for some reason never did. It was the look of desire.

Charlie did not see Lilly again until lunch. Luckily, Evelyn did not share his lunch period. Charlie glanced over at Henry. He was eating alone at his own table, absorbed in a book. Charlie decided to take a chance.

Lilly was already seated at the band table when Charlie approached. "Are you acknowledging my presence now?" she asked.

Charlie ignored her sarcasm and motioned for her to get up. "C'mon. We need to talk." He led her over to the side of the cafeteria hear the hallway.

"Liliana, we cannot be seen together anymore. We can't give the impression that we are involved. From now on, let's just be acquaintances at school."

"What? Why? I'm not even sure how to do that," she said.

"Did you notice the new flute player in band this morning?"

Lilly had. She was a beautiful blonde with striking eyes. "Of course. She had purple contacts. She was kind of hard to miss."

"She *is* wearing contacts, because she's just as blind as I am, but not purple ones. That's her natural eye color," Charlie told her.

"You mean she's Sentrian?" Lilly whispered. "Is every new student who enrolls here from another planet?"

"Just listen, Liliana," Charlie said sharply. "Her name is Evelyn. While we were on Christmas break, she got married to Henry." Charlie looked in Henry's direction, and Lilly followed his gaze. Charlie had pointed him out to Lilly before. The very strange Henry was sitting with his nose in his book. He took a pen out of his pocket protector and underlined something in the text.

"The sophomore?" Lilly asked. It was hard to imagine anyone in their school married. But Henry, the total geek, had that beautiful flute player for a wife? That was an image she didn't need in her head.

"Evelyn has been sent to Earth to monitor the actions of the younger Sentrians, namely the teenagers. Having a supervisor stationed at the school means I will be under intense scrutiny."

Lilly looked at Charlie and rubbed his arm. "It'll be OK," she said.

Charlie pulled away. "No, Liliana. This is serious. We have to be *extremely* careful. At school, nothing but casual contact. I will come and see you in the evenings." The bell rang. Charlie turned and went to his class without even saying good-bye.

Evelyn got out of Henry's car, and they walked into the Conner home together. The story Mr. Conner concocted for the school was that Evelyn was his niece, and she had come to live with them because of problems her parents were having. During school, Evelyn and Henry pretended to be cousins. At home things were very different. The entire second floor had been remodeled as a suite for the newlyweds. It was almost as if they had their own apartment.

"So, how was school, Evelyn?" Mrs. Conner asked. She handed Henry and Evelyn full mugs of coffee.

"Different than I expected. The schoolwork is, of course, simplistic and repetitive, but I do enjoy the band class," she said, taking a sip from her mug. "Umm, real coffee is *so* good."

"Yes, it makes coming to Earth almost bearable," Henry said. "Did you happen to see our fellow Sentrian at school? I know he's in band." Evelyn found it amusing that he wouldn't even refer to Charlie by name.

"Yes, but briefly. He took off right after class." Henry nodded. "It doesn't bother you that we are in band together, does it?" Evelyn asked innocently.

"Not at all," Henry lied. "I know to whom you belong."

As soon as the Grays finished dinner, Charlie excused himself and told his parents he was going to the library to work on a research paper. He got in his car and drove straight to Lilly's house. He realized he would need to think of some other excuses. Going to the library every night was not plausible, especially when he could research almost anything he needed on his PCD.

Lilly was waiting in the den for Charlie, trying unsuccessfully to concentrate on calculus homework. When the doorbell rang, she jumped up from the couch to answer the door. As soon as Charlie was inside, he pulled Lilly to him and held her tightly for several seconds. They sat down on the couch, and Charlie wrapped his arm around her shoulder and kept it there most of the evening. "It is so good to be back here. You have no idea."

"So, aside from missing me every hour of every day, was it nice to be home?" Lilly asked.

"I have very mixed feelings on the subject. It was good to see some of my friends, but I did not miss Sentria as much as I thought I would. I guess I've become Earthanized."

"Earthanized? Is that even a word?" Lilly asked.

Charlie shrugged. "What about you? What did you do besides pine away for me?"

"We celebrated Christmas, and of course, I watched the *Twilight Zone* marathon on New Year's Eve."

"Rub it in, why don't you," Charlie said.

"So, tell me about this wedding," Lilly said. "How does a Sentrian wedding differ from one of ours?"

"Well, I'm not entirely sure. I've never been to an Earthan wedding, only seen them on TV. But I know that instead of standing at an altar, the couple stands in a circle, and the priest ties their hands together to show that God has bound their lives to each other."

"Sounds romantic," Lilly said.

"No. Actually it's quite somber, but then it's supposed to be. God ordains the union. It is the most significant day of our lives; the culmination of God's will for us. A Sentrian wedding is sacred and life changing."

Lilly released herself from his grasp and turned to face him. "Charlie, there's something that's been bugging me. I get that it would be disastrous if Evelyn found out about us, but the whole band knows we're together. You know how people talk. It won't take her long to find out."

"Yes, I'm sure she will eventually. And when she does I'll tell her that we went out as friends a few times. If she finds out about homecoming, I'll say that I asked you to the dance because *I* was curious about the Earthan homecoming tradition. It's going forward I'm concerned about. The rules have changed. Now we are not allowed to socialize with Earthans. It might be a good idea if you let others know that we aren't seeing each other anymore."

Lilly didn't care what other people thought, but she was uncomfortable with lying to Beth. She and Charlie might never have gone out if it wasn't for Beth.

Charlie kissed her on the forehead. "I don't want you to worry about this. I'll handle it. Let me make us some coffee, then I'll help you with your calculus homework."

That sounded great to Lilly. She had only managed to solve one problem by herself.

Charlie and Lilly continued on this way for a couple of weeks: virtually ignoring each other at school and then meeting secretly in the evenings. Sometimes Charlie would say he was going for a walk, and then Lilly would pick him up at the corner of his street. Other times they would meet up at the diner, but most of the time, Charlie made up some story for his parents and went over to Lilly's house.

Unfortunately, all their trouble was for nothing. Ever since the first day in band, the interaction between Charlie and the female horn player had put Charlie on Evelyn's radar. In an effort to gain information, Evelyn began ingratiating herself with some of the other Earthan band girls. She soon learned that Claire and Jana knew a lot about what was going on in the band. Evelyn plied Claire with flattery, and Jana practically vomited gossip. Any information Evelyn wanted to know would flow freely from Jana's mouth.

Claire was primping and preening one day in the bathroom, when Evelyn entered. "Your hair looks so great today, Claire. I wish I could style my hair like that," Evelyn said.

"Thanks. I have a date with my boyfriend tonight. Gotta look good, you know."

"That's right. You told me about him. He doesn't go to our school, does he?"

"No, he goes to Friendswood."

"She used to date Matt, the trumpet player, but he dumped her," Jana explained.

"Jana, he did not dump me. It was mutual," Claire said, giving her a dirty look.

Evelyn saw this as an opening and took it. "So who else in the band is dating?"

"Well, there's Jill and Mark: flute and French horn. They're so cute, it's disgusting. They were band beau and band sweetheart at homecoming." Claire raked the brush through her hair roughly. She was still bitter about that. "Then there's Holly and Trey. She plays the bassoon, and he plays trombone."

"Don't forget, you and Dan went to homecoming."

"Gross, Jana. Don't remind me."

"What about Charlie Gray? Is he seeing anyone?" Evelyn asked.

Claire, who had been applying lip gloss, suddenly spun around to face Evelyn. "Why do you ask? Are *you* interested in Charlie?"

"Well, no," Evelyn said coyly. "My uncle is a friend of his parents. I just wondered…"

"He *was* really into Lilly. She's that short French horn player and Claire's ex-best friend," Jana said. Claire gave her a dirty look. "He gave her, like, the hugest mum for homecoming. Claire was so envious." Claire was now shooting bullets at Jana with her eyes. "But since the start of the new semester, their relationship has sort of cooled off."

"Yeah, like Antarctica," Claire added. "They don't even speak to each other. So if you want a shot at Charlie, here's your chance." She couldn't understand why everyone was so interested in Charlie, but she really didn't care. She turned back to look in the mirror and applied another coat of lip gloss.

Charlie's stomach lurched when he left school after sixth period. Evelyn was standing in the parking lot, waiting for him beside his car.

"Hello, Charlie," Evelyn said. "Would you mind giving me a ride home? Henry has to stay late for a science fair or something."

"I don't know. I don't think Henry would like that very much," Charlie said. Evelyn sauntered over to him with a wicked smile on her face. She leaned over and whispered into his ear. "I don't think he would mind, just this once. We are married now. And it's not like *you* have a girlfriend who might get jealous." Charlie knew then he was in deep trouble.

Beth and Ian were standing outside. Ian's car was in the shop, so they had to bum a ride from Lilly. As they were waiting, Beth saw Evelyn get into Charlie's Mustang. Charlie had been acting even stranger than usual since he came back from Christmas break: not talking to anyone, sitting by himself at lunch. And the way he was around Lilly. It was like he did a complete 180. Before they had been inseparable, but now he was very distant. He didn't just ignore Lilly; he avoided her. Beth had asked Lilly if everything was OK between them, and she was kind of evasive about it. She told Beth, "It's complicated, and I'd rather not talk about it." Beth respected Lilly's privacy and didn't bring up the subject of Charlie again, but with this latest development, she didn't know what to do.

"Did you see that, Ian?" Beth asked, hitting him in the arm.

"See what?" Ian was blasting New Order on his Walkman.

"Evelyn just got into Charlie's Mustang. Do you think I should tell Lilly?"

Ian shrugged his shoulders. If he told her no, she would get mad at him, because he was telling her to mind her own business. If he told her yes, and then Lilly got mad at Beth, well, that would be his fault, too.

"You're such a guy," Beth muttered. "Utterly useless." Beth made up her mind. She would tell her; Lilly had a right to know.

"Hey, guys," Lilly said, walking up. She opened the trunk, and they all put their horns in.

"Lilly, I thought you should know. I saw Evelyn get into Charlie's car this afternoon, and they drove off together." Ian put his headphones back on. He did not want to be a part of this conversation. Lilly put the key in the ignition and started the car.

"Is everything OK?" Beth asked.

Lilly's eyes were wide, and her hands were shaking. "I honestly don't know." Beth was surprised by Lilly's reaction. After telling her about Charlie and Evelyn, she could understand anger or even casual indifference, but not fear.

"Let me just get to the point," Evelyn said to Charlie. "About the Earthan female…"

"Let me save us both time and breath," Charlie decided to take the offensive. "You heard a rumor that I had an Earthan girlfriend, and obviously, you believed it."

"I don't think my informants have any motivation to lie. Unlike you."

"Let me finish," Charlie said. Evelyn crossed her arms but sat back in her seat. "Last semester I became friends with a senior girl in the band. Did I ask her to the homecoming dance? Yes, I did. Because it was an Earthan experience *I* wanted to have. Did we become pretty good friends? Yes, we did. Toward the end of the semester I could sense that she wanted something more. In hindsight, I realize getting friendly with her was not a good idea. Maybe I inadvertently led her on. I was hoping that over Christmas break she would forget about it, but that didn't happen either. As soon as I got back to school, I told her I didn't have those feelings for her, and we agreed it would be best if we didn't socialize anymore, not even as friends. And that's it, end of story."

"Well, that certainly puts my mind at ease," Evelyn said. "*If* it's true."

"What do you mean if? Why would I be attracted to an Earthan, of all things?" Charlie chuckled at the notion.

"The simple answer is you wouldn't be, unless you were mentally ill," Evelyn said. "Even the idea is revolting." She shook her head in disgust.

"Exactly," Charlie agreed.

"But my sources tell me you two were inseparable."

"Inseparable seems like quite an exaggeration to me," he said. "Look, I already told you we were friends. As Earthans go, she's fairly intelligent and interesting. I admit I was lonely. Put yourself in my shoes. I'm light-years away from all my close friends, and it's not like Henry and I were going to start hanging out together."

"It would have been better if you had," Evelyn scolded.

"Oh, right. Henry is locked inside his own little world. He's completely asocial."

"Watch it. You're talking about my husband."

Charlie backtracked a little bit. "OK, I'm sorry. But, Evelyn, you have to admit, Henry is difficult to get to know."

"This I do know, and for that reason I'm willing to give you the benefit of the doubt. I won't say anything to the magistrate or the elders, but no more consorting with Earthan females. Don't test the limits of my patience, Charlie."

"It's a moot point. You're here now. I can simply hang out with you," Charlie replied.

"I'm married. Remember?" Evelyn said.

"Well, invite me over. I'll get to know Henry. We'll probably be great friends."

"Invite my ex-boyfriend over to my in-laws' house? I think not. Look, it does appear that you and the Earthan female are estranged. Just keep it that way. Understood?"

"Understood," Charlie answered.

"Good. Now drive me home."

Lilly was waiting by the living room window for any sign of Charlie. When he pulled into her drive, she ran to the front door. "You had me worried to death," Lilly scolded, holding the door open for Charlie.

"Worried? Why?"

"Beth told me she saw you and Evelyn drive off together. What does she know? Are you in a lot of trouble?"

Charlie put his hands on Lilly's shoulders. "Relax, she did confront me about our relationship, but I handled it." He walked into the kitchen and started the coffeepot.

"Handled it? How?" Lilly asked, following him.

"I told her that we had been friends last semester, but that you had feelings for me that I obviously didn't share. I had to end the friendship, and now we're not even on speaking terms."

"So you told her I was a silly, love-struck girl who imagined a relationship that didn't exist."

It sounded pretty desperate on her part when she put it that way. "Yes," he said meekly. He hoped she wouldn't be mad.

"Did she buy it?" Lilly asked. She didn't care what Evelyn thought about her as long as she believed Charlie.

"Presumably. She agreed not to tell the magistrate, provided I end our friendship. I told her it was already done. But we will have to be careful. Nobody, not even Beth, can know that we're together. If we get caught, I seriously doubt I can talk my way out of it."

Henry was lying on the sofa of their upstairs suite reading a book when Evelyn came in.

"So what happened with Charlie?" he asked.

Evelyn slipped off her shoes and sat down next to him. "Oh, he denied ever being interested in the female; claims she misconstrued their friendship."

"It makes sense," Henry said, putting down his book.

"Yes, he made a very well-reasoned argument, but unfortunately, he did not persuade."

Henry sat up. "You can't be serious. Now, you know I'm no fan of Charlie, but you don't really think he would get involved with an *Earthan*? I mean, it's unheard of."

"Unless," Evelyn suggested, "a person is seriously disturbed."

"You don't believe that, do you?"

"No. Not really. But something's not quite right."

SECRETS AND LIES

A couple of weeks had passed since the confrontation in the parking lot, and Lilly and Charlie shoved Evelyn to the back of their minds. Maybe Charlie underestimated Evelyn. Maybe they grew careless, because they wanted to see each other more. Whatever the reason, they never anticipated crossing paths with Evelyn outside of school. Lilly picked Charlie up on his corner one Saturday, and they drove to Galveston. After a day of walking the Strand, they headed back to Clear Lake.

Evelyn was driving home from League City after dealing with Anthony and Eric, two teens who were giving too much Sentrian video-game access to an Earthan gamer. No harm was done, but she couldn't believe the risks the youth were taking. She was stopped at a red light when she saw a familiar-looking blue Mustang pull up at a diner. A couple exited the car and entered the restaurant. Even with her poor eyesight Evelyn could see it was Charlie, and that Earthan female was with him.

She thought about calling the elders, but they would want to handle things their way. She could confront them: scare the girl and threaten

Charlie. Then she had a better idea. She rushed home to work out her plan before she showed up on the Grays' doorstep.

Helen Gray heard a knock at the door. She got up to see who was there. Evelyn was standing in front of her. "May I come in?" she asked, but even before Mrs. Gray answered, she pushed her way into the entry hall.

"Well, hello, Evelyn. What brings you by?"

"I'm here to see you and Mr. Gray. There's something I need to discuss with you."

"Yes, of course," Helen said, with a sick feeling in her stomach. "I'll put on a pot of coffee and get Louis. Won't you have a seat?"

Louis and Helen were sitting in the living room when Charlie came home. Charlie took one look at his mother and knew something was wrong. "What's going on?" he asked, setting down his trumpet.

Evelyn rounded the corner then. "Hello, Charlie, we've been waiting for you," she said. "That's a nice touch," Evelyn said, pointing to his trumpet case. "It's almost like you really *were* at band practice."

Louis stood up then. "Sit down, Charlie. Evelyn has shared some very disturbing news with us."

Charlie did not sit down. "What did you tell them?" he asked in as even a tone as he could manage. Losing his temper would not be a good idea, he knew.

"Oh, we've been having a very pleasant chat about your little Earthan girlfriend." Her tone went from phony nice to sharp and biting.

"She's not my…"

"Don't even try to deny it," Evelyn interrupted. "I saw you two at the diner this afternoon."

Rage turned to fear. It felt as if all the blood had drained out of his head. All the strength in his body faded as he crumpled into a chair.

"The question to be answered is, what do we do now?" Evelyn asked.

Charlie had a pretty good idea. He was sure Evelyn would involve the magistrate and the elders. He hoped he would not suffer the same fate as Mr. Lassiter, but he couldn't kid himself. This was serious.

"Look, Charlie. We're not upset with you," Louis said. "We're upset with ourselves for not seeing how lonely and unhappy you are. But Evelyn has suggested a solution to the problem."

"What?" Charlie asked warily.

Louis motioned to the coffee table. On the table top were photographs of three girls. "These are the files of Sentrian females who are also in need of finding their One."

"If you agree to start a relationship with one of these girls, then Evelyn won't involve the officials on Sentria," Helen said.

"And what if I don't?" Charlie asked. Helen gasped.

"Then I will have no choice but to tell the magistrate. You will be held in isolation until the ship returns in June. You will likely be sentenced to some sort of behavior modification prison for as long as the judges see fit." It was a terrible pronouncement, yet Evelyn said it without emotion, the way a person might suggest going out to dinner.

Charlie was furious that Evelyn would involve his parents, but it wasn't completely unheard of. Although Sentrians believed that God chooses your One, sometimes parents helped their children locate their One when they were deemed too old to find them on their own. Most of the time these semiarranged marriages worked out perfectly, and if you asked the couple, they would swear that God had used their parents to locate their soul mate. However, Charlie knew that would not be the case for him.

He didn't want this, but what choice did he have? No choice, if he wanted to stay out of Sentrian prison. He glanced over at his mother; she was on the verge of a nervous breakdown. "All right, I'll try," Charlie said, but there was no conviction behind his words. Helen breathed a sigh of relief.

"Excellent," Evelyn said. "Look through these files and give me the name of your choice tomorrow." She left a communicator on the coffee table so that Charlie could talk to his chosen from Earth. "I will make all the arrangements then."

After Evelyn left, Charlie took the files upstairs. He pulled out the information on his prospective wives. He selected a girl named Tamar, because of the three, she was the most unlike Lilly. Charlie had to admit she was pretty, with short red hair and green eyes. According to her bio, she enjoyed sewing and had a degree in education. He hated this. He knew he could never feel about Tamar the way he felt about his Liliana, but for now he had to play along and convince Evelyn that he was done with Lilly.

The next day Evelyn was waiting for Charlie after band practice.

"I choose Tamar," Charlie said simply.

"Fine, I'll arrange a link this afternoon. Tonight you can begin your telecourtship." Charlie turned to leave. "Oh, and Charlie," Evelyn said. "You'd better make this work. If you don't take this seriously, your life isn't going to be worth one Earthan cent."

"I get it, Evelyn."

Not seeing Lilly was out of the question. Charlie just had to be more clever about how. Sneaking out at night still seemed like the safest bet. After dinner he would go upstairs and begin the nightly link with Tamar.

Charlie had to admit that Tamar was really nice and not uninteresting. If he had to marry someone he didn't love, it might as well be her. They spoke for an hour, the amount of time Evelyn had prescribed. After ending the link, it was dark enough for him to slip out of his window. Charlie did not take his car; he ran all the way to Lilly's house. If Evelyn drove by his house, she would see his car in the driveway and assume he was home.

Hopefully, being engaged to Tamar would get Evelyn off his back. He knew he would have to end things with Lilly eventually, but he couldn't give her up just yet. Charlie thought as long as he continued his nightly link with Tamar and gave Evelyn no reason to be suspicious, he could at least see Liliana until the end of the mission. Charlie was wrong.

It had been two weeks since Charlie and Tamar's engagement, and Evelyn was keeping close tabs on Charlie. At school, he gave no sign of interest in the girl, which did not surprise Evelyn. Charlie was a bit reckless, but even he would not be so stupid as to try something at school, right under her nose.

Evelyn spoke with Tamar often and was glad to hear that she seemed genuinely excited about marrying Charlie. She told Evelyn that yes, they were communicating nightly. She even mentioned that her mother and Helen Gray had started making wedding plans. Since all was going well on that front, Evelyn decided it was time to pay Charlie a visit and find out how things were progressing for him. She dropped by unannounced one evening.

Mrs. Gray answered the door. Her hand went up to her throat. "Hello, Evelyn."

"I came to check on Charlie," Evelyn said. "May I come in?" she said and pushed Mrs. Gray out of her way.

"Charlie and Tamar are getting along so well," Mrs. Gray gushed as she poured Evelyn a cup of coffee. "They are thinking of getting married the week we return. I've spoken to Tamar's mother, and she is starting to make the preparations." She turned her head and called upstairs. "Charlie, can you come down? Evelyn's here to see you." She turned back toward Evelyn. "Tamar and her mother are going shopping for the wedding gown next week." She glanced up at the staircase nervously. Charlie had failed to even answer her. "Maybe he didn't hear me, or he might be asleep."

"Uh-huh," Evelyn said. She knew that if Charlie was upstairs, he had heard. Helen got up to go to his room, and Evelyn followed. When she opened his bedroom door, Helen was horrified to find his room empty and his window wide open. The curtains were blowing in the breeze.

"I'm sure there's a reasonable explanation for why he's not home," Helen began.

"Yes, there is," Evelyn said. "The reasonable explanation is that you cannot control your son, and you have no idea where he is or what he's doing. Fortunately, I think I do." She grabbed her purse and got into her car. Helen ran to her room and shut the door. She called Louis, but it was hard for him to understand her, because she was completely hysterical. She managed to tell him that Charlie was gone, and Evelyn was looking for him. Louis promised to come straight home. After she hung up with him, Helen curled up into a little ball on the bed and closed her eyes.

Evelyn drove straight to Lilly's and parked on the street opposite her house. She had to be careful. Charlie's exceptional hearing would make it difficult to sneak up on him. Fortunately, Evelyn knew that even a super-sonos had points of vulnerability.

For one, he had the ability to filter out noises he didn't want to hear. She seriously doubted he would be turning on any filters tonight. He needed to be extra aware in case she was spying on him, as she was now. But there was a second way to catch him off guard. It was distraction. When he was involved in a conversation or activity with another person, he didn't hear the outside world as much. As nauseating as the idea was, Evelyn hoped the

Earthan girl would be enough of a distraction to keep him from hearing her approach.

As silently as possible, Evelyn walked to Lilly's front porch. She was even wary of the grass crunching beneath her feet. With any luck, Charlie would attribute that noise to a squirrel or a stray cat. She sat completely still, breathing as lightly as possible. She could and would wait them out.

Over an hour later, she saw Charlie emerge from Lilly's entryway. Evelyn needn't have worried about him hearing her. He *was* utterly distracted. He held the Earthan girl in a tight embrace and had his lips pressed up against hers. Evelyn wanted to vomit up her dinner, but she repressed the urge. Now was not the time for that. Now was the time for confrontation.

Out of nowhere, Evelyn appeared. She ran right up to the two of them, so close to Charlie that he could feel her breath on his neck. Lilly let out a little scream. She thought her heart was going to jump right out of her chest. Charlie put his arm around Lilly protectively and moved in front of her, standing between Lilly and Evelyn. He tried to remain calm on the outside for Lilly's sake, but inside he was in full panic mode.

"Tell me, Charlie. What exactly is your fascination with this female?"

"Look, Evelyn. What you saw, it's not what you think."

"Liar. I can't see well, but I'm not blind."

"Just leave us alone," Lilly said defiantly.

"It speaks," Evelyn sneered.

"We aren't hurting you. It's not like I'm going to tell anyone who you are or where you're from." Charlie winced. Liliana had no idea who she was dealing with. He silently begged her to be quiet.

Evelyn looked at Charlie. "She knows about us? How many of our other secrets have you divulged?"

"Even if she said something, no one would believe her," Charlie said, as if that made things any better. Evelyn ignored him. She moved around him to more closely examine the creature. She touched Lilly's hair, and Lilly slapped her hand away.

"Feisty, isn't it?" Evelyn examined her, observing the Earthan female from all angles. "What's this?" she asked, seeing a circle-shaped bulge under Lilly's T-shirt. Evelyn pulled the chain on Lilly's necklace out of her shirt to reveal the circle charm Charlie had given her. "You're engaged? Charlie this goes way beyond disgust. You need help."

Lilly snatched the charm out of Evelyn's hand. "What are you talking about?" Lilly's eyes darted back and forth between Charlie and Evelyn.

Evelyn crossed her arms in front of her. "Help me understand, Charlie. You told her you are an alien, but you neglected to mention that this necklace is the Sentrian equivalent of an engagement ring?"

"What?" Lilly asked.

"Yes, girl," Evelyn said in an utterly bored tone. "For whatever reason, Charlie has claimed you as his, and by wearing the necklace, you are agreeing to marry him. Charlie, I must say, I'm disappointed. When we ended things, I never dreamed you would be so desperate as to throw your life away for a low-class, sweaty Earthan."

"You two dated?" Lilly's eyes grew wide.

"Briefly. A long time ago," Charlie answered. "I can't imagine why things didn't work out."

Evelyn gave Charlie a dirty look. "No matter. I'm much better off," she said, flashing her own wedding necklace at Lilly. "But I don't suppose you've told her about Tamar, either."

"Who's Tamar?" Lilly demanded. She was tired of being in the dark. It seemed Charlie had failed to mention lots of things.

"Tamar is Charlie's *real* One. They are getting married this summer, as soon as we return to Sentria," Evelyn said.

"Is this true?" Lilly asked, searching Charlie's face.

"Liliana, this is not my choice. I've never even met Tamar. Evelyn and my parents are forcing me into this arranged marriage."

"But that can't be," Lilly said. "That's not how it works. You told me God selects your One, not your parents."

"Very good, Earthan. It seems Charlie has instructed you on the Sentrian code of law. Evidently, he neglected to mention the one exception to that rule." Evelyn proceeded to recite the law from memory. "If a Sentrian youth has not found his or her One by age eighteen, then the parents may intercede to locate him or her on behalf of their child."

Charlie looked at Evelyn with disgust. "You make it sound so voluntary." He turned to Lilly. "But if I haven't married by age twenty-one, the government may force me to marry someone of their choosing; which in my case, they would definitely do. They distrust older singles."

Lilly wasn't interested in the reasons why. "So you're going to marry this Tamar girl?"

Charlie looked down at his feet. He couldn't look at her; he just nodded.

"Then here," she said. She removed the necklace and handed it to Charlie.

"Liliana, don't," Charlie begged. He didn't care that Evelyn was standing right there. "I love you, not Tamar."

"Charlie, I'm sick of all the lies. I don't know what's true anymore."

"I love *you*. That's the only truth." Charlie reached for her hand, but she pulled away. Evelyn was shocked at his confession. There could only be two reasons for him to say it: he was desperate to keep his hold on her, or he really believed it. She found both possibilities equally disturbing.

"I'm going to make this really easy for you. You're engaged, and I will *not* be the other woman. I never want to see you again." Lilly turned and went into the house, slamming the door behind her. Charlie just stood there, staring at the closed door.

"Let's go, Charlie," Evelyn said, a smug grin on her face. He followed her to her red convertible and got in. Once they were on their way, Evelyn told him, "You, I can't trust. So for your sake, I hope she meant what she said."

"She did," Charlie said somberly. "Jane would rather sacrifice her own happiness with Mr. Rochester than compromise her integrity."

"What does that mean?" Evelyn asked.

"Never mind."

APART

Charlie was expecting Evelyn to run straight to the magistrate, but fortunately she seemed satisfied, even elated, with the way things turned out. Charlie suspected that part of the reason she didn't want to involve her father-in-law was because she wanted to handle the situation herself. In Charlie's mind, Evelyn was a cat, and he was a cockroach that she enjoyed batting around—not to kill it, but to torture it.

When she dropped Charlie off, Evelyn did talk to Charlie's parents about what happened but assured them she would not go to the authorities. "You really must supervise him more closely," she scolded.

Helen flinched. Evelyn was half her age and not even a mother, and here she was criticizing her parenting skills. Louis knew Helen was about to lose it. He put his hand over hers to calm her. "You have our word," he told Evelyn.

"I'm not going to tell Tamar or her mother about this, but I expect you to get your relationship back on track," she told Charlie. She turned her attention back to his parents and spoke as if he wasn't even in the room. "I'm sure once he starts spending more time with Tamar, he'll realize what true love is and forget about this unnatural infatuation he has for the Earthan female."

Charlie crossed his arms and leaned back against the couch. He couldn't stand Evelyn's superior attitude toward Liliana, but he couldn't say anything. She droned on and on about the importance of keeping Charlie away from "the inferior Earthan girl." When Charlie couldn't stand it anymore, he filtered out her words. After an eternity, Evelyn finally rose to leave. "I'll see you all tomorrow for church services."

After she left, Charlie started up the stairs. "Not so fast," his father said. "You are very fortunate, son. Evelyn could destroy us if she wanted to. Your reckless behavior has put us all in danger."

"I am aware of that."

"Then please, for Sonora's sake, give this foolishness up. It has brought us nothing but trouble. Let me make this clear. You will not see the girl again. Tomorrow and until we return, your time will not be your own. We will find things for you to do to fill your day."

Charlie went to his room, but he could hear his parents whispering to each other.

"You don't suppose…I mean, this Earthan girl couldn't be his One, could she?" Helen asked.

Louis glared at her. He picked up a coffee cup and threw it at the wall. "Stop it. I will not listen to such blasphemy in my own house."

Helen's eyes grew wide and she ran to her room. *Great*, thought Louis. He swept up the mess, then went to the kitchen to fix his wife a glass of Instant Smile. It gave him time to calm down. He didn't like that he had lost his temper with her; it wasn't even her fault. But her comment really got to him, mostly because he was afraid it was true.

Helen was curled up in a ball on the bed, sniveling, when he entered. "I'm sorry, my One. I brought you a glass of Instant Smile." He walked over to the bed and she sat up and wiped the tears off her cheeks.

"Listen, Helen. I don't want you getting yourself all worked up about this. She couldn't be his One. It's not possible."

"How do you *know* it's not possible?"

"Because I do." Louis took a breath. He felt his patience waning. After a moment he calmly, but sternly told her, "No one has ever bonded with one of them and our son will not be the first."

"Well, what if he's disturbed?" she fretted.

Louis put his arm around Helen's shoulder. In a softer, more soothing tone, he said, "I don't believe our son is disturbed. I think he's just lonely and confused. "Take a sip. It will calm you down." Helen took a sip of the drink and smiled weakly up at Louis.

"Evelyn's right about this. When he is more bonded with Tamar, this Earthan female will be nothing more than a bad memory."

"You know, I was right," she said. "If we had let him stay on Sentria this past year as I wanted, we wouldn't be dealing with this now."

"Yes, I know that now, dear," Louis said.

Charlie put on his earphones and filtered out their conversation. He couldn't stand to listen to them discuss *his* life anymore. He didn't think he was disturbed, and he knew that spending more time with Tamar would not change how he felt about Lilly. It didn't matter now. He doubted Lilly would ever want to speak to him again. He groaned, put his pillow over his head, and closed his eyes.

Sunday after church, Charlie and his father spent most of the day on home-improvement projects. The first thing they did was nail the windows of the upstairs bedrooms shut.

Lilly spent most of Sunday in bed. She hadn't bothered to even get up and take a shower. She tried to sleep but without success; the events of the night before replayed over and over in her head.

Stop it, Lilly ordered herself. Just stop thinking about him. It's over. She tried to finish a novel she had started. It was no use. Her thoughts kept drifting to Charlie. She threw the book down and curled up in a ball on her bed.

When Michelle came home from work, she was surprised to find Lilly still in her room. She was sitting at her desk staring out her window, still wearing her pajamas from the night before. "What's the matter? Are you sick?" Michelle asked, feeling her forehead.

Lilly knew she would have to tell her mom that she and Charlie were no longer together, but she didn't feel like talking about it yet. "I guess. I've had an upset stomach all day." That was at least the truth.

"Well, if you don't feel any better tomorrow, just stay home from school," her mom told her.

Lilly nodded and when her mom left the room, she lay back down on her bed.

Lilly awoke with a new outlook on Monday morning. The deep hurt she had felt on Sunday gave way to anger. Anger at being lied to repeatedly. Anger at Charlie's betrayal. As wicked as Evelyn supposedly was, she had at least told Lilly the truth.

When the going gets tough, the tough go to work. Isn't that what she had learned from her mother? She wasn't weak. She would not *allow* him to keep her home from school and give him the satisfaction of knowing how badly he hurt her.

"Good morning, Mom." Lilly grabbed a cereal bar and headed out the door.

"Good morning," Michelle yelled after her. "Guess you're feeling better."

She was aware that Charlie was staring at her during band and at lunch. During English class, he even tried to get her attention. She ignored him. It was easy, as if nothing had even happened. It didn't hit her until later.

When she got home, Lilly lay on the couch, sniveling and feeling sorry for herself. After her pity party, she sat upright and wiped her eyes. This was not the way Lilly Garcia comported herself. She wasn't like Claire, who needed a boyfriend the way everyone else needed air. No more letting

Charlie dictate how she felt. She would have to stay incredibly busy so that she had no time to think about him.

The rest of January dragged by. Lilly began going to the gym and swimming so that she had something to do on Saturdays. On Sundays she attended bible study before Mass. But the nights were the worst. She couldn't shut her mind down. After a week or so of sleepless nights, she began taking long, brisk walks every evening and went to the library several times a week. She stopped drinking coffee altogether. After a long walk and reading for an hour in bed, she couldn't keep her eyes open. It helped to stay busy, but *he* was never far from her thoughts. At least marching season was over. It would be unbearable to spend two hours a day so near him without speaking to him.

One night at dinner Michelle remarked, "I haven't seen Charlie in a while. Are you two doing OK?"

Lilly sighed. "You might as well know. We broke up." She didn't want to see Michelle's expression, so she looked down at her plate instead. She shoved the food around with her fork.

"Why? What happened?"

"We're going in different directions. It's for the best."

"That sounds pretty lame," Michelle said. "How does Charlie feel about it?"

"He's not happy about it. But I think he realizes we don't have a future together."

"Well that just sucks."

"Mom," Lilly said.

"Lil, I'm sorry. I know this is between you and Charlie, but I saw how happy he made you. Real love is so hard to find, and it seems like you're just throwing it away. Look, I love you Lil, and I trust your judgment. But I love Charlie, too. He's like the son I never had."

"Don't you mean he's like the *boyfriend* you never had?"

"Yeah, that, too." She looked at Lilly in silence for a moment. "Are you sure there's not more to it? He's not involved with another girl or something?"

"Why would you even say that?" Lilly asked.

"Because it doesn't make sense."

Lilly didn't want to discuss it any further. She turned her gaze away from her mother.

"OK, OK, I'll drop it. But what about you? How are you doing?"

"Mom, I'm fine. Now can we please talk about something else?"

"All right, but I'm still holding out hope for a reconciliation. I'm going to miss him. That boy sure did know how to make a good cup of coffee." Michelle shook her head and took her plate to the sink.

Lilly didn't need her mother reminding her how happy she had been with Charlie. Lilly was the one who had lost everything. Charlie was more than a boyfriend; he was her best friend, someone she always wanted as a part of her life. She shook her head. There was no sense dwelling on it.

When Beth asked her about Charlie a few days later, Lilly simply told her that they had broken up. It was over. End of story. Beth didn't ask for any explanation, and Lilly didn't offer any. At least now she didn't have to keep secrets from anyone anymore.

As bad as things were for Lilly, Charlie had it worse. At least Lilly could come and go as she pleased. Charlie felt like a prisoner. He had to go straight home after school, do his homework, and talk to Tamar for an hour. Talking to Tamar wasn't horrible, but she did not compare to Liliana.

His mother stood over him while he did his homework. She walked upstairs when he started the link to Tamar to make sure he was following through with the arrangement. On the weekends, his father did not let Charlie out of his sight. He always had another project for Charlie to do.

But Evelyn was the worst of all. Charlie noticed that she did drive-bys of his house to see if he was there. Sometimes he would stand at his window and wave at her just to annoy her. At school she would pop up out of nowhere: at his locker, in the halls, in the parking lot before and after school. She even followed him to Thursday night brass sectional practice, even though she was a woodwind and had no reason to be there.

He could hear what others were saying about him, and it bothered him. Most of the band thought Evelyn was his new girlfriend—his new, possessive, stalker-like girlfriend who never let Charlie out of her sight. The girls all believed he was the scum of the earth for dumping Lilly to date Evelyn. The guys were in awe. They couldn't believe Charlie could "snag two hot chicks" in such rapid succession.

Only Beth got it half right. By Charlie's body language and facial expressions, she could tell Charlie did not have feelings for Evelyn other than revulsion. So why did he put up with Evelyn following him around?

The weeks of February passed slowly for Lilly. Valentine's Day was hard, but the second weekend in March was worse. It was a weekend she couldn't stay busy and avoid her problems. It was concert season, and the band had a competition. She would have to see Charlie, both on the bus and during the concert. They were performing a piece Lilly loved, "Pines of Rome" by Respighi. The music was powerful, especially the fourth movement, but Lilly couldn't even enjoy it. She hoped the band would do well, but she couldn't get excited about any of it.

Charlie was hoping for some time alone on the bus ride, but no, Evelyn had to sit down right next to him. He sighed. Liliana was up front sitting by herself listening to music on her headphones with her nose in a book. Did she ever think about him? He wanted to stare at her, study her, but he couldn't even do that with Evelyn in his business 24–7.

Evelyn always had her eyes on Charlie but virtually ignored Lilly. Charlie understood why. It was obvious to Evelyn—and anyone else halfway paying attention—that Liliana wanted nothing to do with him.

The band performed better than they ever had. Afterward, they waited around in the back hall for their scores. When the judges announced they had made the highest possible score, straight ones, the band started shouting. Everyone was jumping up and down and hugging each other.

Dan headed straight over to Lilly. He picked her up and swung her around. "We did it. Isn't that fantastic?"

"It would be more fantastic if you put me down," Lilly said. She thought it was a strange thing to do, until she saw him hugging other girls and giving high fives to the guys. Lilly figured he was excited that they won the competition.

Charlie knew better, and it infuriated him. He wanted to forcibly remove Dan's head from his body, but he couldn't do a thing. He went into the restroom to try to get some control. It didn't help much. He ended up slamming his fist into the cinder block, making a long crack along the wall.

Evelyn watched Charlie's reaction to Dan. She recognized Sentrian jealousy when she saw it. *This could get interesting*, she thought.

There was no way Charlie was riding home on the bus. It didn't matter what Evelyn did to him. If he didn't get out, get away, he knew his head would explode. He told the band chaperone his parents were picking him up and gave his trumpet to Ian to put back in the band hall. Then he started running. He was still wearing his tux from the performance, but he didn't care. He ran the entire twenty miles back to the band hall. His car was the only one left in the parking lot when he arrived.

When Charlie got home from school the following Monday, there was an urgent message from Sentria on his electronic note pad. It was from Tamar. That was strange. What was so urgent that it couldn't wait for their link tonight? He opened the note pad and retrieved the message.

"Silas, I have something I must tell you, and I'd rather not leave it on your note pad. Please contact me as soon as you are able."

Charlie assumed Evelyn had some new requirement for their telecourtship. That would be typical. He set up communications with Sentria, and a few moments later, Tamar appeared on the screen.

"I got your message. What's the matter, Tamar?"

"I truly hope you will not be upset with me, but I have to let you know that I found my One, and I have to break off our engagement."

Charlie sighed in relief. "I'm glad for you, Tamar. I truly am." And of course, he meant it.

"Really?" she said, relieved. "You're not angry?"

"Tamar, I could never be angry with you. You're a wonderful girl, and I wish you much happiness."

"Thanks, Silas. It is just as they say it is. We met at the library. I dropped a book, and he stooped down to pick it up. Our eyes locked, and we just knew. When you meet your One, there will be no doubt."

"I'm sure you're right. So when is the wedding?"

"Not until the summer season. Elias has signed up for the military academy, and that will be his first break. Don't worry about Evelyn. I'll send her word that our situation has changed."

"Oh. So you haven't told her yet?"

"No, I wanted to tell you first. My mother and I thought you should be the first to know."

"Tamar, I have a favor to ask," Charlie said.

"Certainly. What is it?"

"Would you mind not telling Evelyn about your engagement until after we return to Sentria?"

"I suppose I could. But why?"

"You know how it is. If you tell Evelyn, I have to tell my parents. They've been pressuring me for a while now to get married, and I'd rather not go through the whole process of locating another prospective mate until I'm back on Sentria."

Tamar did know about that. Her parents had been pressuring her, too. That's why she had been matched with Silas in the first place. "OK. But how are you going to keep it from her? Evelyn checks the logs, and she'll know we're not in communication with each other."

"I think I have a way around that," Charlie said.

The next day Charlie looked for an opportunity to speak to Lilly alone. He didn't have much free time away from Evelyn, but even when he did, Lilly avoided him. The same for the next day and the day after that. It was discouraging. He even tried to pass her a note in English class, but she ripped it up and threw it away without even opening it. How could he let Lilly know he was no longer engaged if she wouldn't even speak to him?

He was opening his locker and thinking about it when he heard a familiar voice. It was Liliana's. He could hear her from where she was standing on the other side of the campus.

"Thank you for the invitation, but I already have plans for spring break." Lilly loaded her horn into the trunk of her car.

"Aw, c'mon. Come to the beach one day with me. It'll be fun, I promise," Dan told her.

"Like I said, I already have plans."

Dan leaned his arm against the back of Lilly's Jeep. "Well, then how about prom? My Dad's gonna let me borrow his convertible."

Lilly shook her head. "I'm not going to prom."

"Look, baby. Forget about that loser, Charlie. I know what you need." Dan moved closer into her personal space. He reached up and caressed her arm.

Lilly wrenched her arm away. "I said no." Charlie shoved his books into his locker and ran toward the sound of her voice.

Lilly turned to leave, when Dan grabbed her arm. His tone changed. It went from inviting to demanding. "Hey, I wasn't finished talking." The anger in his eyes frightened her. He tried to pull Lilly close to him, but she pushed him away. Charlie tilted his head and listened for her voice to know which direction to go. He started running, but he still had to pass the football field to get to the band-hall parking lot.

"Hey Charlie, where's the fire?" Ian asked as he flew past. "Dude should have gone out for track."

Dan grabbed Lilly then. "Let me go. You're hurting my arm." Lilly dropped her purse so she could use both her hands to push him away. She yelled loudly, hoping someone would come, but all her classmates were too far away to see or hear her.

"Shh," Dan said as he clamped his hand over Lilly's mouth. "C'mon, baby, relax." Lilly squirmed and tried to get out of his grasp, but Dan was too strong. "Let's go for a ride," he said and pushed her toward his car.

Charlie was at an all-out sprint coming into the parking lot. Then he saw Dan, holding Liliana by the arms as she struggled to get away. He zoned out, enraged. His vision was a red haze. All he could see was that lecherous vermin with his filthy hands all over his Liliana. In one swift move, he pulled Dan off of Liliana. He lifted Dan up by his neck and said, "You will never speak to her again, you will never look at her again, and you will never think about her again. If you ever touch her again, I will break every bone in your hand." Then Charlie flung him into a row of parked cars. Dan's head connected with the bumper of a nearby truck, making an unsettling thud. By then, some of the students noticed something was going on and walked over.

"Dude, what happened?" someone asked.

Charlie didn't even register the comment. He put his hand on Liliana's shoulder. "Are you OK?"

She wasn't. Not really. "I'm fine, thank you." Her voice quavered, and her hands were shaking slightly. She smoothed down her mussed hair and stepped away from Charlie.

Dan's friends helped him up and walked with him over to his car. He looked back at Charlie with wide eyes. Now that the excitement was over, the crowd quickly dispersed.

Lilly reached down to pick up her purse, but Charlie grabbed it first. He handed it to her, his hand lingering against hers a little too long.

"Thank you," Lilly said, turning to walk away.

"Wait a minute. I've been trying to talk to you all week. I need to tell you something."

Lilly turned to face him. "I appreciate your help just now, but this doesn't change anything." She was tired. All she wanted was to go home and forget about what had happened.

"Please just listen. I couldn't stand the thought of his hands on you. I won't let anyone hurt my girl."

"*Your* girl? Really? Because I thought *your* girl was in a galaxy far, far away. You forfeit any right you ever had to call me your girl. Like I said, thanks for your help. But don't start with the jealousy act. It's not cute or sweet; it's annoying." Lilly unlocked her car and got in.

"Liliana, I will *always* be protective of you, and I will never stop loving you."

"Yeah, well, sounds like a personal problem to me." She shut the car door and drove off.

Evelyn, who had been standing at a distance, approached him. "I see she still holds you in utter contempt."

Charlie realized something then. "You were here the whole time, weren't you? While I was racing to get to her, you were standing here, watching." Evelyn said nothing. She just smiled.

"I understand that your whole purpose in life is to make me suffer, but Liliana hasn't wronged you. Would it have killed you to help her? Save her from that monster?"

"Like I care what happens to that Earthan girl," Evelyn said. "But Charlie, I thought you knew. By not helping her, I *was* making you suffer."

Later that night, Charlie was in his room, trying to think of a way to get through to Liliana. Even if he could get her alone, and he got her to listen to him, would she believe him? Charlie thought not. He needed proof.

He went to his desk and took out his PCD. He loaded the transmission from Tamar onto it and walked over to the upstairs bathroom. This was the only window not nailed shut, but it wasn't an oversight. Louis never dreamed that Charlie might try to squeeze through it. For that matter, Charlie never dreamed he would either, but desperate times called for desperate measures.

As quietly as he could, he slid the window up. It squeaked and complained. Charlie listened to hear if the noise awakened his parents. Nothing. He reached over the window sash and gently laid the PCD on a flatter section of the roof so that it wouldn't fall. He pulled himself up and through the tight opening. Once he was out, he picked up the PCD and quietly jumped into the soft grass in the backyard. He climbed the fence and ran through the woods to Lilly's house.

Charlie was relieved to see that Michelle's car was not in the driveway. One less thing to worry about. He grabbed the spare key from where Lilly kept it and let himself in through the back door.

"Liliana," Charlie called out so she would know he wasn't an intruder.

Lilly sat straight up in bed. *Him. He* was here. She stomped down the stairs. "What do you think you're doing? Get out," she said.

Charlie grabbed her hand and pulled her over toward the sofa. "Don't talk. Just listen." He showed her the video file of Tamar's break-up message.

After it played, Lilly asked, "So you two aren't getting married?"

"No, we're not," Charlie said with a grin.

"But I thought it was all arranged, and she was your One. You told me that can't be changed."

"In the first place, she was never my One. In the second place, it doesn't matter what arrangements were made. She's found her One, and Evelyn cannot interfere with God's plan, even if she wanted to." Charlie took hold of Lilly's hands. "But that's not the best part. Tamar has agreed not to tell

Evelyn that she's marrying Elias until we return to Sentria. So we can be together."

"No, Charlie, we can't," Lilly said, pulling away. She stood up and moved away from the couch. "If Tamar hadn't broken things off, you wouldn't even be here now. You'd still be planning your wedding."

"Liliana, that's not fair. I wanted to be here all along, but you never let me. The only reason you're listening to me now is because I brought you proof that Tamar ended things."

"You're darned right I wouldn't have listened. Charlie, you were engaged to another girl."

"Not really. I knew she wasn't my One, so we technically couldn't be engaged."

"Now you're just arguing semantics." She crossed her arms. "Be honest. We both know that if she hadn't found someone else, you'd still be engaged."

Charlie approached her slowly and lowered his voice. "Things aren't that simple. It's not as if I had a choice." She lowered her head, and he lifted her chin with his fingers and looked into her eyes. "I thought you'd be happy. Now there's no impediment to our being together. Well, except for Evelyn…"

"And the fact that you're leaving for Sentria in a couple of months, and I'll never see you again."

Charlie put his hands on her shoulders. "Look, I know you're still upset with me and this whole situation. I don't blame you. But I know you still love me. I can see it in your eyes."

Lilly lifted his hands off her shoulders and turned away from him. He put his hands right back and whispered in her ear. "If I could think of any way to stay here, I would."

She didn't turn around. "This is not about good intentions. It's about reality. Walking away from you in January was the hardest thing I've ever done. I don't want to go through that again. Charlie, we have no future together."

She was right, of course, but it was still painful to hear. What had he been hoping for? That she would be thrilled to sneak around with him for a couple of more months and then say good-bye? He walked around until he was facing her. "Here." He pulled out the circle necklace and handed it to her. "I want you to have this."

"No," Lilly said. "That's just a tragic reminder that we can't be together."

"No, it's not. This is proof that I will never love anyone else." He folded her fingers around the necklace and walked out the door.

Lilly tossed and turned. Finally, she got up and walked downstairs. Michelle, who had been sleeping in the recliner, woke up.

"Sorry, Mom," Lilly said. "I couldn't sleep so I decided to make some coffee."

"Make enough for me, too." Michelle stretched and joined Lilly in the kitchen. "So what's got you so worried that you can't sleep?"

"You might as well know. Charlie came over tonight. He wants to get back together."

Michelle tried to contain her excitement. "Is this a good thing?"

"Probably not."

"So what's the problem? Are you addicted to your own misery or something?"

"No, Mom, be serious." Lilly poured the coffee and sat down across from Michelle at the kitchen table. "After graduation, the Grays are moving far away, and Charlie is going with them. What's the point of getting back together?"

"I know I've told you before about how deep down I knew your father and I didn't have a prayer of staying together. But when he asked me to run away with him, I did it anyway. No one could have talked me out of it. Now, you are not me, and Charlie is definitely not Lalo, but…"

"But it doesn't matter because…" Lilly started, but Michelle stopped her.

"What I'm trying to say is, don't give up. You two have way more of a chance than Lalo and I ever dreamed of. Graduation is a ways off. Things could change. Even if the Grays move, Charlie might stay here and go to college. Or, as much as I would hate it, you and Charlie might decide to go to college out of state. Nothing is set in stone."

Lilly wished that were true, but she knew things wouldn't turn out that way. "So you don't regret marrying Dad, even though it ended badly?"

"If I hadn't married Lalo, I wouldn't have you, and that would have been the real tragedy. I think you should give Charlie a chance, at least. Worst case scenario, you spend two happy months together before he leaves, rather than moping around the house all the time." Michelle got up from her chair and kissed the top of Lilly's head. "Now, I'm going to bed, and I think you should too, mi hija."

Lilly thought about what her mother said. Maybe she was right. She could just enjoy the here and now, and let the future worry about itself. At lunch the next day her resolve weakened. She glanced around. Evelyn was nowhere to be seen, so she took a chance. She dropped a note on Charlie's table instructing him to meet her in the hallway so they could talk.

He did a moment later. And that's when they picked up where they left off. Charlie asked her what was new, and she told him about a *Twilight Zone* episode she had recently seen.

SPRING BREAK

Charlie set the timer for his link to Tamar and again slipped out of the bathroom window. Lilly was waiting by the sliding glass door to let him in. He pulled her close and kissed her. Then, he led her by the hand to the couch, where they sat down.

Lilly put her legs up on the couch and leaned against his chest. She tilted her head back to look up at him. He wrapped his arms around her and kissed the top of her head.

"Are you sure it's safe coming over here? Won't your parents check up on you?"

"Nah, they don't come upstairs much, especially now that I'm 'engaged.' They want to give me my privacy in case I'm speaking to Tamar. They won't check on me unless the house is on fire."

"Well, then, let's hope you didn't leave a burning candle around," Lilly said.

"Seriously, there is one place we need to be more careful, and that's school. As much as I loved talking to you at school today, we can't risk that again. We were fortunate no one saw us. If it gets back to Evelyn that we are on speaking terms…"

"I know. I know. No contact at school. Charlie, I've been wondering about something. What *did* your parents say when Evelyn told them you were involved with me?"

"I don't think you want to know," he said.

"C'mon, Charlie. I can handle it."

"Well, they were shocked, of course, and disappointed. My father told me never to see you again, and then he nailed my bedroom window shut. He thinks I just need time with Tamar to get you out of my system. Unfortunately, my mom thinks I might be mentally ill."

"Mentally ill? For real? So even with their intense reaction, you don't think they will check up on you?"

"No, I don't. My father has ordered me not to see you. He can't imagine me disobeying him because I never have."

"Until now?" Lilly asked.

"Until now."

"That bothers you, doesn't it?"

"Well, yes, it bothers me. I have always looked up to my father, and it hurts me to go against his wishes, even when I know he's wrong."

Lilly sat straight up and faced Charlie. "OK, I have another question for you. If your people and my people are related, I mean we're very distant relatives, right? Then why is it your people have such a low opinion of us?"

"It's kind of complicated. We *are* technically related. We're kind of like distant cousins, but when we were relocated to Sentria, God altered our essence."

"Your essence? What's that?"

"You would call it DNA. Let me give you an example. In order to survive on my planet, we needed the ability to stay cool because it's very warm, and to be very strong due to the dense atmosphere and strong gravitational pull. In these aspects we are genetically different. And my people believe that makes us better."

"You call it genetic difference, but aren't they really genetic improvements?"

"Not all of them. Remember we do have a shortened life-span and poor eyesight. On Sentria, the light of our sun is very dim, and with three moons, it's only slightly darker at night than during the day. That's why we're blind as bats."

"Well, what about your super ears?" Lilly asked.

"No, that's actually *not* a trait most Sentrians share. We call it supersonos. The average Sentrian has hearing equal to or marginally better than the average Earthan. About one in a thousand Sentrians is a supersonos. But I am exceptional even among that subset. I can hear spoken conversations up to a mile away if I really concentrate."

"It must make it hard to sleep with all that noise." "It's pretty easy, actually. Supersonos have the ability to filter out extraneous noises and only hear the sounds they choose."

Lilly looked down. "What?" Charlie asked.

"It's kind of embarrassing. Before I knew about your super ears, I had some conversations with Beth that I know you overheard."

Charlie smiled. "Liliana, I don't deliberately eavesdrop. I filter out conversation unless there is something critical I need to know, or danger is involved. Like with Dan attacking you. Occasionally some communication comes through, but I don't go out of my way to listen in to other people's conversations."

Lilly wasn't sure she bought that. If she had that ability, she knew she would use it to her advantage. "OK, but that still doesn't explain why Sentrians have such hostility and disdain for Earthans. I mean I heard Evelyn refer to me as a 'low-class, sweaty Earthan,' and she called me 'it.'"

"You remembered that, huh?" Lilly nodded. "Sorry about that. I'm afraid most Sentrians think they *are* superior to Earthans. Since we are a branch of your genetic tree, we kind of view Earthans as the prototype and ourselves as the second generation. To most Sentrians, Earthans will always be backward, violent brutes." Charlie glanced over at Liliana to see if he had offended her and was relieved to see her smiling.

"So you're really slumming, going out with me," she said.

In an attempt to limit Charlie's free time over spring break, Louis decided to keep him busy with extra projects. On Monday he had Charlie wash all the windows and replace the light bulbs all around the house and in the attic. Helen stayed home to supervise.

That night, as usual, Charlie slipped out to see Lilly. When he arrived, Michelle was still at work. Lilly put in a movie, and they sat on the couch to watch it. Actually, they weren't watching it at all. Lilly was far more interested in Charlie's lips and his warm embrace. He leaned over her and ran his fingers through her hair. Making out with Lilly was the highlight of his day. Charlie was blowing kisses into her ear when he heard Michelle's car driving toward the house. He jumped up, smoothed his hair down, and wiped Lilly's strawberry lip gloss off his lips. Lilly sat up straight on the couch, and Charlie sat down in the chair across from her. They both tried to look interested in the movie.

"Hey, guys," Michelle said. "What are you doing?"

"Watching a movie," Lilly said. She began twirling her hair with her finger.

Michelle looked around at the living room. There was a full bowl of popcorn on the coffee table, obviously untouched, and a freshly made butt impression on the sofa cushion next to Lilly. Michelle touched the cushion and found that it was warm. "What's this movie about?"

Charlie looked at Lilly. He had no idea. "Well, Mom, it's an action movie," Lilly said, twirling her hair faster.

"Who's in it?" Again Charlie looked to Lilly to answer.

"That guy from that other movie, you know. Right, Charlie?" Charlie nodded.

"So why is that guy chasing the lady in the yellow Camaro?" Michelle asked, pointing at the television.

Charlie shrugged.

"You know, Mom. It's not a very good movie. It really didn't hold our interest." She felt her face turn red. Busted.

Michelle nodded. "Look, guys, I allow you two to hang out here because you're both eighteen, and responsible, and because you've never given me a reason to distrust you. And with my work schedule, I really don't have much of a choice. But I wasn't born yesterday. I know that when I'm not here, you aren't just holding hands and making eyes at each other."

Charlie stood up then. "Mrs. Garcia, I'm sorry. I *was* kissing Liliana, but I swear that's all."

"Charlie, I don't mind if you sit on the couch next to Lilly. You are boyfriend and girlfriend. I also don't mind a kiss or two as long as it doesn't go any further than that, and you don't start sucking face right in front of me. But please just drop the Puritan act, because I don't buy it."

"Mrs. Garcia, I can assure you that I have the utmost respect for your daughter and for you, too. And I would never do anything to …"

"Charlie," Michelle interrupted.

"Yes, ma'am?"

"Stop talking and go make us some coffee."

"Yes ma'am," Charlie said, practically running into the kitchen.

Michelle picked up the bowl of popcorn and offered some to Lilly. "You know, you two are terrible liars."

On Wednesday the Grays decided Charlie should paint the upstairs bedrooms. Charlie drove Helen to the hardware store to pick out the paint and supplies.

Evelyn and Henry were eating lunch at a Mexican restaurant across the street when she saw Charlie's car pull into a parking space. "Well, well," she said. "I knew he had to leave the house sometime."

"Who had to leave the house sometime?" Henry asked.

"Charlie," she said, getting up from her seat. "I'll be back."

"Wait," Henry said. "I'll go with you."

"Better not, dear. I know how you detest confrontation." Evelyn darted out of the restaurant before Henry could protest.

Charlie was standing at the counter waiting for the paint. He looked up when he heard the bell on the door ring and saw Evelyn walk through the door.

"What are you doing here, Charlie?"

"Well, let's see. I'm standing here with a paintbrush in one hand and color swatches in the other, waiting for the clerk in the back to mix up some colors in metal cans. I don't know, this is just a wild guess on my part, but maybe, just maybe, I'm buying some paint."

Evelyn was not amused. "All right, where is she? Where's your little girlfriend?"

"Tamar's on Sentria, Evelyn."

"Very funny. You know you're not supposed to be out unsupervised. I suppose I'm going to have to speak to Louis and Helen again."

"It's Mrs. Gray," Helen corrected, appearing from behind the paint aisle. "What exactly did you want to speak to my husband and me about?" Charlie was impressed. Instead of cowering at the sight of Evelyn, his mother was actually standing up to her. But then, Evelyn was the one person who really got under his mom's skin.

"Oh, Mrs. Gray, it is so good to see you again," Evelyn said, fake smiling. Her tone became sugary sweet. "I thought Charlie was here alone."

"No, Evelyn. That would be a violation of the rules. Charlie is doing some painting in our home over spring break. We were just picking up the supplies."

"That's good, that's good, staying busy over spring break." She turned to Charlie. "So how are things going with Tamar? Are you speaking often?" she asked innocently.

"Why don't you tell me? I know you check the logs," Charlie replied.

Evelyn's tone changed. "You don't need to get defensive. If you don't like being monitored so closely, you shouldn't have broken the rules."

"What's going on, Evelyn?" Henry asked as he walked over to stand next to her.

"Your wife is checking up on me and my mother. She seems to think that hardware stores are havens for Sentrian lawbreakers."

Henry pulled Evelyn aside. "Were any rules broken?"

"I told you to wait at the restaurant." She spoke softly, but of course, Charlie could hear.

"You didn't answer my question," Henry said.

"No rules were broken." Evelyn frowned at her husband. Charlie was amused by their exchange. Maybe Henry wasn't such a dweeb after all.

Henry approached Charlie and his mother. "Evelyn and I will be on our way. We'll leave you to your work." He led Evelyn out of the store by the elbow. When they were outside, Evelyn wrested her arm out of his grasp. "What are you doing? I wasn't finished with him."

"Yes, you were. I'm not sure why you're so fixated on Charlie, but I'm getting tired of it."

"You can't seriously be jealous. You are my One, not Charlie. I just can't stand people who think they don't have to follow the rules."

"Then go harass Ben and Micah in League City. They're constantly testing the limits here on Earth. Look, you told me yourself that Charlie's talking with Tamar nightly, and that the Earthan female will have nothing to do with him. Unless you have incontrovertible proof of wrongdoing, leave Charlie and his family alone."

"You know, your father put me in this position, because he knew you were a pushover. You want proof, fine, I'll get your proof. But when I do, I will come after Charlie with everything I can avail myself of in the Sentrian punishment code, and you won't be able to stop me."

"So what chores did your dad have you do today?" Lilly asked.

"Paint the upstairs bedrooms," Charlie said.

"Wax on, wax off," Lilly said.

"Huh?"

"Never mind, Karate Kid. You were telling me about your run-in with Evelyn at the hardware store."

"The strange thing was that Henry seemed to be on my side. He basically told Evelyn to back off and leave me alone."

"Do you think he's jealous? I mean, you and Evelyn did date."

"True, and we Sentrians do have a bit of a jealous streak."

"Yeah, I kind of noticed."

"His was not the typical jealous reaction, though," Charlie said.

"Meaning, he didn't try to throw you across the parking lot?"

"Very funny. But still, for Henry to be jealous he would at least need some sort of provocation. He's kind of a bore, but he is definitely level-headed, not one to fly off into a jealous rage. Even a Sentrian without corrective lenses could see I have no interest in Evelyn, and now that they are married, she could never be unfaithful."

"So, what are you saying? No Sentrian has ever cheated?"

"No, there have been cheaters, but for most of us, the idea is utterly repulsive. It's not just a solemn vow that keeps Sentrian couples together. The pronouncement of the union at the end of the wedding ceremony itself causes a chemical change in the brains of Sentrians. It would be physiologically impossible to love someone else. Remember, unlike you, we have limited free will."

"That's so bizarre," Lilly commented.

"That is why finding your One is sacred. The elders once tried to separate a married Sentrian couple. The results were disastrous."

"What happened?" Lilly asked.

"A few centuries back, the Sentrian elders tried to arrange marriages on a large scale—not just for problem cases like me. The elites, government officials, and elders tried to keep their sons and daughters from having contact with commoners so that their children would only bond with elites like themselves. "Here." Charlie took out his PCD. "Why don't you read some Sentrian literature for a change?" Charlie pushed a few buttons and some undecipherable text appeared on the screen. He pushed another button and the text became English. Charlie made some coffee and sat down next to Lilly as she read.

The Tragedy of Arina and Paltiel

Arina was the only child of an aristocratic Sentrian couple. Her parents doted on her and they wanted their daughter to marry a man worthy of her elite status. She was a smart, friendly girl, but she lived like a prisoner in her parents' palatial estate. Tutors were brought in to teach her, and friends would come over to see her, but she wasn't allowed to leave.

Her parents located a suitable male named Cale. He was a senator's son from another province. Plans were made for them to wed in a year, when Cale turned sixteen. But Arina was already falling in love with Paltiel, her parent's servant. He brought her books and music. He talked with her and listened to her when she had problems or just wanted companionship. They fell in love and knew they were meant to be together. Shortly before Arina was to be married, the governor was called to the capital on business. He and Arina's mother left for a short trip, leaving Paltiel in charge of things while they were gone. Paltiel knew this was their only chance. He took Arina out of her home, and they ran away to a small village where some of Paltiel's cousins lived. Paltiel and Arina got married and were very happy.

When her parents came home and found her missing, they hired locators to find her. It didn't take long for them to find out about Paltiel and bring them in from the village. Arina's father had a friend who was a judge. He was more than happy to declare the marriage illegal and voided it from the public record. Her parents took Arina back home, and they continued to make preparations for her marriage to Cale.

Paltiel was heartbroken and followed his One back to her home. He made many desperate attempts to see her. Arina's parents forbade her from seeing Paltiel, but she repeatedly defied them. Her parents had him declared a criminal and he was imprisoned. But Arina ran away and visited him in prison. When her parents realized that they couldn't keep them apart, they used their high position to influence the elders to impose a penalty of death on Paltiel. He was given poison and died. Arina was inconsolable. On the eve of her wedding to Cale, they found her hanging from a noose made out of a bed sheet.

Lilly looked up at Charlie. "I can see why they call it a Tragedy. Did this really happen or is this some sort of Sentrian legend?"

"It really happened. Before Arina and Paltiel, it was always understood that you didn't question God's choice for a soul mate. After Paltiel's execution and Arina's suicide, the elders decided to pass a law that made it illegal for a person to interfere with God's plan. The law states that once a person finds their One, and the marriage ceremony is complete, regardless of the circumstances, no one may nullify it. The judge who declared the marriage illegal and both of Arina's parents were sentenced to three years in prison. The elders, of course, absolved themselves of any wrongdoing. So you see, even if Henry is jealous, deep down he knows that Evelyn belongs to him and could never love anyone else."

"This is exactly what I don't get. Why are Sentrians jealous at all? Fidelity is not a problem on your planet."

"Because of the way our brains are programmed, we are suspicious and paranoid that others will try to steal away our One. It's not just the physical act that defines fidelity for us. Even spending too much time with another's One could set off a really jealous Sentrian, and there are those who test the limits. We call them seducers. They try to make other Sentrians jealous by striking up conversations with their One, flirting, or having some other type of casual contact. And it's not usually out of carnal desire. Usually the seducer is trying to obtain something from the victim or cause pain to the victim's mate. Seduction is a crime on my planet punishable by prison time, and for good reason. There have been seducers who have been killed for trying to lure away a person's spouse. In most of these cases, the spouse of the victim was absolved of murder or just given a light sentence."

"Whoa. So adultery is worthy of death on Sentria?" Lilly asked.

"Under the right circumstances, yes. But it doesn't happen very often."

"Why is that?"

"Because cheaters don't get the circle. That's reserved for your One."

"You mean the necklace?" Lilly asked, looking down at her own.

"No, I'm referring to something different," Charlie said and smiled.

"What?" Lilly asked.

"Nothing," he said, still smiling.

"You have to tell me now."

Charlie shook his head. "Maybe someday, but not today."

Lilly gave up and returned to the previous topic. "But there are cheaters, right?"

"Yes. It's rare, but it does exist. If the offended mate doesn't kill the seducer outright, the state may put the person to death as an example to others. But if you get too close to a person's One, regardless of your motives, there is typically a beating handed out."

"Is Evelyn a seducer?" Lilly asked.

"That's a strange question," Charlie replied.

"That's no answer, Charlie."

"Well, I suppose in the strictest sense of the word she might be, but she knows where the line is, and she won't cross it. She may flirt with men, but it's more to get them to fall in line with her wishes than to actually lure them away from their Ones."

Lilly grew quiet, lost in thought.

"What are you thinking?" Charlie asked.

"I was just thinking about Henry. If you haven't given him any reason to be jealous, then maybe it's not so much jealousy on his part as it is anger on Evelyn's."

"What do you mean?"

"You told me once that when you two were dating, it was you who broke it off, right?"

"Yes, but she would have soon realized that we weren't meant to be."

"That's beside the point. Think about it from her perspective. She's a beautiful, intelligent Sentrian woman who is going places, but you dump her and start dating an inferior Earthan girl. You really insulted her."

Charlie thought about it. "You know, in a weird way, that makes sense. When did you become such an expert on the Sentrian psyche?"

"I'm not an expert on Sentrians, but I do have some personal experience with how the female mind works."

PROM

Spring break ended, and the entire senior class was gearing up for prom and graduation. Prom posters were hanging up all over the school. A couple of times Charlie noticed Lilly staring at them, but she never said anything.

Lilly had bigger things to worry about than a silly dance. Two more months and school would be over. It made her sad to think that Charlie would be leaving then. Seeing Charlie only in the evenings was not enough. Plus, the whole sneaking around thing, trying not to get caught by Evelyn, was getting really old.

One evening Charlie asked her, "Why don't you go to prom? I know you want to."

"No way. It wouldn't be any fun without you."

"Well, of course that's true," Charlie said modestly, "but I don't want you to miss prom because of me. This is your senior year. I don't want you to regret not going."

"I won't regret it. It's just a stupid dance," Lilly said. "I can't imagine you'd want me to go anyway. I mean it's not like you'd want me to dance with someone else."

"Oh," Charlie said. "I didn't think you'd want to dance with anyone else."

"Well, of course. I'm not going to stand around and drink punch all evening. Going to prom and not dancing isn't my idea of a good time," she said. Charlie looked worried. "It's OK, Charlie; I'm not going."

Evelyn still didn't believe that Charlie was staying away from Lilly, but she could never catch either of them doing anything improper. Charlie was too smart to get caught driving over to her house, and after the incident at the hardware store, Henry wouldn't let her go to the Grays' home to check up on Charlie in person. After a drive-by of Charlie's and Lilly's houses, Evelyn went home. She was surprised to find her father-in-law there when she arrived.

"So how are things with the youth? No problems, I trust?"

"No," she lied. She had never told the magistrate about the situation with Charlie, and she had no plans to do so. He would handle things differently, and she did not want his interference.

"I'm glad to hear it. Some of the other team leaders are having difficulties, and I need some help from those who are managing well. Come speak to me after dinner."

"Certainly." Evelyn smiled and excused herself. She really did not want to help out; dealing with Charlie was a full-time job. But she would do whatever it took to get ahead in the Sentrian hierarchy. After dinner she returned to the magistrate's study.

"Evelyn," he said. "The records department is very far behind. I need your help at the off-site facility until we return. You will be in charge of the day-to-day running of the facility, and I've pulled Andy and Linda from the NASA complex as your aides. Here is the contact information for your secretary, Sylvia. She will coordinate with you to set up the workstations. Any questions?"

"Yes, Magistrate. But what do you want me to do about my other responsibilities?"

"Oh, you are referring to the supervision of the youth. You've done such a splendid job keeping them in check that we can afford to pull you for this assignment. Don't worry about the school charade. I've already telephoned the principal and informed her that you are going back to live with your mother."

"Oh," Evelyn said.

"Your expression is odd. I would have expected you to be elated over the promotion."

"Oh, I am glad," Evelyn quickly said.

"I see," the magistrate said. "You are concerned about being separated from Henry. That is completely understandable. Rest assured that you will be able to communicate with each other via PCD, and Henry will, of course, stay with you on the weekends. You will find that sometimes you have to make sacrifices for the good of the state. That's what leadership is all about." The magistrate turned around in his chair and faced his computer screen. That was his signal for Evelyn to leave; he was done speaking with her.

Evelyn went to her room. She began pacing across the floor. This was a terrible development. It would be virtually impossible to continue surveillance of Charlie, considering the hours she would be putting in at the records facility. If she couldn't keep an eye on Charlie, then someone else would have to. She thought about Henry. It *would* be convenient to have Henry watch Charlie, but he was not apt to pay attention to what Charlie did or who he was talking to. Besides, he was kind of naive and trusting when it came to stuff like this. No, she needed someone who *would* notice; someone who was always looking for the worst in others. The names Jana and Claire immediately came to mind.

An hour later Evelyn was waiting in the mall at the food court for Jana and Claire. She waved to them when they walked in.

"What's wrong?" asked Claire. "You sounded so anxious on the phone."

"It's my mom," Evelyn lied. "She and my stepdad got back together, and she wants me to move back in with them."

"Now?" Jana asked. "At the end of the semester?"

"I know, I know. That's what I told her. But she convinced me it's for the best. I just hate missing out on the band trip and all the other end-of-school stuff. You two have *got* to promise to keep me updated on what's going on here. I want to know about the band trip, prom, graduation, and any other juicy tidbits that come up."

"Of course we will," Jana said.

"And most important, I want to know all the gossip on the band couples: who are together and who are broken up."

"Well, yeah," Claire said. "That's the most interesting gossip of all."

"Oh, I'm going to miss you guys so much," Evelyn said, giving them each a hug. She hoped she didn't sound too phony.

"Morons, incompetents," Evelyn grumbled as she slammed down the phone. She had asked the two dim bulbs to report back to her on any gossip from the band trip to Dallas. She specifically asked them if there was any indication of Charlie and Lilly getting back together.

Claire really couldn't be bothered. She told Evelyn she barely even saw them on the trip. Evelyn had come to realize that if it didn't have an impact on Claire directly, she wasn't interested. All she wanted to talk about was how hard it was to be away from her boyfriend for the whole weekend while they were in Dallas, and how she thought Matt wanted to break up with his girlfriend and get back together with her. This was not the kind of gossip Evelyn was interested in.

Jana didn't remember ever seeing Charlie or Lilly together on the trip, but she had heard that Lilly wanted nothing to do with Charlie about a month ago. A month ago Evelyn was still tracking Charlie. A month ago was old news.

This wasn't going to work. Jana had the intellectual capacity of a doughnut. But what choice did she have? She started pacing the floor again. There had to be a better way to monitor Charlie. She realized she would have to make the time to follow him again.

"It's going to be hot soon," Lilly remarked. "We'll be able to use the pool. Do you like to swim?"

"Not too much," Charlie said.

"So, is it a Sentrian thing? You don't swim on your planet?"

Charlie cleared his throat. "Well, uh, yeah, I mean we do swim, but it's different. On Sentria, swimming is not a…co-ed sport." He tried to get the image of Lilly diving into the deep end out of his head.

"Co-ed sport? I'm not talking about swimming laps, Charlie. I'm talking about hanging out in the pool on a hot summer day."

Charlie squirmed in his seat. "We have some different ideas than you do. For a Sentrian male, seeing a female in water, or especially with her hair wet, well, it's like an Earthan male looking at a *Playboy* magazine."

Lilly arched her eyebrow. "So that's why you made such an effort to keep me out of the rain that day last fall. It would be indecent for me to show my wet hair in public."

"Yes, completely indecent. I mean, not you. You're not indecent. But for me to see you that way, yes," Charlie explained awkwardly. "I think I'll just go check on the pizza." They were splitting a crappy pizza and studying for their English exam on *Ethan Frome*.

"You know," Lilly said, motioning to the novel, "I would like this story better if it wasn't so depressing."

"Unfortunately, we can't all have happy endings," Charlie said. He felt like he was an expert on that subject.

"But couldn't they have come up with a better solution than suicide? And they couldn't even get it right."

"Don't judge them too harshly. I know things didn't work out, but they were at least trying to do *something*. They were trying to find a way to be together, even if it was in death."

"Well, they succeeded, although not the way they intended. He would have been better off with the hypochondriac wife," Lilly said.

"Every story can't be wrapped up into a nice pretty little package like *Jane Eyre*. I mean the fire that killed Rochester's wife was rather convenient, wasn't it?" Charlie asked.

"Considering that the fire was set by the crazy wife herself, and it practically destroyed Mr. Rochester's home—and left him blind—doesn't seem too convenient to me," Lilly said.

"The problem wife was gone, and no one thought any worse of Jane or Mr. Rochester," Charlie said. "And Ethan will always be seen as a cheater and Mattie a seducer. To most people, they both got what they deserved. And you even feel kind of sorry for Ethan's wife, Zeena, at the end."

"So what's your point?" Lilly asked. "That I'm silly to wish for a happy ending?"

"No, not at all." Charlie brought the plates with the pizza over to the table. "I guess my point is that things aren't always so cut and dried. Ethan and Mattie aren't as bad as they seem, and Jane and Mr. Rochester aren't total saints either. Both couples made tough choices. For Jane and Mr. Rochester things turned out well, but not for Ethan and Mattie."

"I know. You're right. But maybe I just feel better reading stories that do turn out right, because I don't have any hope for us. We have less of a future than even Ethan and Mattie."

"Don't, Liliana."

"Don't what? Don't face the facts? You're leaving right after graduation."

"C'mon, Liliana." He encircled her with his arms and held her tightly.

"Charlie, it scares me how much I love you. I don't want to be without you."

Charlie kissed her forehead. He had no words of comfort. "Neither do I."

Charlie crawled back in the bathroom window later that evening. He was surprised to hear the sound of his parents talking. It was well after ten; they were usually in bed by now.

"I guess I was just hoping things would be different now than before Christmas break. We worked ourselves to death back then, and here we are again, trying to play catch up," Louis said.

"At least you don't have that witch, Evelyn, for a supervisor," Helen complained. "She's constantly watching me. It's unnerving. I guess she thinks she has to keep tabs on me because of Charlie."

"I'm sure that is why. But I do have some good news. On the third weekend of this month she is going with the leadership team out of town for a conference. I overheard Mr. Conner discussing it with his secretary."

"Why out of town? That seems strange," Helen said.

"I thought so, too. But I heard from Fred that they are combining the conference with a visit to an Earthan research facility in San Antonio."

"That's wonderful," Helen exclaimed. "Evelyn will be gone for a few days."

"Shh, you know how Charlie can hear," Louis cautioned.

"Yes, but when he sleeps, he's dead to the world. He doesn't even stir. You know, it still seems odd to me that all of the leadership would go now, with all this work we have left to do," Helen said.

"Well, Fred also mentioned that if all of the departments aren't ready to go after graduation, we'll stagger our departure and possibly send replacements down for some of our people."

"What does that mean for us? Are we going to have to stay through the summer now?"

"I doubt it. I agree with Evelyn on this point. I want Charlie back on Sentria as soon as possible and married to Tamar."

"It figures," Charlie grumbled.

"Now, Helen. Not a word of this to your co-workers. This is not common knowledge. C'mon, let's go to bed. We have a long work day tomorrow."

Charlie pulled out his calendar and looked at the date for the third weekend in April. The timing couldn't be more perfect.

Evelyn was annoyed. She did not want to go to this conference, even though she knew it would help advance her political career. The conference would last almost four days. That would give Charlie way too much time for mischief. She supposed it could be worse. At least Charlie had no idea she would be out of town. She sipped her coffee. Most of her day was spent at the records facility and at least part of the night staking out Charlie's house. That was where she was now. Not that all this surveillance did her any good. She never caught him doing anything, and his car was always in the driveway. Lilly's car was in her driveway, too. But Evelyn didn't buy for a second that Charlie was following the rules; he just hadn't been caught yet.

"I have great news," Charlie said excitedly as Lilly let him in the back door.

"What? Tell me," Lilly said. She plopped down on the sofa next to him.

"OK, Lilly, I know this is kind of short notice, but would you go to prom with me?"

Lilly brightened at the thought. But then reality hit, and she frowned. "What about Evelyn?"

"I found out Evelyn and the entire leadership council will be out of town that weekend. It's supposed to be a big secret, but my father found out."

"And he told you?" Lilly asked.

"No, not exactly. I overheard him talking to my mother. So what do you say? Will you go with me?"

"I still don't see how we can. I mean, that's a huge risk. If she happens to find out that we went to prom together…"

"Don't worry about that. I'll figure something out. In the meantime, why don't you let it slip that you're going to prom with someone from another school, a friend of a friend or something."

"OK," Lilly said. She was curious about what he was planning and how he was going to pull it off.

The prom's theme was retro. The music would be from the fifties, sixties, seventies, and eighties. The students were encouraged to dress up for the prom from any one of those decades. Lilly knew immediately she would dress from the fifties for Charlie.

She was sitting at the band table at lunch when Claire brought up the subject of prom. "I hate that retro theme. That is *so* lame. They are going to play all that old music, and the clothes from the sixties and seventies—U-G-L-Y. I'm going to prom with Darren in Brazoria instead."

"I'm going to prom," Lilly said.

"Wait," Claire said. Jana leaned in to hear. "Did you and Charlie get back together?"

"No, I'm going with a guy from Spring, a friend of a friend. You don't know him."

"So what's his name?" Jana asked.

"Jimmy. Uh, Jimmy Smith," Lilly answered. It was the first name that popped into her head. She cringed. It sounded so fake.

"So are you two friends or boyfriend-girlfriend?" Jana began her cross-examination.

"We're just getting to know each other," Lilly answered. Michelle was right. She was a terrible liar. She couldn't even fabricate a story about a make-believe boyfriend.

"So it's too soon to know if you two are a thing or not?"

Lilly nodded.

"What does he look like?"

"Well, he's pretty cute." How vague could she get?

The bell rang, and Lilly jumped up to get out of there. She hoped Jana didn't notice her strange behavior. Luckily, Jana was not very bright.

"We'll talk later, Lil. I want to hear more about Jimmy," Jana called out to her as she left.

Jana dialed Evelyn's number. She was quite proud of herself. This would be some news Evelyn would actually want to hear.

"Lilly's going to prom with a guy named Jimmy," Jana told Evelyn when she picked up the phone.

"Really? Are you sure?" Evelyn asked.

"I'm positive. She told us all about it at lunch," Jana said smugly.

"Well, what did she say?" Evelyn asked. Jana related what she knew. Then she proceeded to bore Evelyn with the other school gossip. Finally Evelyn found an opening and hung up with her. She sat down on the bed. She didn't know quite what to make of this news. If Jana had told her that Lilly wasn't going to prom at all, that would have made Evelyn more suspicious. But she knew how devious Charlie could be. If they were really still together, he would never want anyone else to know. Would he go so far with the ruse as to let her take another male to prom? Would he even be capable of allowing it? Evelyn didn't think so, considering what had happened to Dan. Maybe it was less complex than all that. Perhaps Charlie's precious little pet was a typical, fickle Earthan, and she had simply moved on.

Lilly didn't have a lot of time to shop for her prom dress. After one frustrating afternoon of dress hunting she gave up and called Dana, since she had been a lifesaver for finding her homecoming dress. Dana, of course, knew exactly where to go.

"Meet me at Vintage Couture after school tomorrow. If they don't have your dress, then no one will."

Lilly was overwhelmed when they arrived at the store. It occupied the space of a former grocery store and was filled with rows and rows of clothes in styles dating back to the early nineteen hundreds.

"They have everything here," Dana told her. "This is where I got my dress for prom."

"From which decade?" Lilly asked.

"Late sixties. It's a floor-length, neon-paisley thing," Dana told her.

"It sounds pretty," Lilly said.

"I wouldn't say pretty, I'd say pretty loud. You won't be able to miss me, even in the dark." They began walking down the rows of dresses. "I wish the retro theme had extended to the forties. That was such a glamorous era."

"Or even the twenties," Lilly said, thinking of Abuela.

"So, Lilly, did you have a decade in mind?" Dana asked.

"Definitely the fifties." Dana nodded and motioned for Lilly to follow. The clothes were arranged in rows by decade. Dana showed Lilly to the row of fifties clothing.

"I knew you were going to say the fifties," Dana said. "Charlie's such a throwback from that time: the way he acts, the way he dresses. And you seem more mature than your age, almost out of place with the rest of the seniors. The fifties suit you two better."

Lilly had not seen much of Dana this semester, but she assumed that Dana knew she and Charlie had broken up. "Actually, I'm not going with Charlie." Lilly concentrated on the rack of clothes and did not look at Dana's face. She didn't want Dana to see she was lying.

"What? Why not?" There was true surprise in her voice.

"We broke up a few months ago. I thought everyone knew."

"No, I didn't. Lilly, I'm so sorry."

"It's OK," Lilly said, trying to change the subject. "I'm going with a friend from Spring. His name's Jimmy."

"Whoa. For real? I am disappointed by the news about you and Charlie. You two seemed like the perfect couple."

Lilly looked at Dana. She was dead serious. Dana, one of the most popular and beautiful girls in school thought that she and Charlie, a couple of band geeks, were the perfect couple.

"Thanks. But it really is OK." Lilly started rummaging through the racks again. She picked up a dress she thought might work. "Hey, Dana, what do you think?" she said, holding it up. It was a beautiful tea-length, royal-blue dress with an A-line skirt.

"It's gorgeous. Go try it on."

Lilly immediately knew it was the right one. It fit her like a glove. She and Dana headed over to the handbag section and found a clutch that would go with her dress. Lilly thought the black flats she wore for homecoming would work for this dress, too.

After Lilly paid for her dress and handbag, Dana handed her a business card. "Here, you'll need this. Cheryl knows how to do retro hair and makeup. She's doing mine."

"Thanks, Dana. I'll call her."

Dana was right; Cheryl knew retro style. It was the day of prom, and Lilly was sitting in a chair in Cheryl's beauty shop having her hair teased to be put up in a beehive. After Cheryl styled her hair, she applied Lilly's makeup. Lilly was impressed. Cheryl had transformed her from an eighties teenager to a fifties-era young lady. She went home to get dressed.

Charlie thought it best if he met Lilly at the hotel where the prom was being held rather than pick her up. It would be safer, and if anyone grew suspicious, they could just leave in their separate cars. Also, it eliminated the need to answer questions from Michelle about Charlie's strange appearance.

"You mean I don't get to take pictures of you two in front of the fireplace?" Michelle complained.

"Didn't you take enough for homecoming?" Lilly asked.

"But this is prom. At least promise me you'll get some pictures at the dance," Michelle said.

"I'll think about it," Lilly said. She still wasn't sure how Charlie was going to pull this whole Jimmy persona off.

Charlie had just finished getting ready. He had his hair greased back and even put in a few blond streaks. Charlie took out the case that held the contacts Lilly had convinced him to buy last fall. He struggled but finally got them in. The change was dramatic. Without glasses, Charlie really did look completely different. He put lifts in his shoes as the final touch. Hello, Jimmy.

His parents were both working late and wouldn't be home until morning. That worked in Charlie's favor. He could take Helen's car so that no one would recognize his Mustang. Charlie parked at a nearby shopping center and walked over to the hotel. He waited by a fountain outside the main entrance where they had agreed to meet.

Charlie saw Lilly first. He didn't make his presence known but admired her from a distance. Charlie smiled at the sight of her. Audrey Hepburn paled in comparison to his Liliana. When she stopped at the fountain, he walked up beside her. "Good evening, Liliana," he said. Lilly turned at the sound of the familiar voice. Her eyes grew wide. It was Charlie, but it wasn't. The absence of his glasses, combined with the other changes, made him virtually unrecognizable. And with the lifts in his shoes, he was taller even than her beehive hairstyle.

She didn't know what to say. "Jimmy, you're so tall," she finally managed.

"So, what do you think? Can we pull this off?" he asked, taking her arm. Lilly was pretty sure they could. She knew it was him, but she doubted anyone else would. It was dark in the hotel ballroom, and no one would be paying attention to them anyway.

"I think so." She leaned over and whispered in his ear. "Don't tell my boyfriend, 'cause he's the jealous type, but I think you're pretty cute. If things don't work out with us, maybe you and I could get together."

Charlie smiled. "Shall we?" He motioned to the hotel entrance.

"Yes, let's."

They got confirmation pretty quickly that the disguise would work. As they entered the hotel, a guy who was in their English class approached them. "Hi Lilly," he said. "Are you just getting here?"

"Yes. How's the dance?" Lilly asked.

"Pretty cool. The music's great. The DJ's really good." He looked at Charlie then and extended his hand. "I'm Nathan. I'm in one of Lilly's classes."

"Nice to meet you, Nathan. I'm Jimmy," Charlie said, trying out his alter ego's name.

"You, too. Well, I won't keep you. And uh, Lilly, you look really pretty," Nathan told her.

"Thanks," Lilly said. Charlie frowned at him and pulled her closer.

They bypassed the picture stand and headed straight for the dark dance hall. A strobe light was spinning overhead, and some of the guys were doing really bad John Travolta impersonations to "You Should Be Dancing."

As soon as that song ended, "The Promise" by When in Rome began to play. Charlie led Lilly to the dance floor. A few people mouthed, "Who's he?" Lilly just smiled. The DJ went back to the sixties with "I'm a Believer."

It was getting crowded on the dance floor. They decided to take a break, and "Jimmy" went to get them some drinks. Lilly found a table right next to Dana and Ryan. Dana looked every bit the flower child. She wore her long, red hair perfectly straight. A crown of flowers completed the look.

"You were right. Your dress really is loud," Lilly told her. It was hot pink with a brown-and-green paisley design. Dana was wearing brown suede boots that poked out from underneath the long gown. The simple line of the dress made her look even taller, if that was possible.

"You like?" She did a quick turn to model the ensemble for Lilly.

"Oh yes. The flowers are a nice touch," Lilly said.

"Thanks. Lilly, you look stunning. I saw you with Jimmy. He's cute. And a good dancer."

"I think so."

"You look really happy," Dana said, smiling. "San Francisco" began to play and Dana grabbed Ryan's hand. "C'mon, honey. This is our song." Ryan followed her out to the dance floor. He was wearing a powder-blue tux with flared pant legs and ruffles on the front of his shirt. In Lilly's opinion, wearing that awful tux for Dana's sake was the epitome of true love.

Charlie/Jimmy came back with two Cokes, one without ice. "They didn't have coffee," Charlie explained.

"I'm glad they didn't. Charlie may drink a lot of coffee, but I doubt Jimmy would. That would be too much of a coincidence."

"Good point," Charlie said. The Cure's "Friday I'm in Love" played, and Lilly practically dragged Charlie to the dance floor. After it ended, Charlie took her hand and led her to a more secluded part of the dance floor. There were only a few couples dancing here.

Lilly was confused until "Earth Angel" began to play. She smiled. "You arranged this."

Charlie shrugged. "Didn't you notice it was taking me a long time to get our Cokes?" He pulled her close, and she wrapped her arms around his neck. He was so tall she had to stretch and tilt her head up to look at him. He was beautiful. And perfect. And dancing with her. Ten, twenty, even sixty years from now, Lilly would remember this moment in her life. It was just Charlie, Lilly, and the music. Nothing else. She leaned in closer to Charlie and rested the side of her head on his chest. Listening to his galloping heartbeat, she knew she was home: safe and well-loved in Charlie's embrace. Charlie leaned over and tenderly kissed Lilly on the top of her head.

The music ended, and the class president walked to the front of the room and took the microphone. "Now it's time to announce the prom king and queen." The room erupted in applause. Lilly looked up at Charlie.

"You want to go now?" he asked.

She nodded. She would much prefer to spend the remainder of the evening alone with Charlie than endure this tedious ceremony. As they were leaving, the class photographer walked up to them and said, "Smile." Before they had a chance to object, she snapped a picture.

They exited the hotel, and Charlie said, "I wish she hadn't done that."

"Are you worried Evelyn will find out?"

"I don't know. Not really. That photo is not likely to end up in the yearbook, and even if it does—"

"You'll be long gone to Sentria by then," Lilly finished for him. Charlie looked down at his shoes. Lilly did the same. They were having such a wonderful evening, they didn't need a dose of reality to ruin it.

Charlie lifted up her chin with his fingers. "Let's go to the diner. I'm not ready for the evening to end." They walked to their separate cars—another unpleasant reminder that they were not allowed to be like other couples—and drove off.

Lilly thought about it all the way to the diner. Why were they going along with this? Why weren't they even trying to do something? Yes, the Sentrian elders were pretty scary, but Charlie was on Earth's turf now. Why did the Sentrian rules have to apply here?

They entered the restaurant, and the hostess showed them to a booth. Charlie could tell Lilly was preoccupied; she hadn't spoken a word since they arrived. "What's wrong?" he asked.

"I'm wondering how you can accept it. Just let them take you away. You were the one who was praising Mattie and Ethan for their determination to stay together and yet, you aren't even trying to find a way to stay here."

"What are you suggesting?" he whispered. "A suicide pact?" His voice was low, but his tone was harsh.

"No, of course not. I just don't see how you can be OK with letting others dictate how you live your life and telling you who you can fall in love with. I don't know. Maybe you don't feel the same way about me that I feel about you. This would be an easy out for you."

"No, Liliana," Charlie said, raising his voice. "That's not true, and you know it. If I thought I could get away with it, I'd hide until they left. But that just isn't realistic." There was no way Lilly could know. She hadn't grown up under the oppression of his government. She had no idea what they were up against or the dangers of trying to rebel.

"Well, don't get mad at me," Lilly fired back. "This isn't my fault. It's *your* stupid planet that's ripping us apart." Lilly folded her arms across her chest.

Charlie started laughing. "It's not funny," Lilly protested, but soon she was laughing, too.

Charlie and Lilly walked to her Jeep, hand in hand. There was a big, brilliant full moon, a perfect circle in the night sky. "I promise I won't give up," he told her. "I'll keep trying to find a way for us to be together." He said it to make her feel better, and he would try, but he didn't have much hope.

"I know you will," Lilly said. She stood on her tiptoes and kissed his cheek. "I'm not giving you a choice. In this situation I think you should follow Mrs. Hartman's advice."

"What do you mean?" Charlie asked.

"Brainstorm!" Lilly said.

He grabbed her around the waist and lifted her onto the hood of her Jeep. "I love you, Liliana." He traced the side of her face with his index finger. "More than tongue can tell."

"I love you, too, I love you—" She looked up, thinking about it. "I love you—infinity."

"Infinity. I like the sound of that. I love you—infinity, too." Then he pulled her close for a kiss.

When Lilly came home she found Michelle snoring in the recliner. The TV was still on. Michelle had made a futile attempt to stay up. Lilly knew that tomorrow her mom would expect a play-by-play of the evening, and she would give it to her. But tonight she wanted to keep the memories to herself.

Charlie needn't have rushed home. His parents were still out of the house. He went up to his room and put on his music. He was able to think better with his music playing. When he told Lilly at the diner that he didn't have a solution to the problem of leaving, it wasn't *exactly* true. No matter how he thought about it, he always came back to one solution to the problem. It was the *only* solution. Charlie took out his PCD and accessed the Sentrian code of law. He read through the entire document that night to be sure he was correct. Now he had found a way for them to be together, but Liliana might find it too extreme. He wasn't sure if she would go for it.

COURSE OF ACTION

Lilly woke up and ambled into the kitchen in her PJs. A bowl of cereal sounded good to her. On the kitchen table she found a note from her mother.

Mi hija,

I didn't want to wake you, but I'm dying to hear all about prom. I'll make us dinner tonight, and you can tell me all about it. Invite Charlie, too.

Love, Mom

Lilly glanced up at the clock. It was nine fifteen, later than she thought. Her mother had left for work over an hour ago. She was pouring cereal into a bowl when she was startled by a rapping sound on the sliding glass door. She pushed back the vertical blinds and saw Charlie waving at her. He had washed the blond streaks out of his hair and was wearing his glasses again. She hadn't even run a brush through her hair. Quickly she tried to smooth her out-of-control mane as she opened the door.

"What are you doing over here in broad daylight? Are you trying to get caught?" she scolded.

"Evelyn's still out of town, as are most of the leadership and elders. The rest of the Sentrian adults are already at work."

"Oh." Lilly relaxed. "I was just about to have a bowl of cereal. Do you want some?"

"No, but I will make us some coffee." He filled the carafe with water and returned to the coffee maker. "Remember last night when I said I would try to find a way for us to stay together?" Lilly looked up from pouring milk in her bowl and nearly spilled it all over the table.

"I think I've found a way," he said.

"Tell me," she insisted.

"Well, OK." Charlie sat down at the kitchen table across from her. He hesitated. "But I'm warning you, it will seem very radical to you."

Lilly stared across the table at her alien boyfriend. "I think I can handle it."

"Remember the story of Arina and Paltiel?"

"Yes, of course."

"Well, I think I mentioned that the Sentrian laws changed after their death, because the elders realized that after a couple gets married, it can't be undone." He paused then, trying to read her expression. "Liliana, we would have to get married. It's the only way we could stay together."

Lilly's eyes widened in surprise. She was only eighteen years old. Her plans for college didn't include being a freshman wife. Charlie looked down at his hands. He didn't want to look at her face in case she was repulsed by the idea.

"OK, let's do it," Lilly said.

Charlie looked up at her then. He wasn't expecting an answer so quickly and certainly not such an easy yes. "Are you sure?" he asked.

"Yes, I'm sure. Getting married straight out of high school isn't my first choice, but if it's a way for us to stay together, then I'm all for it."

"Well, I don't want you to marry me for the wrong reasons," Charlie told her.

"I wouldn't be," Lilly assured him. "If circumstances were different, and we had the luxury of time, I could envision marrying you after college anyway. We'll just be moving it up a few years."

"Wait, you need to consider a few things first. With my shortened lifespan you are going to be a very young widow."

"Charlie, there are no guarantees in life. I could die before you do."

"Not likely," he said. "And there's another thing. Liliana, I will never be able to impregnate you. You and I are different enough genetically that we could never procreate together."

"That doesn't matter," Lilly said, smiling at his rather clinical way of stating the situation.

"You say that now, but in a few years it very well might. I don't want you to regret not having children."

"Charlie, do you want to get married or not? Because it sure sounds like you're trying to talk me out of it."

Charlie got up from the table and leaned against the counter. "Liliana, whether you marry me or not, I will never love anyone else. Of this I am sure. But I want to be fair to you. You need to be sure, too. Because if you decide to do this, you will be giving up a lot."

Lilly got up then and walked over to him. "No, I won't. I'll be getting exactly what I want. I can deal with not having children. I know we won't grow old together, and I accept that. What I can't handle is you leaving for Sentria in a few weeks and never seeing you again."

Charlie looked into her eyes. He saw that she was serious. "OK. We'll have to keep our plans a secret. Even from your mom. We'll have to elope, because if the leaders find out our plans, they will do everything in their power to stop us."

"Elope? Well, OK," Lilly said, thinking. "You know, there's a justice of the peace a few miles from here."

"No, Texas has a seventy-two-hour waiting period. The Sentrian information systems are very much integrated into Earth's computers. As soon as we apply for a license, I guarantee Evelyn will be notified. We won't have a prayer. We'll have to get married somewhere that doesn't have a waiting period. I've researched it, and I believe Las Vegas is our best chance."

"Vegas?" Lilly asked. Charlie nodded. "So when did you want to go?"

"It would be great if we could leave right now while Evelyn is still out of town. Unfortunately, I have too many loose ends to tie up. I need to get some money together for the trip. Plus, I want to wait until after graduation for your sake," Charlie said, thinking aloud. "We don't leave for Sentria until the fourth of June. Maybe we could sneak out the night of graduation. I'm sure Evelyn will be working at the records facility up until the moment we leave for Sentria, anyway."

"So, we'll need to get married as soon as we get our license."

"Yes," Charlie said. "We can't go for style. We just have to go to a chapel that can accommodate us quickly. I realize this is probably not what you envisioned for your wedding day."

"No, it's fine for me." Lilly may have daydreamed a time or two about marrying Superman, but she hadn't been one of those girls who spent all her spare time looking through bridal magazines and fantasizing about the fabulous wedding she would one day have. It was Charlie who would be losing out. "What about you, Charlie? I know this isn't how you wanted it to be. We're not going to have the sacred service that is so important to you." Lilly could tell by the look on his face that she was right.

"With my blatant disregard for His will, I doubt God would want to be in attendance at our wedding anyway."

"A civil service will work," Lilly said, trying to make him feel better. "I don't need all the fanfare."

"Sentrian law states that no one can intervene once we're married. A civil service is just as legal on this world as a religious one." Charlie looked at Lilly. "So it really doesn't bother you? Not having a traditional wedding?" He thought most girls, even Earthan ones, dreamed about having a fairytale wedding.

"No, my only worry is my mom."

"She's going to be really angry, isn't she?"

"Definitely. But mostly she'll be hurt that I just took off and did this." Lilly had always been the good girl. She didn't sneak out. She didn't drink or smoke. Even though she was eighteen and legally old enough to get married, it didn't seem right. She still felt like a kid. This would be the most irresponsible thing she had ever done. Just as irresponsible as when Michelle and Lalo had done it. For most of Lilly's life, her mom had warned and lectured her about what a mistake it had been to run off with Lalo. And now, Lilly was about to do the exact same thing with Charlie. Her mom would be so disappointed in her. Lilly worried her necklace with her fingers. Charlie reached over and stopped her by grabbing her hand.

"I don't want to pressure you. If this is not something you want…"

"No. I am one hundred percent OK with this." She smiled to reassure him and herself.

Charlie glanced up at the clock. It was nearly ten. Evelyn and the elders would return in a few hours. "I've got to go now."

"You can't stay just a little bit longer?" Lilly asked.

"It's very tempting, but I have some shopping to do before we're back under surveillance again."

"Shopping? For what?"

"You already have a Sentrian engagement circle. I think you need an Earthan wedding band." He kissed her on the forehead and then left through the sliding glass door.

Evelyn called Jana as soon as she got back from the conference. She had to suffer through several minutes of boring details about the primitive Earthan dance they called prom before Jana finally got to the point. Yes, Lilly had been in attendance. No, Charlie was not her date. She came with someone named Jimmy. Yes, they seemed pretty serious. No, Charlie had not been there. Satisfied she had gotten as much useful information out of Jana as was possible, she made an excuse and hung up. There was only one thing that bothered Evelyn. Jana wasn't the brightest. It would be better if she had a more reliable source.

"Now will you let it go?" Henry asked. He had been standing at the door to their room.

Evelyn turned around to face him. "Oh, so you've started eavesdropping on my conversations?"

"Don't try to deflect the question."

Evelyn sighed. "You were right. The Earthan female has a new boyfriend. It looks like Charlie is out of the picture, whether he wants to be or not."

"And?"

"And what?" Evelyn demanded.

"You're going to quit harassing Charlie and quit spying on the Earthan girl."

"No way. Not until we are all safely back on Sentria. You don't know Charlie like I do. He's devious. I know he's up to something. I will not be his fool."

"One day, when you're not too preoccupied with Charlie, it would be nice if you got back to being my wife."

Henry walked off, and Evelyn just rolled her eyes.

For the next two weeks things went back to the way they were before the elders went out of town. When Charlie came over at night, they made their preparations. Charlie had been saving the money his parents either gave him or just left lying around, and Lilly raided her piggy bank. Right before they left she would take most of the money out of her checking account. That should get them to Las Vegas and get them started wherever they ended up. They only had one worry: that Evelyn might find out. Unfortunately, she had started staking out Charlie's house again, but more stealthily than before. Charlie wasn't sure what this could mean.

Evelyn had put in a busy day at the records facility. She started at five in the morning and would be there until at least six o'clock that night. Thank goodness for Earthan coffee. Although coffee had no stimulative effect on her

Sentrian system, something about the warm drink revived her. The one thing she took comfort in was that by this time next week she'd be on a shuttle headed for Sentria. She decided to take a break and get a late lunch. While she was sitting at a café in the mall, she heard a small voice ask, "Evelyn?"

She turned around and saw a tall, plain-looking Earthan female sitting at the table behind her. The girl looked vaguely familiar to Evelyn, but she couldn't be sure. These Earthans all looked alike.

The girl spoke again. "It's Shelby. From English class."

"Yes, of course," Evelyn said. She couldn't care less. Then she noticed the girl had a camera case slung across her shoulder.

"Aren't you in yearbook or something?"

"Uh-huh," Shelby said.

"You must be busy this time of year, what with prom and graduation," Evelyn noted.

"Yes, well, it's part of the job. The trouble is, I've got so many pictures, and I can only use a few in the yearbook. Like at prom, I had to take pictures of every couple as they were leaving in addition to the dance photos and prom king and queen. You can just imagine how many photos I've got to sift through. But what about you, Evelyn? Everyone wondered what happened to you."

Evelyn didn't want to discuss her sudden absence from school, but it looked like she would have to in order to continue this conversation with the yearbook girl. "I went back to live with my mom and stepdad. I'm just here for the week visiting my aunt and uncle. Did you say you took pictures of *all* the couples at prom? That's a lot of pictures. What are you going to do with the extras?"

"They'll be tossed as soon as we decide on the final ones for the yearbook, but I have a lot of sorting to do between then and now," Shelby said.

"Do you think I could see these pictures? I had to leave before prom, and I won't be here when the yearbook comes out."

"Well, I guess that would be OK. I've never done it before. I mean, I've never shown someone the pictures before the yearbook comes out. Seeing as you won't get a chance to see them otherwise, I suppose I could make an exception. I was just headed back to school to do some of the layouts. Do you want to come with me?"

"I'd love to," Evelyn said, smiling.

Evelyn convinced Shelby she could help with the sorting process, so she was sitting at a corner desk with huge stacks of raw photos in front of her.

"Take out the pictures that are no good because of technical factors, such as blurriness or lighting issues. Later, our editors will decide which of the good pictures will make it into the yearbook."

"Will do," Evelyn said.

Evelyn had to admit that Shelby was a good photographer. She had to remove very few poor-quality pictures from the stack. It seemed to Evelyn that the yearbook staff had a preference for a few select individuals: cheerleaders, drill team, and athletes. *These must be the beautiful ones by Earthan standards*, Evelyn thought. By comparison, there were very few photos of the band. After looking for about half an hour, she finally found what she was looking for: a picture of the Earthan girl Charlie was so smitten with, and her date. Evelyn squinted and pulled the picture closer to get a good look. It was Charlie, of course. He had altered his appearance, but he was still recognizable to Evelyn. "I knew it," she said under her breath.

"Did you say something, Evelyn?" Shelby asked.

"I just looked at my watch. I didn't realize it was so late. I'm afraid I'll have to go, but I did finish these two piles." Evelyn slipped the incriminating photo into her purse and got up to leave.

"OK. Well, thanks for your help." Shelby thought it was odd that Evelyn had seemed so insistent on seeing the photos and then decided to leave before even looking through a quarter of them.

When Evelyn got home, she ran up to her room. This photo was the proof she had been looking for, but it didn't explain *everything*. Evelyn had been checking the logs and knew that Tamar and Charlie were speaking every night. Was he such a slime that he would deceive Tamar just so he could date his annoying, tawny-haired wench? Unspeakable. In the whole history of her planet she had never heard of anyone doing such a thing. She pulled out the logs to examine them more closely.

That was when she noticed something she hadn't before. Every night they spoke at the same time and for the same length of time—there was no deviation. She used her security clearance to override the password code and opened a log from the last month. This was considered a breach of privacy, but she knew if she found evidence against Charlie, the elders would overlook it.

Evelyn began watching. She should have been looking at a video feed of Charlie and Tamar, one on each side of the screen. Instead, she saw a side-by-side view of their empty bedrooms. She flipped through several days' worth of entries but always found the same thing: two empty bedrooms with no sign of Charlie or Tamar.

What is going on? Evelyn asked herself. She picked up her PCD and put in a link to Tamar. She could understand Charlie's motivation to lie, but why would Tamar go along with it?

Tamar appeared on the wall screen. "Hello, Evelyn," she said meekly.

"I'll get to the point. I've been going through the communications, and I know you and Silas are recording empty logs. The evidence is irrefutable, so don't bother trying to deny it. What I want to know, Tamar, is why?"

"Well, the truth is, I found my One a few months ago. I told Silas right away, and to my relief, he wasn't even mad."

I bet he wasn't, Evelyn thought. "Why didn't you contact me with this information? I could have found a suitable replacement for Silas."

"I...I...was going to," Tamar stuttered. "But Silas asked me not to. He told me if his parents found out that our engagement was over, they would be disappointed and would try to set him up with someone else right away.

He wanted to wait until he returned to Sentria. Elias and I weren't planning to announce our engagement until later this summer, so I saw no harm in complying with his request."

"I see," Evelyn said.

"Evelyn, what's going to happen to us?" Tamar asked.

"Tamar, do not worry. You are not in any trouble. I wish you much happiness in your upcoming marriage." Before Tamar could respond, Evelyn terminated the link. She had no interest in punishing Tamar. She was an innocent pawn in Charlie's twisted game. Evelyn decided to focus all her wrath on the person who did deserve it.

When Charlie got home from school, he went upstairs to set up the nightly link with Tamar. He saw he had a message from her on his electronic note pad. He hadn't spoken to Tamar since she told him of her engagement. His heart sped up as he opened the link.

"Hello, Silas. I'm afraid Evelyn knows that our engagement is off. She did some in-depth investigation of our logs. She told me she wasn't mad at me, but she seemed angry. Watch yourself, Silas. I don't trust her."

Charlie's mind raced. He knew he didn't have much time. He grabbed a pen and a piece of paper and quickly wrote Lilly a note. He hoped he could get it to her before it was too late.

He ran out to his car and headed straight to McDonald's. Luckily Beth and Ian were still there. Charlie ran over to their table. "Beth, please, I need a favor."

"Calm down, Charlie. What is it?"

"I need you to get this message to Liliana. It is imperative that she read this today."

"OK, Charlie. Sure thing. We'll leave now." Beth grabbed her purse, and Ian followed her out to his car. With great relief, he watched as they backed out of the parking lot. The easy part was done. Charlie got back in the Mustang and mentally prepared himself for what he would face when he got home.

There was a knock on the door. Lilly peered out of the peep hole. Ian and Beth were standing on the front porch. Lilly opened the door, and Beth shoved the note in her face.

"Here," Beth said. "You need to read this now. It's from Charlie."

"Yeah," Ian said. "He acted like it was some kind of emergency. I wanted to read it on the way over, but Beth wouldn't let me." Beth hit him in the arm, but Lilly wasn't paying attention. She was engrossed in the note. Her knees grew weak. She had to sit down.

"Go get her a glass of water," Beth told Ian. "Is everything OK?"

"No, not really," Lilly said. Evelyn *knew*. This was *no bueno*. Lilly didn't know how much trouble Charlie was in, but she realized that Evelyn would never let him out of her sight until they returned to Sentria.

While Ian was in the kitchen, Beth whispered a question to Lilly. "You and Charlie are back together, aren't you?"

Lilly was in a fog, but she managed to nod. "I knew it," she heard Beth say. Lilly continued reading the note. At the end of the note, he asked her to be prepared for a change of plans and look for messages from him in her French horn case. She read the last line of the note: Do not worry and do not be afraid. We will get through this. Love, Charlie.

She wanted to believe Charlie, but she didn't know how anything was going to be OK ever again.

"Lilly, what's wrong?" Beth asked.

Lilly didn't answer her question. Instead she said, "Look, guys, I'm going to ask you for some rather odd favors in the next few days. Please just trust me."

Charlie had gotten out just in time. On his way home he spotted Evelyn's red convertible tailing him, but he was sure she hadn't followed him all the way from McDonald's. Charlie pulled into his driveway, relieved that at least Lilly had been forewarned. Evelyn got out of her car and approached him.

"Charlie, I don't suppose you know why I'm here," Evelyn said.

"I don't have the faintest idea," Charlie lied, wanting to protect Tamar. "But I'm sure you're going to tell me."

"Let's go inside and wait for your parents."

An hour later, Louis and Helen arrived. For Helen it was like a sick sense of deja vu: Evelyn sitting in their living room, telling them what Charlie had done wrong.

"Hello, Louis, Helen," Evelyn greeted them.

"Evelyn," Louis said. Helen refused to speak to her.

"Sit down," Evelyn commanded. "We need to talk about Charlie."

"What's the matter now?" Louis glared at Charlie. Charlie looked down at his shoes.

"Charlie's no longer engaged to Tamar, *if* he ever was."

"What? What happened? You two seemed to be getting along so well," Helen exclaimed.

"*Seemed* is the operative word. They have been pretending to speak. He has programmed the logs to open automatically and shut down after an hour. They have been recording some pretty scintillating scenes of their empty bedrooms."

"You had no right to check our logs. That's a breach of privacy—completely illegal." Charlie's voice rose as he stood up.

"Sit!" Evelyn commanded him as if he were a dog. "Once the elders see all the proof of wrongdoing I have, they will commend me for violating your privacy, and you know it."

"What have you done?" Helen's hand went to her mouth. She was shaking badly. Charlie said nothing and leaned back against the couch.

"Tamar found her One," Evelyn answered for him. "Charlie asked her if she would pretend they were still engaged, supposedly to keep from being set up with someone else. Of course, it was really so he could continue his relationship with the Earthan girl."

Charlie started to object but then looked up. Evelyn placed a picture of him and Liliana at prom on the coffee table. Charlie cringed. Now Evelyn had tangible proof that they were still involved. Louis picked up the photo and stared at it, squinting. Then he put it down. He shook his head in disgust.

Evelyn sneered. "It seems you two have been doing an excellent job of supervising Charlie. He went to prom with her right under your noses."

"Well, if the leaders wouldn't make us work sixteen hour days, maybe we could." Helen said. Louis hushed her.

"Charlie, how could you?" Louis stood up and walked over to where he was sitting. "I thought I made myself clear. You were not to see this girl again."

There was nothing to say. He had disobeyed. But he didn't regret it. Rather than look down in shame, Charlie lifted his head and stared his father in the eyes.

"I really did not want to do this, but I had to involve the elders and the magistrate," Evelyn said, knowing she would likely be in trouble for not reporting Charlie's relationship with the Earthan girl sooner.

"No, please," Helen begged. Louis hushed her again.

"I've already contacted the magistrate. He will be here shortly."

Helen was about to lose it. "This can't be happening." She grabbed Louis's arm. "You have to make them see…"

"Does my wife have to be here for this? She can't take this kind of stress. She has the Bernalian trait," Louis told Evelyn.

Evelyn pointed at Helen. "She's a weak one?" Louis nodded, and Evelyn rolled her eyes. She didn't have a lot of patience for those with the

Bernalian trait, even though by law she had to show compassion for their condition. "Very well. She may lie down in her room until the magistrate arrives, but ultimately it's up to him if he wants her to be present for the meeting. You knew of your wife's frailty; you should have made more of an effort to keep Charlie in line."

"Yes, Evelyn," Louis said respectfully. "You're right. May I at least bring her a cup of coffee with Instant Smile?"

"Go ahead. I'll keep an eye on your wayward son. Oh, and I'd like a cup of coffee myself. Why don't you make us all some?"

Louis nodded. He went to the kitchen to prepare the coffee, and Helen jumped up and ran to her bedroom. Evelyn picked up a magazine and started flipping through it. Charlie leaned back against the couch. The way he was feeling, he doubted he could swallow even a sip of coffee right now. Charlie thought about his mom. Right now she was probably taking her tranquility medicine to calm down. Then she would crawl under the covers and hide from the world. He had always just accepted his mother the way she was. But now, knowing what he had to face, he couldn't decide if he envied or pitied her.

For the next twenty minutes, Charlie and his father sat in silence, waiting for the magistrate and his advisers to arrive. There was no point worrying about it; they would punish him however they saw fit. While he was concerned about what they would to him, Liliana was foremost on his mind. Separation from her would be unbearable.

There was a knock on the door, and Evelyn got up to let them in. Mr. Conner had a scowl on his face. Although he was as short as Louis, he had a very intimidating presence. The two elders were dressed identically in dark-gray suits. The only distinguishing feature was that one was thin and the other fat. They greeted Charlie and his father in a cursory fashion.

"I want the two of you to wait upstairs. We have much to discuss with Evelyn first," the magistrate said to Charlie and his father.

They got up and went to Charlie's bedroom. Louis sat on the bed, and Charlie leaned against the window seat. They said nothing to each other. There was really not much to say. Charlie looked out the window. Everything was as it should be. Dogs were wagging their tails and barking. Kids were riding their bikes. Fathers were arriving home from work. There was no indication in the outside world of the hell going on inside his home. Charlie overheard the elders grilling Evelyn, and his focus shifted to the conversation downstairs.

"Why didn't you bring this to our attention sooner?" the thin elder asked Evelyn.

"I thought the problem was solved. He seemed to be working the prescribed program, and he was, by all appearances, connecting with Tamar on Sentria."

"You still should have told us. We could have taken the necessary steps to ensure Charlie's *full* cooperation," the thin elder rebuked Evelyn.

"Can we continue this conversation outside? He is a supersonos, you know."

So Evelyn didn't want Charlie to overhear her being reprimanded by one of the elders. Well, too bad. It made Charlie smile.

"No, we can't go outside. We can't leave him alone. He cannot be trusted. And you haven't answered the question."

"Look, I know what you would have done to him to ensure his cooperation. I was simply trying to give my fellow Sentrian a second chance," Evelyn said.

"Hah!" Charlie scoffed, and Louis looked up at him. Evelyn wasn't fooling anyone. She wasn't trying to give Charlie a second chance. She just wanted to make his life hell.

The thin elder and Evelyn bickered for a while until finally the magistrate spoke up. "Enough. Evelyn, while I admire your initiative in attempting to solve the problem yourself, all the leadership must be notified when an offense of this magnitude is committed. Now, let's get down to business."

The thin elder grumbled but said nothing more. Charlie agreed with him that Evelyn was getting off too easy. Being a daughter-in-law of the magistrate obviously had its benefits. It was too late for Charlie, but he had been hoping Evelyn would get what she deserved.

"Now, what to do with Silas? Any suggestions?" the magistrate asked. They proceeded to go through a litany of possible punishments. Charlie filtered them out. He concentrated on the original plan: eloping with Liliana. Unfortunately, sneaking away would be much more difficult now.

"What about the Earthan girl?" Evelyn asked.

Charlie's heart sped up. He didn't expect them to go after her. He was prepared to face the consequences of his actions, but he didn't want his Liliana to suffer for his mistakes.

"Evelyn, how confident are you that she is the only Earthan who knows of our existence?" the magistrate asked.

"Very confident."

"You were also very confident that Charlie had given up this strange Earthan romance," the thin elder countered.

"I attended high school with *them*. These creatures are not just intellectually backward, they are savagely cruel. If she had confessed to anyone that she thought there were aliens living among them, she would have become the object of vicious ridicule."

"Yes, but you have not been in this high school for the last two months. How would you know?" The thin elder wouldn't let it go.

Evelyn sighed. "They may be unintelligent, but the manner in which they gossip about one another is highly sophisticated. If there was a rumor going around about Charlie being an alien, my sources would have informed me."

They spent the next few minutes analyzing the incriminating prom photo and going over the empty logs to Tamar. Then Mr. Conner started giving out instructions. To the two elders he said, "You will go to the school tomorrow and inform the girl that she will stay away from Charlie, or she will face very unpleasant consequences. Scare her if you need to, but try not to harm her. We don't need a police investigation on our hands."

That should have made Charlie feel better, but somehow it didn't. Charlie heard footsteps coming up the stairs. The fat elder knocked on the door. "You may come down. The magistrate will speak to you now. And bring your wife," he said to Louis. They followed the fat elder down. Louis ducked into his bedroom and got Helen up. He led her by the hand into the living room.

"Sit." The thin elder motioned toward the sofa. The Grays did as they were told. Helen put her face in Louis's shoulder and closed her eyes. Louis put his arm around her and gently patted her hand.

"Silas Gray, I'm sure you are aware that these are serious charges," Mr. Conner said. "Evelyn believes, as I do, that you are mentally and emotionally ill, but that doesn't mitigate your guilt. You have broken multiple laws. When we return, you will be handed over to the Great Council."

Charlie wasn't surprised that they were going to file charges against him, but it still hurt to hear. He had never thought of himself as a criminal. They made what he and Lilly had—something beautiful and pure—seem dirty and wrong.

"You will be detained in your home until our ship leaves next week."

The fat elder leaned over and whispered into the magistrate's ear. "Sir, remember the awkward questions we were asked when Evelyn withdrew midsemester? I believe we have to let him finish the last three days of school and graduation. If we pull him out now, the Earthans will want to know why. We wouldn't want them poking around, meddling in our affairs."

The Earthans *would* think it strange if a senior didn't complete the last few days of school and attend graduation. They might even ask for a reason why, but Charlie knew they wouldn't launch an investigation over it. The Sentrian elders, however, did not know that. They mistakenly assumed that the Earthans were as suspicious and paranoid of their own citizens as the Sentrian government was. This gave Charlie a glimmer of hope and an idea.

"Agreed," the magistrate said. "What precautions can we put in place to ensure he will have no contact with the female?"

"Remember, we are going to speak to the girl," the fat elder said. "These beings are primitive and ignorant, concerned more for their own survival than for anyone or anything else. Threatening her with physical harm should be all it takes to keep her away."

"Yes. But we still need someone to watch Silas so that he doesn't try to contact her," the magistrate said.

"I could return to the high school," Evelyn volunteered.

"No, reenrolling for the last few days of school would be more suspicious than pulling Silas out at the end of the year," the thin elder said.

"He's right," the magistrate said. He paused in thought. "I think I have a solution. Henry is still enrolled at the school. He can monitor Silas."

"With respect, sir," Evelyn said. "Henry and Charlie are in different grades. It will be impossible for Henry to guard him at all times."

"You are also in different grades," the thin elder pointed out.

"Yes, but at least I'm in band with Charlie and the girl. It will be much easier for me than for him. Henry is too trusting. He doesn't understand how manipulative Silas can be."

"You are his wife. I think it is your duty to make him understand. That is all," the magistrate said and departed.

"I'll be back shortly," Evelyn told the Grays. "I will be staying here every night until we return to Sentria. Charlie won't be sneaking out on my watch." While she was gone, she left the two elders to stand guard outside the house, one in the front and one in the back.

Charlie expected a proper chewing out from his father, but Louis had nothing to add. He gave Charlie a look that conveyed his disappointment and then went into the den and turned on his PCD. Charlie ran upstairs and furiously scribbled out a note to Liliana before Evelyn returned.

Evelyn packed in a hurry. Henry stood in the doorway holding a mug of coffee and watching her fill her overnight bag with clothes and toiletries.

"Henry, this is very important. Do you understand what you need to do?"

"Yes, Evelyn, I get it. I'll drive him to school in the mornings. I'll follow him between classes and sit with him at lunch. Then, I'll drive him back home again in the afternoons to your waiting arms," Henry said. "Oh, and I almost forgot. I guess I should go with him to the bathroom and watch him relieve himself."

"This is not the time for vulgar jokes," Evelyn said. "This is serious. Charlie is in a desperate place. He may try anything."

"Does it really matter at this point?" Henry entered the room. "I mean we are returning to Sentria next Monday. What difference does it make if he says hi to the girl in the hall? He'll be gone soon, problem solved."

Evelyn shook her hairbrush at Henry. "You know, it's that kind of lax attitude that got us into this mess in the first place. Remember, you *are* a seminary student and the son of the magistrate. How can you think it's OK to break our laws with impunity?"

Whenever Evelyn, or the elders, or even his father brought up the point about all these laws Charlie had broken, it made Henry nervous. The Sentrians had a noninvolvement *policy* in regard to their Earthan missions. That was true. But Henry was a student of Sentrian religion and law, and he couldn't see any actual laws Charlie had broken. The sacred text did not mention relationships with Earthans. They were not expressly forbidden or allowed. On the other hand, Evelyn had breached Charlie's privacy by inspecting the logs, a clear cut violation, but no one seemed to care about that.

"Just don't let him out of your sight," Evelyn warned. "I'm counting on you."

HENRY

The next morning Henry drove to Charlie's house. Evelyn and Charlie were waiting in the driveway for him to pull up.

"Ready?" Henry asked.

Charlie nodded and got in the passenger side of the car. Henry was quiet on the ride to school, and Charlie was thankful for that. Charlie was focused on only one thing. He had to find a way to get his note to Lilly.

When they arrived at school, Henry followed Charlie to the band hall. He watched as Charlie got his trumpet out of the case and sat down. Then he left and went to his class. Charlie couldn't believe it. He looked around, expecting to find Henry spying on him, but he was really gone. Charlie saw him walking toward the math department, his backpack slung over his shoulder.

Charlie got up from his seat, ran over to Lilly and pressed the note into her hand. Mr. Patterson tapped on his music stand to indicate he was ready to begin. There was not time to talk. Charlie grabbed his trumpet and ran to his seat. Lilly put the note in her pocket and joined in playing the chorale.

After band, Lilly pulled the note out of her pocket. It was folded in quarters with writing on the outside. It said, "Read this note *in private* as soon as you can."

Lilly didn't have a chance before her next class. By third period she was dying to see what it said. She told Mrs. Hollins she was feeling sick and asked if she could go to the nurse. Mrs. Hollins nodded, and Lilly headed straight for the girl's restroom. She went into an empty stall and opened the note.

Dearest Liliana,

So many things have happened since yesterday afternoon. I'm in a lot of trouble, as you can well imagine. Henry is guarding me during the day at school, and Evelyn is my warden at night. The elders plan to put my case before the Great Council on Sentria. The punishment will likely involve incarceration and reprogramming for who knows how long. We will have to move up our plans. We cannot wait until Friday evening. We'll have to sneak out during the graduation ceremony itself. But don't worry, I've got a plan for that, too. See if you can get Ian and Beth to help. We'll need them to pull this off. Tomorrow I'll send another note with more details. I'm so sorry about this huge mess I've dragged you into. I know I'm asking a lot, but once we're married, they'll have to leave us alone. The magistrate is sending two elders to see you today. They will threaten you to stay away from me. Please don't let them frighten you. They will not hurt you. Just agree with whatever they say and tell them what they want to hear. Please leave me some sort of message that you are still prepared to go through with this.

I love you,
Charlie.

Lilly quickly penned a note back.

Dear Charlie,

I was scared when I read the note Beth gave me. I didn't sleep all night worrying about what they might do to you. I was so relieved to see you in school today. Of course I still want to marry you. How can you even ask? The elders don't scare me. I can handle them. I will wait for your instructions. I love you—infinity.

Liliana

She stepped out of the bathroom and walked over to Charlie's locker. She checked that no one was looking, and then she slipped the note through the slats.

Charlie found the note just before lunch. Henry had been following Charlie from class to class, but he always stood at a distance. Charlie stood in front of his locker with his back turned to Henry and quickly looked over the note. He could hear Liliana's voice in his head as he read it. Charlie slipped the note into his pocket and turned around.

"Ready?" Henry asked.

"Yeah, let's go," Charlie said. They headed to the cafeteria and sat in Henry's usual spot, a corner table close to the entrance. Lilly walked in and saw Charlie sitting with Henry. She glanced at him before sitting at the band table.

Henry ate quickly and then pulled out a book for the remainder of lunch. Charlie was shocked at Henry's inattention. He could have gone over and kissed Lilly on the lips, and he doubted Henry would have noticed. Why would Evelyn leave Henry of all people with the responsibility of being his guard? The bell rang then, and Henry got his backpack and left. Charlie took the opportunity to reread Lilly's note, more slowly this time. He paused at the end, smiling.

As Henry and Charlie were walking out to the parking lot that afternoon, Charlie saw them. The thin and fat elders were standing next to Lilly's car, talking to her. Charlie froze. He wanted to go over there and rip their limbs from their bodies. He had never felt so helpless. He couldn't even protect his girl.

Henry grabbed his arm. "C'mon, Charlie." He pulled him toward his Honda.

"Henry, I…" Charlie began to speak.

Henry shook his head and motioned for Charlie to be quiet. He reached over and pulled something out from under Charlie's wrist. It was a Sentrian bug. Henry flipped a switch on the tiny device to off.

"Your conversations are being monitored. It's a secondary precaution. Evelyn attached it to you last night while you were asleep. It's activated when you speak, but it's audio only. No video."

No wonder Evelyn allowed Henry to guard him. He really didn't have to do anything. Charlie supposed it could be worse. At least she couldn't *see* what he was doing.

Henry started the car. Charlie was still staring over at Liliana. "Charlie, I realize you are fond of the girl, but going over there right now with the elders talking to her is a *very* bad idea."

Charlie knew Henry was right, but it was so hard to watch her over there alone with them. His fists were still clenched.

"They won't hurt her," Henry said. Although Charlie told Liliana the same thing in his note, now he wasn't so sure. He could hear their raised voices and threats. The thin one pounded his fist on the hood of Lilly's Jeep.

Henry tried to distract Charlie. "The girl—I'm sorry, I don't know her name."

"Liliana, her name is Liliana."

"Is Liliana unintelligent, reckless?"

"No," Charlie said. "Just because she's an Earthan doesn't mean…"

"Calm down, Charlie. I was just pointing out that she won't say or do anything foolish. She'll be fine."

"Oh," Charlie said. He had assumed Henry was like his fellow Sentrians—believing Liliana was a stupid, inferior Earthan. But Henry spoke about her the way he would speak of someone his equal. All the others referred to Liliana as the Earthan girl or Earthan female, but Henry had actually asked her name. He, at least, recognized her as a person. "Why are you doing this?"

"Doing what?" Henry asked.

"Telling me about the bug. Trying to keep me out of trouble. You're not even following me very closely. Didn't Evelyn warn you about me?"

"Repeatedly," Henry said. "Look, Charlie, this isn't fun for me, either. I'm just counting down the days until we return to Sentria. I don't want to follow you around. And I'm *really* not crazy about my wife staying at her ex-boyfriend's house, in his room, every night."

"If I were in your shoes, I wouldn't like it either."

"I ought to beat the crap out of you just on general principles," Henry said and shrugged. "But this is my reality now. Yours, too. Let's just try to get through these last few days of school."

Henry drove them to Charlie's house and switched on the bug when he pulled into the driveway. Evelyn was waiting by the front door for him. Charlie slung his backpack over his shoulder and entered the house.

From the time he got home until the moment he left in the morning, Evelyn wouldn't let Charlie out of her sight. The only privacy he had was in the bathroom, but even then, if she thought he was taking too long a shower, she'd start banging on the door. She sat beside him at dinner and hovered over him while he did his homework.

The first night, Evelyn didn't sleep; she sat in a chair while Charlie lay in his bed. Tonight she decided to do something different. She rearranged the furniture in his room, putting the dresser against the already bolted window and pushing the bed against the door. She slept on the bed and made Charlie sleep on the floor. Still, Charlie was sure she slept with one eye open.

The next morning, after Henry picked Charlie up he switched off the bug again. "So how was your evening in lock-down?" he asked Charlie.

"Not much fun," Charlie said. He didn't think Henry would want to know the details of the sleeping arrangements. "Can I ask you something, Henry?"

"Yeah, sure," he said.

"Why do you keep turning off the bug?"

"The bug is for you and is your punishment. Why must I endure having my conversations monitored simply because I've been assigned to take you to school and follow you around?"

"Good point." Charlie was realizing that Henry wasn't so bad. He had Henry pegged all wrong. He kind of reminded Charlie of himself when he first arrived. The only difference was that Henry fell in love with the right kind of girl. "Yesterday afternoon, you said you were counting down the days until we return to Sentria. Have you got big plans when we get back?"

"Yes, I'll be starting my second year of seminary in the summer season. I had to take off a year for this mission, and I'm really looking forward to going back."

"Seminary? I had no idea." Charlie had imagined the son of a magistrate would go into politics. But then, Charlie was discovering that Henry was nothing like his father.

"Yeah, not too many people do know. My father was kind of disappointed that I didn't want to follow in his footsteps, but he got over it when I gave him a very ambitious daughter-in-law. I think he realizes that Evelyn is better suited for his world than I am."

"I must admit, I was surprised to find out you two were engaged. I mean, how did you two—oh, never mind, it's none of my business," Charlie said.

"But you want to know how we got together," Henry finished.

"Well, yeah. You two seem like opposites."

"Trust me, you're not the first one to notice. We met at university. I had to leave for this mission, but we decided we wanted to continue our friendship. We communicated through a link and talked almost every day. One day I was sitting quietly in prayer, and God told me to marry her. And well, you know the rest."

Henry pulled into the school parking lot. "See you at lunch." He leaned over and turned Charlie's bug back on. He didn't bother following Charlie to the band hall.

Charlie put a note with detailed instructions in Lilly's French horn case. In the note he warned her not to speak to him, because he was wearing a bug. He watched her as she read it. After she finished the note she looked at him and gave him a thumbs up.

Henry was the first one in his class to finish his test during first period, giving him a chance to consider things. He had been oblivious to Charlie and Liliana, mostly because he and Charlie weren't friendly, and he really didn't care what Charlie did. And he had no interest in spying on others like most Sentrians.

Now he couldn't help but notice. This thing between them was not some crush or puppy love. This was the real thing. Separating them would not fix Charlie. If she were Sentrian, there would be no problem, but because she was Earthan, Charlie was considered an outcast and worse. He was regarded as a criminal and deeply disturbed.

That day at lunch, Charlie was already sitting at the table, watching Lilly, when Henry arrived. When she thought no one was looking, she would sneak glances in Charlie's direction. Henry felt like he was intruding on a private moment. He reached over and switched the bug off. "Now we can speak freely."

"You know something," Charlie said.

"What?"

"I don't regret or apologize for the way I feel about Liliana, but I am sorry for the difficulties I am creating for you."

"I forgive you," Henry said. "Thank you for acknowledging it."

They finished eating, and Henry pulled out a book again. *He sure does read a lot,* Charlie thought. Yes, of course, Henry reads a lot. A lot of Earthan books. Like Charlie, Henry realized Earthans were not savage or unintelligent, as the teachers on Sentria had always taught, and just like Charlie, he had come to this conclusion from reading their own books in their own words. The bell rang, and Henry went on his way.

After school, Henry drove Charlie home to Evelyn's custody. She was standing in the driveway waiting for them.

"Charlie, go inside," she ordered. "Henry, I need to speak with you *privately.*"

That was her way of telling Charlie she didn't want his sensitive ears listening in. He didn't care. He would listen in if he wanted to. She could control many things, but not his superhearing.

Charlie went into the house, and Henry got out of the car. He walked over to where Evelyn was standing.

"Have you noticed any suspicious activity from Charlie?" she asked.

"No, why?"

"I haven't heard him have any conversations with the girl, and I realize that in class he won't be talking much. But there are longer stretches of time, like before and after school and at lunch time, when I hear nothing. It's like he's not even speaking. These are times when you should be with him."

"If that's an accusation, I don't appreciate it," Henry said defensively. "Look, you wanted me to guard him, and I am. But if you're asking me to be friends and make small talk with your ex, well, you're asking too much."

"Oh," Evelyn said. Of course Henry wouldn't want to speak to Charlie. When he put it in that context it made perfect sense. "I'm sorry I doubted you."

"You're forgiven." Henry rubbed her arm tenderly. "Call me later if you get a chance." Evelyn nodded. Henry kissed her cheek and after she walked in the door, he drove home.

Lilly asked Ian and Beth to meet her at the mall later. It was time to make the final preparations, and she needed their help. Before she met with both of them, she wanted to talk to Beth alone. She felt like she owed Beth some sort of explanation. Lilly picked up Beth at her house. Ian agreed to meet them at the mall.

On the drive over, Lilly said, "Beth, I know I can trust you not to say anything, but there's a reason we need your help." Lilly paused. "Charlie and I are running away to get married."

"What?" Beth asked. "Why?"

"Charlie's parents don't approve of our relationship. They want to separate us. They're taking him away right after graduation."

"Not approve of you? That's crazy."

"Well, they have some different ideas about who Charlie should date. Look, Beth, I can't ask you to keep secrets from Ian. He is your boyfriend, after all, but…"

"You don't have to ask me. I won't tell him. Is this what all this secret note passing has been about?"

Lilly nodded. "The day you brought over the first note, he was letting me know that they were taking him away sooner than he thought. We had to change plans and move up the time frame."

"How soon?"

"After graduation," Lilly said.

"Whoa. That's the day after tomorrow. Are you sure about this? Is this what you really want?"

"I don't want to be separated from Charlie. If this is the only way to stay together, then I'll do it," Lilly admitted.

"Charlie can be pretty intense. Are you sure he's not pressuring you into this?"

"No, of course not. This was as much my decision as his," Lilly assured her.

"I'm not trying to upset you or make you mad, but I want you to be sure. This is a big, life-changing decision you're contemplating, and you've never been real objective where Charlie's concerned."

"What do you mean?"

"Look Lil, I like Charlie. You know that. But there's something about him. Something off. I can't explain it, but if you distanced yourself from your feelings about him, you might see it, too. He's really weird."

Here we go again, Lilly thought. Well, they say love is blind. In her case it was mentally impaired as well. Lilly snickered at Beth, "You're one to talk, Goth Girl."

"Yeah, I know," Beth said with a smirk. Then her expression grew grim. "What about your mom? Does she know?"

"No, she doesn't."

Beth gave her a disapproving look.

"I know, I know," Lilly said. "I hate not telling her, but this is something we have to do without any interference."

"Well, OK then. I'll have to figure out something to tell Ian about the reason you're sneaking out that he will believe."

Thursday was the last day of school, and it was only a half day. Lilly was getting ready for school. It was seven o'clock in the morning and already approaching ninety degrees. Summer was here. She had no idea where she'd be next week. This could be the first summer she didn't spend in Texas.

She walked into the band hall and found another note in her horn case. It was short.

Liliana,

Tomorrow we start our life together. I can't wait to see you again and be able to talk to you like we used to. I am so blessed to have you as my wife. All the love in my heart,

Charlie

Lilly smiled as she read it. She folded it up and put it in her purse.

At the last bell, Charlie walked out to the parking lot with Henry. Liliana was standing under the eaves by the band hall. He was staring at her, and she was looking back.

"Here," Henry said as he reached over to turn off the bug. "Go tell her good-bye, but don't take too long. Evelyn's aware that today we have early dismissal, and she's expecting us home."

"Are you sure?" Charlie asked.

"Yes, go."

Charlie ran over to Lilly and swung her around in a big bear hug. "What are you doing?" Lilly asked. "Henry is watching."

"It's OK. Who do you think gave me permission?" Charlie showed her that the bug was turned off. Henry gave them a little nod. Then he turned his back to give them a little privacy.

Charlie hugged her again. "I've missed you."

"Me, too," Lilly said, glancing nervously in Henry's direction. She looked at Charlie. "Are you all set for tomorrow?"

"I am. Is my backpack ready to go?"

"Yes, it's where you said to leave it. I'll pick it up before I leave today."

"Thanks," Charlie said. "What about Ian and Beth? Are they all set?"

"Yes, and don't get mad, but I told Beth that we are eloping. Ian thinks we are sneaking out of graduation early to go party, and he approves."

"That's OK. Beth, I trust. I'm glad you told her," Charlie said. He pulled Lilly close and kissed her forehead. "Just one more night apart." Reluctantly, he pulled away. "I better go. Henry's doing us a huge favor, and I don't want to get him in trouble." Lilly nodded, then walked over to the band hall. Charlie got into the passenger seat of the Honda.

Once they were on the road, Charlie spoke. "I don't know why you allowed me to talk to her, but thank you."

"You're welcome," Henry said.

"I have something for you," Charlie said.

"What's this?"

"It's called *Atlas Shrugged*. I know you like to read, and I thought you might enjoy it." Charlie wished that he had known Henry before. He thought they might have been friends.

Evelyn was standing in the driveway as usual when Charlie arrived.

"Well done, Henry. You can relax now. I'm taking over." Henry nodded and drove away.

"It's over, Charlie. All you have left is graduation, and I will be there, watching you every minute."

"Well, then you won't mind taking this off." Charlie pointed to his wrist.

"How do you know about the bug?"

"You must have hit a nerve when you put it on. It's been bothering me for the past three days." He lifted his wrist up so she could remove it.

Evelyn scowled as she did so. "Go inside and pack for the trip home."

TOGETHER AGAIN

As they planned, Lilly picked up Charlie's backpack from the slot where he stored his trumpet. Inside were some changes of clothes for Charlie and other things he had packed for their trip.

There was still a lot left for Lilly to do. First, she drove by the bank and withdrew $320 dollars. She had sixty dollars in cash in a coffee can at home. With what Charlie was able to scrape up, it would have to be enough.

She reserved one hundred dollars, her birthday money, for a few personal things. Lilly pulled into the mall parking lot and headed for the petite dresses in her favorite department store.

She didn't need something real formal, but she did want a dress that looked halfway decent on her wedding day. On the sale rack she found a cerulean-blue formal dress in size zero. It looked pretty when she tried it on. After paying for it, she left the department store and headed out into the main corridor of the mall.

Lilly hesitated in front of Victoria's Secret. Did she really have the nerve to walk in there and buy lingerie?

"Grow up," she said to herself. "You're getting married the day after tomorrow. If you can't handle this, then you shouldn't get married at all."

She walked into the store and a sales clerk showed her to the section where the nighties were displayed. A short dark-blue satin nightie grabbed her attention. She held it up and looked in the mirror. It barely hit the top of her thigh. If she bought it, it would be the most suggestive nightie she ever owned. She knew Charlie wouldn't care if she slept in his old T-shirts as long as they were together. Still, she wanted to make a special effort for her wedding night. Lilly used the remainder of her money to pay for it.

As soon as she got home, she took her purchases and went inside to finish her preparations. She didn't notice the red Honda that had been following her ever since she left the bank, which was now parked across the street from her driveway.

After packing the rest of her clothes and toiletries, she laid the dress, still in its plastic wrap, on top of her other things and zipped up the bag. Then she placed the bag in the hatch of the Jeep next to Charlie's backpack.

Finally, she went to the kitchen, grabbed a Diet Coke, and sat down to do what she dreaded most. She wrote a good-bye note to Michelle.

The next morning her mom made pancakes, Lilly's favorite breakfast food.

"You took the whole day off?" She was hoping Michelle would go to work after the graduation.

"Sure, I thought we could go celebrate afterward. We could go to Bradley's, if you want."

"Actually, Mom, I sort of have plans. I was going to go out with some of the band afterward."

Michelle was disappointed, but she understood. "No, that's fine. You probably want to spend every last minute with Charlie. I remember wanting to go out with my friends after graduation. Of course that included Lalo, so Abuela had something to say about that. Just call me if you'll be late. And mi hija, I probably don't need to say this, but I'm your mother, so I will. Don't do anything stupid. You've got your whole life ahead of you."

"Sure, Mom," Lilly said. She walked away before her mom could see the guilt written all over her face.

Charlie was stuck riding to graduation with his parents and Evelyn. The two elders followed them in their black Blazer for extra security. At this point he could really do nothing. He wouldn't be able to get away from Evelyn to get any more messages to Lilly. It was up to Lilly, Beth, and Ian now.

One good thing was that Lilly had been playing in the band at high school graduations since she was a freshman and knew both the layout of the pavilion and the graduation protocol pretty well. After receiving their diplomas, the graduates would file off the stage and down a rather dark hall. They would reenter the pavilion from a side door to return to their seats. It would give them approximately two minutes when they would be out of Evelyn's view. Lilly arrived at the pavilion early and went over to where the band was warming up. She gave a few last-minute instructions to Beth and Ian and then went to join the rest of the graduates.

Evelyn was determined to keep Charlie and Lilly apart so she made sure Charlie was one of the last students to line up. By the time she left his side, the only seats left were at the very back. So Evelyn, Charlie's parents, and the two elders were seated as far away from the stage as you could possibly get.

Watching paint dry or organizing a sock drawer is always more interesting than sitting through a graduation, even if it's your own. For Lilly there was an added layer of anxiety on top of the monumental boredom.

She was fidgety. Her necklace was buried deep under her graduation robe, and her long hair was pinned up under her graduation cap. She had to settle for wringing her hands. Finally, the band began to play "Pomp and Circumstance," and the students headed toward the floor of the pavilion.

Charlie drummed his fingers on his lap. It seemed like an eternity before the introduction and requisite speeches by the principal, class president, and valedictorian were completed. At long last, the principal began announcing the names of the graduates. "Allison Marie Abbott," Mrs. Martin called out. The second row rose to line up behind the first row. Lilly was on the sixth row. Midway through the Fs, Charlie saw Beth stand up and head for the back hall. *Good girl,* Charlie thought to himself.

"Jack William Foster," the principal continued. Lilly's row rose and lined up. Her stomach was doing flip-flops. She stole a glance at Charlie. He smiled at her, and that gave her all the reassurance she needed.

"Liliana Elsa Garcia," the principal called out. Michelle jumped to her feet and started clapping. Evelyn leaned in closer as if that might help her see better. With her already poor vision, and sitting so far back, she doubted she would be able to make out an elephant walking across the stage.

Beth was already waiting for Lilly in the bathroom in the back hall. Lilly took off her graduation gown and Beth put it on. Then Lilly helped Beth pin her much shorter locks under the graduation cap. From a distance it would match Lilly's updo. Beth gave Lilly a hug.

"Good luck and congratulations," Beth said, handing her an envelope. She ran and caught up with the seniors in Lilly's row with plenty of time to spare. Lilly unpinned her long hair, slipped off the skirt she had worn under the gown, and put on a pair of jeans and sneakers from the bag she had hidden in the bathroom before the graduation started. There was nothing left to do but wait. Lilly leaned against the bathroom wall and said a little prayer.

Charlie watched as Lilly's row filed back in. There was Beth in Lilly's place, dressed in her cap and gown.

"Carrie Sue Garrett," the principal called out. Charlie glanced nervously over at the band. Ian was still sitting there looking bored. What was he waiting for? They hadn't come this far for Ian to blow it now.

Charlie's row stood up. He stared intensely in Ian's direction as if he could somehow get his attention by glaring at him.

"Brandon Ethan Gore," Mrs. Martin said. Ian looked up suddenly. He quickly stood up and ran to the back hall. "Charles Silas Gray."

Evelyn sat at the edge of her seat, straining to see Charlie. He walked across the stage and into the dark hallway. Lilly and Ian were waiting for him inside the boy's restroom.

"Cutting it a bit close, weren't you?" Charlie said as he took off his cap and gown.

"It was all part of the plan," Ian said. "I wanted to keep you on your toes."

"You certainly did that," Lilly told him.

"Won't your parents notice I'm not you? I am a lot taller than you." Ian said. Lilly smiled. On a good day, Ian was maybe five six.

"I don't think so. You'll be sitting between two basketball players. Anyone would look short between those two," Charlie said. He was also counting on Evelyn's poor eyesight. She would notice if Charlie's seat was empty, but she wouldn't be able to see any details that would distinguish Ian from Charlie.

"I hope Mr. Patterson won't be mad at you and Beth for cutting out in the middle of the graduation performance," Lilly said as she adjusted his cap. As part of the band, they were still needed to play "Pomp and Circumstance" one more time as the graduates filed out.

"Don't worry about it," Ian said. "He's got the whole summer to get over it."

"We've got to hurry," Charlie said. He gently pushed Ian out the door. "Now go." Ian ran down the hall and sandwiched himself between Brandon Gore and Sam Grayson, both of whom were over six feet tall. He got there just in time to reenter the floor of the pavilion. When they sat down, Brandon and the girl next to him stared at this guy who was so obviously not Charlie.

Ian waved and said, "How's it going?" The girl giggled, and Brandon shook his head. Sam didn't seem to notice that Ian was not the same person who walked across the stage with them a few minutes earlier.

Evelyn sat back in her seat and relaxed once she saw Charlie reenter the pavilion. Now all she had to do was collect him after graduation. That would be his last opportunity to try to see the girl.

Charlie grabbed Lilly's hand, and they ran out of the dark corridor into the bright sunlight. They headed toward Lilly's Jeep. Charlie figured with over half the alphabet to go and closing remarks they had at least a couple of hours before Evelyn realized anything was amiss.

Lilly was opening the back hatch of the Jeep to put in her tote when a guy in a red Honda drove up and rolled down the window. It was Henry. Lilly's heart began to pound. Her suspicions about Henry were right; he was a lackey for his wife.

"What are you doing here?" Charlie asked calmly.

"You'll never make it in her car. The minute they realize you two are gone, they'll be searching for her Jeep. Here," he said. He threw Charlie a set of car keys. "It's a rental. I made sure they can't trace it to you or me."

"How did you know we were going to run? Does Evelyn suspect?" Charlie asked.

"No. I mean, she always thinks you're going to try something, but she doesn't know your specific plans to run off together today," Henry said.

"Then how did *you* know?" Charlie asked.

"Yesterday, after you said good-bye to Liliana, I expected you to be more subdued. You were, in fact, cheerful. After I dropped you off, I saw Liliana's vehicle at the bank, and I followed her to the mall and then home. I watched her put your backpack and her bag in the back of her Jeep. I figured the graduation ceremony would be your best and last chance to get away. Now, you'd better get going. Take advantage of the head start you have."

"Thank you, Henry," Charlie said, pulling on Lilly's arm.

"No, wait," Lilly said. "Why are you helping us?"

"Liliana," Charlie complained.

"No, it's OK. In your shoes I'd be suspicious, too. Look, I don't know if it's right—your relationship with Charlie. But I do know what my father and Evelyn are doing is wrong."

Charlie picked up Lilly's bag and his backpack and they got into the rental car. Henry watched as they drove out of the parking lot. "May God go with you," he said. "You're going to need Him."

Lilly looked out the window, watching Houston fly by as Charlie headed for I-10. It made her sad to see all the wonderful familiar sights in the rearview mirror. She should be attending a graduation party with her friends tonight. She should have a fun summer and get ready to start college in the fall. Instead she was on her way to a place she'd never been before to get married, with no idea when she might see Texas again. Lilly moved closer to the passenger-side window and farther away from Charlie.

"Am I the enemy now?" he asked.

Yes. No. Maybe. Lilly sighed and said, "I don't know. I mean, no."

"If you're having second thoughts…" He was giving her a way out if that's what she wanted, but he hoped she wouldn't take it.

"I'm not," Lilly said. "It's just very hard to leave everything and everyone behind."

"And you wouldn't have to, if it wasn't for my stupid planet," Charlie said, trying to get Lilly to smile.

It had the desired effect. "You're darned right," Lilly said. Charlie pulled her over close to him, and she rested her head on his shoulder.

As soon as Charlie drove passed Katy and into Brookshire, Lilly picked her purse up and pulled out a disc Charlie had made her. It was a mix of songs by the Cure, Depeche Mode, and New Order. The card Beth had given her fell out.

"What's that?" Charlie asked.

"It's a card from Beth," Lilly said. She opened the envelope and the card. "Congratulations on Your Wedding" was written in flowing black script on the front. This was the only wedding present she and Charlie would receive. Inside were two twenty-dollar bills. Forty dollars was a lot of money for a sophomore without a job. Lilly wished she could give Beth a great big hug.

"Wow," Charlie said, "Forty bucks. Let's add it to our stash. What does the card say?"

"Wishing you all the happiness on Earth. Love, Beth."

"How fitting. But I suppose all the happiness on Sentria doesn't mean much."

"Considering what they want to do to us, definitely not," Lilly said.

Depeche Mode's "Never Let Me Down Again" began to play. Lilly settled back against Charlie's shoulder for the long ride ahead.

They passed through one small Texas town after another. Charlie wanted to put as much distance between Evelyn and them as possible. Finally, when it was starting to get dark, Charlie pulled over at a small diner to eat.

The waitress took their order and brought Charlie a cup of coffee and Lilly a Diet Coke. When their burgers arrived, Charlie dug in, but Lilly just picked at her food.

"Not hungry?" Charlie asked.

Lilly shook her head no. She started worrying her necklace.

"What's wrong?" he asked.

"Nothing," she replied as she rolled the circle charm between her fingers.

"I don't buy it. Look, I'm trying not to take it personally, but I was kind of hoping you wouldn't be so miserable on the eve of our wedding."

"Very funny. If I'm miserable, it's because I'm thinking of my mom. By now she's read the note. She's probably worried sick." Lilly pushed her plate away.

Charlie looked into her eyes. "As soon as we are married, and I think we are safe from Evelyn and the elders, you can call your mom. I promise. You can even let her yell at me if you want."

Lilly smiled. "OK, I will."

"Seriously, you're not nervous about getting married, are you?"

"Not the wedding so much as the marriage," she said truthfully. She loved Charlie with all her heart, but she was practical. She knew love wouldn't pay the bills. "Charlie, how are we going to survive? Neither one of us has a job." Lilly thought that after a month or two, Michelle might have calmed down enough to allow them to come back to her house. Maybe they could work out an arrangement to live with her and pay rent. But that was a long way off. They needed income now.

Charlie laughed. "You're worried about *that*? Liliana, I was able to get about twelve hundred dollars, and with what you have, we can make it last for a while if we're careful. Besides, I'm not planning on being unemployed for long. If I have to work three jobs, I will. You don't honestly believe I would have asked you to marry me if I didn't know I could provide for you?"

"Twelve hundred dollars?" Lilly was shocked. Charlie had mentioned that his parents always had money lying around, but she never expected it would be so much.

"It's a Sentrian thing," Charlie said. "We like to have cash around in case of an emergency."

"Well, you know, I can work, too."

"Absolutely not. You're going to college in the fall just as you planned. Maybe you don't understand, because it's not the way things are done here on Earth, but Sentrians get married younger than eighteen all the time. It's normal for us to be out on our own at an early age."

"How? What will you do to earn a living?" She needed specifics.

"I already have a couple of degrees, remember? With my skills I should be able to find a decent job. We can rent an apartment, and you can go to school full time. You're not going to have to sacrifice college to marry me."

"Oh," Lilly said. She didn't want to admit it to Charlie, but she was greatly relieved. Charlie convinced Lilly to eat a few bites of her burger. Then they got back in the car and drove for a few more hours. He was planning to arrive in Las Vegas late tomorrow evening. They would need to find a place to rest for the night and then get up early for the long drive ahead of them. Fort Stockton seemed like as good a place as any. They stopped at the Walmart there to pick up a few supplies. The weather was pleasant, so they decided to sleep outside and save their money for the hotel tomorrow. Lilly was happy about that. Her wedding would not be a formal affair, but she at least wanted to take a shower before she walked down the aisle.

Charlie found an open field surrounded by trees and pulled the car in. He fully unzipped a sleeping bag he had bought at Walmart and spread it on the ground to give some cushion to the hard earth. Then he put a blanket over it. Charlie lay down on top of the blanket. She snuggled up next to him, using his shoulder as a pillow. It was a warm, clear night. The stars twinkled in the expansive Texas sky.

Charlie pointed out a star. "We call it AV12. Its solar system only has three planets, but it does have twelve moons. And RS30 over there, the planets in that system are all covered with poison gases. I wrote a paper on it for an astronomy class.

"Are you going to miss it?" Lilly asked.

"Miss what?"

"Sentria. After we get married, you'll never be able to go home again." She realized that while she was giving up a lot, Charlie was giving up more. She at least had the expectation of seeing her mom one day and going back to Texas. Charlie would never see his parents, friends, or home again.

"Sentria is not my home anymore. My home is with you." He hugged her tight against his chest. "Besides, it's just a stupid planet anyway."

Charlie told her more stories about the different planets and stars until she fell asleep. The tension of the day gave way to drowsiness. Not even the noisy crickets could keep her awake.

Lilly awoke to the sound of birds chirping. Yes, they were definitely out in the country. In the distance she heard a cow moo, low and long. It was still mostly dark, but a bit of pink light could be seen peeking over the horizon.

She was still exhausted from the long drive and would have gone back to sleep, but she really needed to go to the bathroom. Unfortunately for this city girl, there wasn't one in sight. She walked across the field to a secluded area with trees, hoping she wasn't squatting in poison oak.

In the short time she was gone, the sky had lightened up considerably. Charlie was awake now, sitting up on the blanket and rubbing his neck. "Oh, good, you're back. I thought you got cold feet and ran off."

"Not cold feet, full bladder." Lilly yawned and stretched.

"C'mon, let's pack up and go. I'd like to get an early start," Charlie said. Lilly helped Charlie fold up the sleeping bag and blanket, and they headed out.

O

ON THE RUN

Evelyn was livid. How had Charlie slipped through her fingers? She had no clue where he was. Out of desperation, she made the decision to activate the locator chip in Charlie's neck. By her estimation, Charlie had a two-to-three-hour head start. The locator chip technology had never been used on Earth, but it was their only option. The Sentrians hadn't used the chips to locate people in decades. Most Sentrians forgot they even had tracking chips. Charlie was one of them.

One drawback of the device was that it had a limited range. Sentria was much smaller than Earth, necessitating a detection area of only about two hundred Earthan miles. They would have to be at least that close to Charlie before the device would register his movements.

A search of the pavilion yielded two graduation gowns in the bathroom trash and a Jeep that belonged to the girl, Lilly. They didn't even know what type of getaway car to look for. Evelyn hoped the girl's parents could give them some useful information and made Louis call them.

Michelle stopped by the store before returning home from the graduation. As she was putting away the groceries she noticed an envelope lying on the kitchen table with the word "Mom" written on it. She opened the letter and began reading.

Dear Mom,

Charlie and I have decided to get married. I know it's sudden, but if we don't get married now, Charlie will have to move away with his parents. Please don't think I'm getting married just to keep Charlie here. I love him with all my heart, and we would have married eventually anyway. I'm sorry if I'm disappointing you. You know I love you very much, and it's not my intention to hurt you. I remember you telling me that when you eloped with Dad, no one would have been able to stop you or talk you out of it. I feel the same way about my decision. Try not to worry. I'll call you when I can.

Love,
Lilly

Michelle slumped down into a kitchen chair. She thought back to that night a couple of months ago when she told Lilly not to give up on Charlie and told her about running off with Lalo. Could she have inadvertently encouraged Lilly and Charlie to do this? When she had eloped she had been an impetuous, rebellious teen. Lilly was neither of those things. But Lilly and Charlie were both eighteen. There was nothing she could do to stop them.

The phone ringing startled her out of her thoughts. She jumped up to answer it. "Hello, Lilly?" she asked.

"No, I'm afraid not." A male voice sighed. "I guess this means Lilly's not home. Are you, by chance, Mrs. Garcia?"

"Yes, to whom am I speaking?"

"Mrs. Garcia, my name is Louis Gray. My son Charlie is missing, and I was wondering if your daughter might know where he is. Has she ever mentioned him?"

"Mr. Gray, Charlie has been over here many times. Lilly and Charlie have been dating for most of the year." She was shocked that Charlie's father had no idea his son and Lilly were dating.

"You were aware of their relationship, and you approved?" Louis was incredulous.

"Yes, I was," Michelle said defensively. "They are both eighteen. They're responsible young adults. I didn't see a problem."

Louis blew out his breath. He wanted to scream at this brainless Earthan woman, but he knew he had to keep his cool. If he made her mad, she wouldn't cooperate, and he needed her cooperation if he wanted to find Charlie.

"Yes, of course. You're right." Louis tried to sound reasonable. "But I'm still concerned. It seems Charlie went missing after graduation, and there's a Jeep here that some of the other students have identified as your daughter's. Is she driving your car?"

"No, she's not. But I did get a note from Lilly, and I think you should know what it says. It seems Charlie and Lilly have run off to get married."

"*What!*" Louis yelled. He covered the phone and whispered to Evelyn. She clenched her fists and motioned to the elders to come over. All efforts by Louis to be reasonable went out the window. "That's terrible. We've got to stop them. Where did they go?"

"Calm down, Mr. Gray. Lilly didn't say where they were going. Look, I'm not thrilled about this either, but they are eighteen. There's really nothing we can do about it."

"No, that's unacceptable. Charlie cannot marry your daughter. We must find them and stop them. Mrs. Garcia, I'm going to give you my number. If you hear from them, please call my wife, Helen. I'll be checking in with her."

Michelle took down the number and agreed to call if she heard from Lilly, but she wasn't crazy about Mr. Gray's attitude. It was as if he thought Lilly wasn't good enough for his son. Getting married so young was the last thing she wanted for Lilly, but still, she didn't believe Charlie was no good for her daughter.

She called a friend and made arrangements to pick up the Jeep. After that she didn't plan on leaving the house. She wanted to stay home in case Lilly called.

"OK, where would an Earthan couple go to get married quickly?" Evelyn asked no one in particular.

"Definitely out of state," the fat elder named Bob said. He had been researching popular wedding locations and laws for marriage licenses while Louis took Helen home to wait by the phone. "Texas has a waiting period. I'm sure Silas is aware that as soon as he applies for a license, we will be notified immediately."

"Well, they must be at least two hundred miles away from here, because his locator chip hasn't pinged," Evelyn said.

"I believe Las Vegas, Nevada, would be the most likely destination," Bob said. "There is no waiting period for a marriage license, and weddings can be performed at any time of day."

Evelyn grabbed her PCD and input Las Vegas, Nevada. "Louis, you ride with Bill, and I'll ride with Bob. Keep your PCDs on so that we can share information. C'mon people, let's go," Evelyn ordered.

In a matter of minutes Evelyn and the others were flying down I-10. Evelyn had contacted the magistrate and told him what had happened. He was staying behind to coordinate the arrival of the ship from Sentria that would be landing on Sunday. He gave the order to bring Charlie back with or without his cooperation. That included killing him, if necessary. Evelyn decided to keep that bit of information to herself.

"This is very clever of Charlie, in a sick, twisted way," the thin elder named Bill said. "He knows we can't do a thing to them once they're married." They were speaking to each other through their PCDs.

"Oh no, it's not going to get that far," Evelyn said. To emphasize her point she depressed the accelerator and sped ahead. "Now hand me my coffee," she said to Bob. "We've got a long drive ahead of us."

It was still very early. The sun had not yet peeked out over the horizon. Evelyn decided last night that they would drive straight through and try to catch up to them. Bob and Louis drove the cars last night so that Evelyn and Bill could sleep. Now rested and on her third cup of coffee, Evelyn took the wheel again.

Evelyn's PCD began making a chirping sound. "We've got a signal, we're in range," Bob announced excitedly. A green blinking dot appeared on the screen.

"Bill, Louis," Evelyn said. "Did you get that? We've found his tracking signal."

"Is he on the move?" Bill asked.

"No, he's still," Bob said. "Maybe he's asleep. It is very early."

"Keep me posted on his position," Evelyn instructed. "I'm going to try to close the gap."

An hour later Bob made an observation. The green blinking light was no longer stationary. "They're moving now. Heading west."

"That's OK," Evelyn said. "They won't get far."

Charlie and Lilly stopped at a gas station for fuel and then headed to McDonald's for coffee and breakfast. El Paso was the next big town coming up before they crossed into New Mexico.

When they got back to the car, Lilly loaded her CD into the player. "Road music," she said. "We'll be back in your old neighborhood soon."

"Huh?" Charlie asked.

"New Mexico. Roswell."

"Oh yeah," Charlie said absently. She snuggled up next to him, and he put his right arm around her. A moment later he had to move it to rub the back of his head and neck.

"Is something wrong?" Lilly asked.

"I've had a headache ever since I woke up this morning. In fact, it's what woke me up. My neck's kind of bothering me, too."

"That's probably from sleeping on the hard ground last night," Lilly told him.

"Probably," Charlie agreed. But there was something else bothering him. He could hear a high pitched squeal he didn't recognize, and unlike most things, he wasn't able to filter it out. It was almost as if it was emanating from inside his head.

"You want me to shut the music off?" Lilly asked.

"No, that doesn't bother me," Charlie said. Actually, it helped muffle the shrill, piercing siren in his head. He smiled at her. "You seem in a more cheerful mood today."

"Well, you have to admit, yesterday was pretty stressful. That getaway was pretty intense."

"Yeah, I really thought Ian was going to blow it for us. At least they don't know about this car; that will certainly slow them down."

"Do you think they've figured it out yet?" Lilly asked.

"I'm pretty sure they are aware we've left Houston. I just hope they don't know where we're headed or what we're planning."

Lilly hoped so, too. She started playing with her necklace again. "Just Like Heaven" by the Cure played, and Lilly leaned into Charlie's side. He winced and grabbed his head as a sharp pain shot through his neck.

"Charlie, are you OK?"

No, he *definitely* was not OK. Now he realized what was causing the pain and the squealing noise in his head. It was like a bad nightmare. "No, it can't be. I'm so stupid," he said.

"What? What's wrong?"

"The chip. I forgot about the chip." He struck the steering wheel with his right hand.

"What are you talking about?"

"On Sentria, when you're born they put a chip in your neck, so that the government can keep track of you. It was designed to catch criminals, but all the lawbreakers soon realized they would be caught anyway and just stopped running. Now it's mostly a deterrent, since no one has tried to run away from the Sentrian authorities in about fifty years. It just lies dormant in our heads. They haven't had to activate the chips in decades."

"Until now?" Lilly asked.

"Until now," Charlie confirmed.

"What can we do?" Lilly's voice shook. "How much time before they reach us?"

"I don't know. I've had this piercing sound in my ear for a while now, and it just got louder. That probably means they're getting close. Maybe, if we can get to a store to get a knife, you can cut the chip out of my neck." He wasn't sure if that would work, or if they would have the time to get that far.

Lilly cringed. The idea of cutting Charlie's neck was not appealing, but getting caught was not an option.

Out in the country, stores were few and far between. Charlie pulled in the first one he saw and bought a little pocket knife. He checked. The blade was sharp; it would have to work. He drove off the main road and into a field where his car would be obscured from view, not that it would help them much.

Half an hour had elapsed. Lilly was sitting on the ground sobbing, Charlie's blood all over her hands. She had been sawing on his neck for the past several minutes, but had been unable to locate the chip. Charlie couldn't pinpoint the exact location of it. She knew she was hurting him. And the blood. So much blood.

"Just try one more time," Charlie said, holding the knife out to her.

Lilly shook her head, tears streaming down her face. "No, I could nick an artery. It won't matter about the chip, if you bleed to death," she said, wiping her eyes with the sleeve of her shirt.

Charlie looked at her. He knew she was right. With no idea where the chip was, she could cut all the way down to his spine and still never find it.

They were out of time. "C'mon, let's go." He gave her a hand up and got back in the car.

"What are we going to do?" She couldn't keep the fear and worry out of her voice.

"The only thing we can do. We're going to try to outrun them."

The green dot had stopped for about thirty minutes. Now it was moving again. "How close are we?" Evelyn asked.

"According to my calculations, we should overtake them in about twenty minutes," Bob said.

Evelyn nodded and turned her attention to the flat Texas highway ahead.

Charlie pulled out on the road and drove as fast as he could toward the Texas/New Mexico border. Lilly had found a rag in Charlie's glove box. Her hands were shaking as she rolled it up and applied pressure to stop the flow of blood from his neck. They drove in tense silence. Charlie was concentrating, speeding down the road as fast as he could. About twenty minutes later he noticed someone tailing them.

"They found us," Charlie said simply. A black Blazer was coming up on them quickly. Lilly turned to look. It was the same vehicle the two elders drove when they came to school to threaten her a few days ago. Charlie swerved off the main highway and onto a farm-to-market road. The black Blazer followed. Behind the Blazer, Charlie spotted his father's sedan.

Now they were really out in the boondocks. Charlie sped up and turned down every county road and farm-to-market road he came across in a futile attempt to shake them. But every turn he made, they made, too. "Hold on," Charlie said as he made a sharp U-turn and sped off in the opposite direction. The Blazer took the turn and was right behind him.

"Bill," Evelyn said. "I want you to turn around and block the road. I'm going to try to cut them off on the other side." She stayed on Charlie's tail, and he finally had to whip around again to get away. Now Evelyn had him where she wanted him.

Charlie saw his dad's sedan blocking their way up ahead and Evelyn hot on their tail behind. They were trapped. There were no roads on either side to turn down. If he went off the road into the grass, they would catch them in no time. The only thing standing between them and imminent capture was a telephone pole. Charlie looked over at Lilly. In as calm a voice as he possessed he asked, "What do you want me to do?"

"Floor it," she said, squeezing her eyes shut and holding tightly to his arm. Charlie aimed the car at the telephone pole and punched the accelerator as far down as it would go.

"No," Evelyn shouted when she realized what Charlie was doing. She sped up and managed to get close enough to Charlie to sideswipe his car, knocking him off his intended target. Bill drove his car up on the other side and hemmed Charlie in. Evelyn and Bill forced Charlie's crippled car off the road and into the tall Texas grass. They were at a dead stop.

"Are you OK?" Charlie asked. Lilly nodded. She was a little shaken up, and there was a laceration on her forehead, but she was otherwise unharmed. "I'm going to go talk to them. Stay here; you'll be safe." He hoped it wasn't a lie. As he turned to open the car door, Lilly grabbed his arm.

"Charlie, I love you—infinity."

He turned back and squeezed her hand. "I love you—infinity." Then he got out of his car and walked over to Evelyn.

Evelyn was already out of the Blazer and walking toward Charlie. The two elders and Louis followed close behind.

"That was a valiant effort, Charlie, but you never had a prayer of evading us."

"Please, Evelyn. We are not a threat to you. I swear we won't ever tell your secrets. Just leave me here. Go back to Sentria without me."

"Enough, Charlie," Evelyn said. "This so-called romance with the Earthan is over." On Evelyn's order, Bob came up behind Charlie and restrained his hands. Evelyn signaled to Bill. "Take care of that loose end over there."

"No!" Charlie yelled. Bill pulled Lilly out of the car, and she fought and struggled against him. She kicked Bill in the nose, which infuriated him. "Stop kicking me, you sweaty Earthan." Bill grabbed her left ankle and squeezed down hard. The sound of cracking bone was audible to Evelyn and the elders, but it resounded like thunder in Charlie's sensitive ears. He closed his eyes and steeled himself for the screams that were sure to come.

Lilly did scream. The pain spread through her body like a wildfire. She was vaguely aware of Charlie and the others shouting and making gestures, but she couldn't understand what they were saying. The pain was too intense.

Charlie could have filtered out her screams, but that didn't seem fair. He was the reason she was suffering now. "No, please. No more. Just let her go," Charlie begged Evelyn. He looked over his shoulder at Lilly. She had stopped screaming and was just moaning softly. Either she was in shock or had come to the realization it would do no good. He looked back at Evelyn. "Do whatever you want to me."

"Oh, believe me, I will. I have orders to bring you in dead or alive, and frankly, I don't care either way."

"No," Louis objected, rushing up to Charlie's side. "That was not part of the arrangement."

"There was never any agreement," Evelyn said. "I will do whatever is best for the state."

"Look," Louis said. "Let's just take him back with us. We'll kill the girl and make it look like an accident."

"*No!*" Charlie screamed. He flailed against the fat elder who had restrained his arms behind his back.

"Charlie, better her dead than you," Louis told him.

Bill, who was holding the now still Earthan girl, repositioned her so that he could more easily snap her neck the moment Evelyn gave the order.

It was over. There was no talking them out of it. Charlie was so tired—tired of running, tired of fighting. It didn't matter how hard he tried, they were always one step ahead of him. Charlie did the only thing he could do. He called out to her in his strong, steady voice, "Liliana, look at me." From somewhere in her fugue of pain she heard his voice—the melodious way he always pronounced her name. She made an effort to focus her eyes in his direction. "Look at *me,* Liliana. Don't look away. That's good. That's good. I'm sorry. I'm so sorry. Don't be afraid. I'll be with you until the end." That was the last thing Lilly heard. Her world went from gray to black.

HOPELESS

Evelyn nodded toward Bill, and he moved his hands to Lilly's throat. "Wait," Bob said. "I have a better solution." The fat elder, the more reasonable one, had a better solution.

Charlie released his breath. "Thank you, God," he whispered.

Evelyn motioned for Bill to stop. "I'm listening."

"They're in our custody now; it's not like they can run. Let's put them in a sleep state. Take Charlie back to Houston without a fight. We'll stage an accident scene and stay here until the Earthans pick the girl up. Then, we'll head back to Houston too."

Evelyn considered this. An injured Earthan was easier to explain than a dead Earthan. If they put her in a sleep state, she wouldn't remember much about what happened, and no one would be the wiser. As long as Charlie and the girl were permanently separated, she had no issue with leaving her alive. "Do it," Evelyn said and turned to go back to her car. She was already leaving a message to the magistrate to let him know the problem had been taken care of.

Bob pressed his fingers along the ridge of Charlie's skull, and he crumpled into a heap on the road. Lilly, who was barely conscious, went limp after Bill pressed his fingers against her skull.

Louis picked up his son and put him in the backseat of the Blazer. Then he and Bob lifted up the rental car and slammed it into the telephone pole, shattering the windshield and leaving a huge dent in the driver-side door. Bill shoved Lilly into the driver's seat and then ran over to the Blazer. Evelyn and Bill drove off with Charlie in the backseat.

Bob and Louis stayed behind to report the accident and wait for the emergency response vehicles. "You saved my son's life," Louis told Bob. "I don't know why you did that, but thank you."

"As an elder I have taken an oath to uphold the Sentrian code of law, and I will. Those who break the law must be punished. But Silas is mentally ill, not a hardened criminal. I don't think he needs to pay for his transgressions with his life."

After receiving a call from Louis, Michelle was on her way to the Texas Medical Center where Life Flight was taking Lilly. As it turned out, Louis didn't have to stop the wedding. Before they had a chance to marry, Charlie and Lilly got into a terrible car accident that left him dead and her severely injured. Michelle prayed all the way to the hospital that Lilly would not die, too.

Michelle's boss, Dr. Maxwell, made a few phone calls and was able to get Dr. Morris to examine Lilly when she arrived. He was the best trauma surgeon in Houston. When Michelle arrived she was escorted back to the examination area to wait for her daughter.

Lilly was unconscious but stable when she was rolled off the helicopter. The staff gave Michelle a moment with Lilly before they rolled her into a trauma room. She looked peaceful, but Michelle immediately saw her left leg was grotesquely swollen and discolored. The foot was hanging at an unnatural angle to the lower leg.

They rolled Lilly away, and Michelle sat down. She felt weak and had a sick feeling in her stomach. A nurse tried to get her a cup of coffee, but she refused and spent an anxious few hours waiting for all the tests to be done. Finally, Dr. Morris came out to speak to her. Michelle stood up, but Dr. Morris motioned for her to sit and pulled up a chair in front of her.

"First of all, the good news. The head CT is clear and shows no sign of intracranial trauma or hemorrhage. Lilly is still unconscious, but we can really find no reason for it. Her vitals are strong, and we are optimistic that she will come out of this without any lasting neurological problems. Now the bad news. I'm sure you saw Lilly's left leg. The X-rays show that the bones aren't just shattered, they're pulverized. I've never seen such a severe crushing injury from a car accident. The limb is cold and we can't get any pedal pulses. Mrs. Garcia, there's no way I can save her leg."

Michelle was upset but not surprised.

"With your permission, I'd like to proceed with the amputation. I will try to preserve as much of the leg as possible."

Michelle nodded. "Thank you, Doctor." Dr. Morris excused himself and went to scrub for surgery. A nurse led Michelle over to a desk to sign the papers. It didn't seem real. Yesterday morning she was fixing Lilly pancakes before her graduation, and now her daughter was undergoing surgery to amputate her left leg. Her hands were shaking as she signed her name.

"Is there someone I can call to be with you?" the nurse asked.

Michelle shook her head no. The nurse escorted her to the surgical waiting room. She alternated between sitting in the uncomfortable chairs and pacing the floor with the other family members waiting for word about their loved ones. She was used to being the caregiver, not the waiting family. She didn't much like being on this side of the hospital bed.

The waiting gave her time to think. It was still hard to take in. Yes, she had been upset with Lilly and Charlie for running off the way they did, and she believed they were making a terrible mistake. But she would have learned to accept their decision. When she was sitting at home, waiting to hear from Louis, she had already decided that she would be there for Lilly and Charlie and help them any way she could. She would give them the support she and Lalo never had from Abuela.

Now it didn't matter. It was going to be difficult when Lilly learned she had lost her leg, but Michelle was really dreading telling her that Charlie was dead.

Charlie was caught in that dream state between sleep and wakefulness. Vivid, tortuous images filled his mind. And the screams—her screams. Maybe it was all a bad dream. He could hope so, right?

Then he heard voices in the distance. Voices discussing what should be done with him. Voices that destroyed any hope that this was all a nightmare. He opened his eyes and saw that he was in a small, stark room. The walls were a light gray. In fact, everything was gray. Charlie sat up and looked down at the small cot he was lying on and the plain pants and shirt he was wearing: prison attire. He felt around for his glasses. On a bedside table he found a pair. They were not the ones Lilly had picked out. These frames were solid black and rectangular with oversize lenses. Charlie could just imagine what Lilly would think of these, but he did need to see, so he put them on. Everything came into focus. He looked out the small window at the familiar violet horizon. It was early morning, and he could still make out two of the three moons.

Charlie got up slowly and took a look around at his surroundings. There was a sink on the side of the room and a small bathroom in the corner. In addition to the cot, there was one plain chair that was bolted to the floor. The room was lit with harsh overhead lighting similar to Earthan fluorescent lighting. The gray monochromatic tone of the room was only broken up by the small window and a portrait of a Sentrian landscape on the wall opposite his cot. Charlie supposed it was someone's feeble attempt to cheer the place up.

He examined the door. It was very large and composed of thick metal, obviously designed to be soundproof. Charlie tilted his head and looked up at the ceiling. The door did make it more difficult to hear, but he could still make out some of the conversations of the staff outside of his room.

He heard footfalls coming toward him and someone pressing a code on a keypad outside the door.

The door opened, and a man and a woman entered his room. They appeared to be in their early thirties. They were dressed in all black, definitely Sentrian medical personnel. The woman had a severe look about her. She placed a glass of warm liquid on his bedside table. It was still steaming. Charlie knew what it was immediately. Instant Smile. His mother drank it whenever she was upset, which was often.

"It seems patient 29379 is awake," the man said. "How are you feeling?"

Charlie ignored the question and posed one of his own. "Where am I?"

"The Babylon Institute for the Criminally Insane: your new home," the woman told him.

"I'm Dr. Lot and this is Nurse Rahab. We'll be overseeing your psychological care during your incarceration."

His incarceration? "How long have I been here?"

"One day since you got off the ship. You've been unconscious for the last three days. While you were in your sleep state, Eve Royal and the elders presented your case to the Great Council. You've been sentenced to ten years in this facility," Nurse Rahab said with a smile.

Charlie wasn't surprised. On Sentria, the accused need not be present for their own trial. He wouldn't have been allowed to mount a defense anyway.

"We will let you rest today. Tomorrow we begin therapy," Dr. Lot said. "Oh, and by the way, your father wants to see you. You are permitted a thirty-minute visit tonight, if you'd like. After that you will only be allowed visits once a month."

Charlie considered it. One the one hand, he was still angry with his father. The last time they spoke, he was telling Eve to kill Liliana. On the other hand, a month was a long time to go without seeing anyone he knew, and he had one question he had to know the answer to. He thought his father would at least tell him the truth.

"Yes, I want to see him," Charlie said, rubbing his neck. Although the chip was deactivated, and he could no longer hear its high pitched squeal, the memory of it was very strong.

"I thought you might. He's in visitor processing right now. That will take about thirty minutes. Then he will be brought here, to your room." Dr. Lot and Nurse Rahab left him alone.

The gravity of his situation hit him. He would be in here for ten long years, a full quarter of his life. That kind of sentence was reserved for only the worst of Sentrian criminals. You can't thwart God's will, Charlie thought. He had disobeyed, and as a consequence the Sentrian officials had carried him off to this place, the Babylon Institute. Liliana. He would never see her again. He lay down on the cot and stared at the cold gray wall.

The sound of his father's footfalls roused him. He turned to face the door as he watched Louis/Lucien walk in.

"Hello, Silas," Lucien said as he took a seat. Charlie thought his father looked older, frailer, and very, very tired.

"Father? Are you all right?"

"I'm fine," he said. "When your only son is tried, convicted, and sent to prison for ten years, all in the span of three days, it takes a toll. Your mother…well, she's not up to a visit yet." The way his father said it, Charlie wondered if his mom would ever be up to seeing him in here.

"I have to ask you a question, and I need you to tell me the truth," Charlie paused. "What did they do to Liliana?"

"Silas, they are monitoring our conversations."

"I don't care," Charlie said, getting up from his cot. He turned to face Lucien. "Please, I need to know."

"All right." Lucien looked over his shoulder, as if he expected someone would burst into the room at any second. "They didn't kill her, if that's what you're wondering. They put her in a sleep state just like you. We staged an accident scene and called emergency services. I watched them load her into one of the air ambulances myself. Afterward, I called her mother and informed her of the girl's condition. I also told her you were dead."

The sleep state affected Earthans differently than Sentrians. Lilly wouldn't remember much about what happened that day. Maybe she wouldn't remember the car chase at all. His father said she was receiving medical care. Although Earthan medical treatment was crude in comparison to Sentrian standards, they would be able to treat her injured leg. He knew it was probably best that she believed he was dead, but the thought troubled him. Charlie sighed. At least Liliana was alive; that was the important thing. He would never see her again, so he might as well be dead to her.

"Silas, listen to me," Lucien said. "Now is the time to think about your own situation. Please cooperate fully with the doctors and staff here. Do whatever they ask. If you complete your therapy successfully, you can spend the last years of your life a free man. If not, you'll die in here."

Charlie filtered out his father's words. He turned his head and stared out the little window in his cell. It didn't matter what they did to him, and he honestly didn't care. Without Liliana, his life was already over.

Michelle had been by Lilly's side day and night for a week. Every day she prayed this would be the day Lilly would wake up, and every day her hopes were dashed. She talked to her, read to her, even watched TV with her. At night, she pulled her chair up close to Lilly's bed and slept with her hand wrapped around Lilly's. The only time she left the hospital was to shower.

On the eighth day after the accident, Lilly opened her eyes. She was surrounded by monitors and bags of fluid connected to tubes that drained into her arm. Her throat was sore and she was groggy. It took her a moment to process her surroundings. She was in a hospital. What happened? How did she end up here?

Michelle looked up from her crossword puzzle. "Mi hija, thank God you're awake. How do you feel? Are you in pain?"

"No, Mom. I'm fine." Lilly swallowed; it hurt to talk. "Why am I here? And where's Charlie?"

"I'll tell you everything in a little while, but right now I need to let the nurses know you're awake." Michelle got up to go to the nurse's station.

Lilly grabbed her hand and stopped her. "That can wait." Michelle sat back down. "What happened?"

"You were in an accident, a very bad accident. Do you remember?"

Lilly shook her head. She couldn't remember much of anything. "How bad was the accident, Mom?" Michelle lifted the sheet. Where her left leg should be was a rounded bandage, and there was no ankle or foot. Lilly looked at her mom. Then she looked down at the stump, horrified. She covered her mouth with her hand to keep from screaming.

"It's not as bad as it looks. Dr. Morris was able to save part of your lower leg."

Lilly was crying now. "Well, great. That makes me feel much better." She searched her mind, trying to remember what happened. The trouble was, there were gaps in her memory—big ones. Perhaps Charlie could fill them in. "I want to see Charlie. I need to talk to Charlie," she said through her tears.

Michelle took Lilly's hand and shook her head. "I'm sorry, mi hija. Charlie did not survive."

This time Lilly could not contain the screams. Michelle wrapped her arms around her daughter and held her tightly, rocking her back and forth.

Lilly was hoarse and exhausted from crying. The audible screams had subsided. It would be months before the screams inside her head did. Michelle brushed the hair out of her face and kissed her forehead. Then, she got up and went to get the nurses.

Lilly looked down at the bed. The sheet was still lifted up, exposing what remained of her left leg. Funny how a person's perspective could change so suddenly. She no longer felt any sense of loss for her missing limb now. Her broken heart wouldn't allow it.

End of Book One

BIBLIOGRAPHY

Rudolph, the Red-Nosed Reindeer. Director, Larry Roemer. Rankin/Bass Productions, 1964.

Karate Kid. Director, John G. Avildsen. Columbia Pictures Corporation, 1984.

"Number 12 Looks Just Like You." *The Twilight Zone.* Columbia Broadcasting System, January 24, 1964.

Made in the USA
San Bernardino, CA
16 November 2014